THE PRODIGAL PROJECT

BOOK 4
KINGS

KEN ABRAHAM
AND
DANIEL HART

A PLUME BOOK

PLUME
Published by the Penguin Group
Penguin Group (USA) Inc., 375 Hudson Street, New York, New York 10014, U.S.A.
Penguin Books Ltd, 80 Strand, London WC2R 0RL, England
Penguin Books Australia Ltd, 250 Camberwell Road,
Camberwell, Victoria 3124, Australia
Penguin Books Canada Ltd, 10 Alcorn Avenue,
Toronto, Ontario, Canada M4V 3B2
Penguin Books India (P) Ltd, 11 Community Centre, Panchsheel Park,
New Delhi – 110 017, India
Penguin Books (NZ), cnr Airborne and Rosedale Roads,
Albany, Auckland 1310, New Zealand
Penguin Books (South Africa) (Pty) Ltd, 24 Sturdee Avenue, Rosebank,
Johannesburg 2196, South Africa

Penguin Books Ltd, Registered Offices: 80 Strand, London WC2R 0RL, England

First published by Plume, a member of Penguin Group (USA) Inc.

First Printing, September 2004
10 9 8 7 6 5 4 3 2 1

CIP data is available.
ISBN 0-452-28520-8

Printed in the United States of America
Set in Janson Text

PUBLISHER'S NOTE
This is a work of fiction. Names, characters, places, and incidents are either the product of the author's imagination or are used fictitiously, and any resemblance to actual persons, living or dead, business establishments, events, or locales is entirely coincidental.

For Adam and Philip Barnes.
He's not heavy, he's my brother.
—D.H.

ACKNOWLEDGMENTS

I thank God for those who guide, teach, and encourage me: Ken Abraham, Gary Brozek, Jane Gelfman, and my family. Always in faith.

—D. H.

"The kings of the earth did not believe, nor did any of the inhabitants of the world, that the adversary and the enemy could enter the gates of Jerusalem."

—LAMENTATIONS 4:12

PROLOGUE

John Jameson knew he was drowning.

He knew because he felt himself immersed in embracing liquid, lying on his back with arms outstretched, falling gently into blue-green depths. It was the water of the earth, he thought, the water of the womb, the water of life—and here he would find death. The idea of death troubled him more than he thought it should. Surely death was victory, release from the pain-racked, heartbreaking physical realm. With death, he contemplated, all things would be resolved, all questions answered, all loss regained. Why should he struggle?

But he did struggle, and a sea change came over the waters. Gone were the warm, placid blue greens, the quiet fullness. In their place were roiled and boiling waves, slate gray and frothy, ripping the surface, the spray flung like hail against the winds of the howling night. Below the surf, where it had been calm, he was now shoved and bumped, pulling, turning, driving him down in a tumble of arms and legs. His mouth was open, and he knew he was calling her name. *That* was why he struggled now, because of *her*. He could not slip away selfishly to his own death and leave her to the night. No . . . She was there in the maelstrom because of him, had come on her own, somehow knowing where he'd be, to help him. She had stood beside him as they plunged into the terrible night of raging sea and ashen skies, her strength becoming his, her will to survive becoming *theirs*. She was why he could not give himself over to the siren call of darkness, why he had to live—even as he drowned. He relaxed and let himself fall into the blue-green depths, knowing she waited.

"John?" asked her voice, sending soft vibrations rippling around him. "John?"

He smiled in answer, safe within the water.

Water is a gift of God.

Like so many parts of the earth that are also of God, water seems a simple ingredient of life; pure, nurturing, necessary. It flows through the sand and rock of the earth, through the veins and flesh of man. It covers great areas in oceans of brine or lakes of sugar. It trickles in dripping rivulets or rushes in forceful torrents, changing and shaping, eroding and building what it touches. It leaps in a raging rush over the precipice of innumerable rocky falls, enveloped in a constant thrumming roar, throwing up a rainbow in its own mist. In wide and deep rivers it solemnly sweeps rocky shores, in mossy shadowed streams it trips and dances, bubbling and burbling down through the green. Water is a constant, while moment by moment, it causes change. The brook becomes the stream becomes the river, and where once was high plateau is found deep canyon. The golden stretching beaches on the edge of oceans, seemingly serene, passively forever, are changed with the easy caress or crashing assault of each unending wave. The waves bring, and take, spread out, pull away, tumble in, carry off. In its hypnotic repetition, in its time-less rhythm, before water, nothing remains of what was—but a moment ago.

The human tear, squeezed from the well of emotion, shed in numbers countless like the grains of sand or stars in the night sky, is but a single drop. It rests like a quiver-ing diamond on a fold of soft skin at the corner of a mother's eye as she stares down at her child. Her child knows water, of course. The child formed and grew, softly enveloped in the water within. The mother's tear leaves a silver trace on her cheek, until falling away to hang for a moment in the precious air between them. In almost per-fect silence, it patters against the newborn's skin, and as the mother's fingers brush the salt and water against the child's lips, it once again becomes part of both.

Throughout the millennia, man has used water for his needs, harnessing it, routing it, damming it to take from its power, to live from its sustenance. The hard, hot, gritty earth beneath the first bare steps as they left the garden, this land so cruelly different, signified in a heartbeat what water was to man's survival. There could be no life without it, and even as the pull of a high moon draws the water close to it, man is forever pulled to water's fullness. Where water was in abundance, he channeled it; where it came dear, he captured it—and saved it. Even before the time of Jesus, the people of the desert jealously fought for, or cautiously shared, the oasis that must have appeared as a leaf of the garden miraculously dropped onto the hot sands. In the city of al-Quds, or Yerushalayim, or Jerusalem, the holiest of cities for the three major religions of the world, water came from a spring called Gihon. The spring lies outside the walls of the Old City, but an ancient king, Hezekiah, had a channel cut through the rock, directing the water inside to the Siloan pool. Thus was formed one of the earliest sources of water for Jerusalem.

Jerusalem, at once special and unique on earth and among the souls of men, sits between the Mediterranean and Dead Seas. It lies like a sun-baked earthen chalice, filled to the brim with history, hope, hatred, and spirituality. The Old City, the heart, has been coveted, crowned, and quartered by men zealously and jealously seeking God. The quadrants include the Armenian, the Jewish, the Muslim, and the Christian. Leading in, leading out, are the New, the Damascus, Herod's, Saint Stephen's, Golden, Dung, and Zion Gates. The Christian Quarter shares the Damascus Gate with the Muslim Quarter. The Christian section surrounds the Church of the Holy Sepulchre, site of the crucifixion, the burial, and the resurrection of Jesus. Here also lies the Via Dolorosa—the mute and sorrowful path of hallowed earth Jesus Christ walked from condemnation to the cross, the mile in another man's shoes every person should walk.

In the southeastern part of the Old City sits the Al

Haram ash-Sharif, Har Ha-Bayit, or Temple Mount, believed to be the site of Mount Moriah, where Abraham was asked to sacrifice his son, Isaac. During the tenth century B.C., King Solomon built the first Jewish temple on these grounds. That temple was destroyed by King Nebuchadnezzar around 587 B.C., but rebuilt by Herod less than one hundred years later. Remnants of that temple's walls still stand. On that site, toward the end of the seventh century, the Muslim Caliph Abd el Malik Ben Merwan built the Mosque of Omar, or Dome of the Rock. The mosque emerged from a human mix of devotion and rivalry, as Merwan desired Jerusalem to be as important to the followers of Mohammed as Mecca, where preached another caliph. The Dome of the Rock is considered the most exquisite Muslim shrine in the world, with a metal alloy dome that catches the golden sun, but the light reflected from it cuts into the hearts of many reverent Jews, who wait for the day the Mosque of Omar will no longer stand. In its stead, the Jews will rebuild their temple.

CHAPTER ⊕NE

The water on his fevered brow felt cool and light, like magic feathers that swept away the hot pain. His skin felt stretched and parched, and in his mind it was spider-webbed with cruel dry cracks like the arid desert floor. The wet cloth that lay against his forehead and the left side of his face was pulled away, and he heard soft splashing as it was dipped into a pail. He heard her sharp intake of breath, felt the shadow of her nearness as she leaned over him. Then the wet cloth was back, laid across the torn skin around his left eye, and he gave himself over to the healing sensation of it. He knew he lay in a bed, flat on his back, his arms heavy at his sides, his legs a great distance away, leaden, unresponsive. He knew it was morning, because of the ethereal light bathing his right side. He was aware of the fragrant scent of an unknown flower, the sharp tang of medicinal soap, the beckoning tendrils of strong coffee, and he was aware of her. She smelled like woman, the weight of her hip against his as she leaned over him. She smelled like summer to him—fresh, warm, comforting.

He wished he knew where he was. That *she* was there, still with him, caring for him, was a gift, and even in his pain-racked mind, he thanked God for it. During the times he could keep his thoughts coherent for a few moments, he also asked God, implored Him to let him sit up, open his eyes, move his body, have some *control* over his days. He knew he had been wounded, but even during the elongated micromoment the bullets spattered and ripped around him, he understood he had only taken pieces, like shrapnel, which had peppered the left side of his face, head, and eye. *Superficial,* his operational inner voice had advised him then. *Move, move . . . you'll be okay.* But within a few hours, while fleeing the scene of the shooting, a heavy numbness began to take over. He sensed it first in the blood that seeped around his eye. The blood was too thick, and it kept coming. The dizziness he accepted, the swelling, the racking headache . . . all part of shrapnel trauma around the eye. But then his arms and hands turned to wood, and his legs became clay, and he couldn't stand without her help. He thanked God for her.

"John," said Cat Early softly, her lips almost touching the warm skin of his left ear.

Cat! Cat! He thought, *We made it out of there, huh? We made it and you've taken us to a quiet place, and I've got to get up out of this bed. . . . Cat! Cat?* He fought to make his lips form the words, his tongue a papery, fluttery thing. "Uu-unnnh," he said.

"Sssshh, John," she whispered, "It's all right—it's okay now. I'm here, and we're okay. You have to rest."

"Uuunnnh."

"I'm here, John."

Cat! You've got to be careful. . . . They'll be out there, every-where, looking for me. Cat, I've got to get up, get moving. . . . We've got to keep moving. Where are we, Cat? Where is this place?

"John."

Cat . . . where are we?

He felt the cool, easy weight of the wet cloth on his skin again and forced himself to relax, giving himself over to the water, and to her touch.

"Would you like me to read to you a bit, John?" she asked.

"Unh." He felt her move beside him, heard the soft rustle as she turned the pages of the book he knew she would read. The room hushed in anticipation.

"Here's one," she said, and she began: "God is our refuge and strength, and ever present help in trouble. Therefore we will not fear, though the earth give way and the mountains fall into the heart of the sea, though its wa-ters roar and foam and the mountains quake with their surging."

Cat, he thought, *Where are we?*

+   +   +

Cat Early watched John Jameson sleeping. He lay on a rough bed with worn sheets and a thin blanket. He was naked under the top sheet, his cleaned and folded clothes waiting on a small stool nearby. She was glad he had stopped thrashing around, but saw that his skin still shone with sweat from the fever. The loose bandage she had wrapped around his head, covering the left side of his face and eye, remained in place, the blood that seeped from his torn flesh turning it rust brown. The small house, on the outskirts of a village a few miles from Turin, in northern Italy, was quiet. She felt enveloped in a warm stillness as she sat there, the afternoon sun coming through the open windows and hugging her back. The house was so quiet, she heard a petal hit the wood surface of a table when it fell from a flower that stood in an old olive-oil bottle. She felt she might sit there forever, watching him sleep in peace, embracing the sweet moment as it was given to her. *Let this man rest*, she thought, *and let me watch over him until he's whole again.*

She knew it was a miracle they had made it that far, knew with certainty it was by the grace of God. They had left the ramshackle fishing wharf that lay forgotten on the southeastern edge of Nice, France, in a howling storm. She had stood beside him as he piloted a decrepit old wood-hulled boat, defiantly named *Dulcinea*, across the harbor, past the marker buoy, and into the enraged waters of the coastal Mediterranean Sea. The loose field-dressing he had clumsily applied to his wounds were soon soaked with blood, and he became too weak to stand without her help. He turned over the helm to her and shouted instructions above the roar of the wind and spray as they headed east toward Portofino, Italy. She felt the fear again as she thought of that night.

John had begun to phase in and out of consciousness, and she doggedly clung to the wheel, fighting the lurching boat to keep it on the course he had given her, the dim compass swinging wildly. The night hung close around them, with heavy leaden skies streaked with the colors of Revelation, the stinging rain flailing them like buckshot. Once he moaned and fell to the deck, and she helped him clumsily to his feet as the small vessel swung against the waves. On his orders, she wrapped a line around his hips, and he lashed himself to the port bulkhead, his face ghastly pale in the lightning. She did not know how he did it, but he checked his watch, checked her compass course, and after what seemed like a month of nights, shouted and pointed at a barely discernible flashing light in the distance. She managed to turn the wheel left and the bow of the boat swung bit by bit as it was assaulted by the waves, until the flashing light lay before them. Too late she realized they had a following sea, and she watched in horror while the boat drove headlong into the flashing buoy as they came up on it. The bow caromed off the swinging buoy with a jolting screech, Jameson swung unconscious against his restraining line, and she remembered screaming against the wind, enraged at the night and her helplessness. Then, suddenly, the seas were behind them, *Dulcinea* seemed to take a jaunty attitude, her small diesel engine puttering and sputtering confidently, and they slipped into the small harbor of Portofino.

She heard him moan now, and say her name. She went to his side, ran her fingers softly across the skin of his brow, checked his bandage, waited, then returned to the straight-backed wooden chair she had been sitting in. She let her mind go back to that night again. She shook her head, thinking of how she had literally crashed into a wooden dock on the northern edge of the small harbor, away from the breakwater and the marina where several fine yachts lay. The winds and rain still raged above them, but it was relatively calmer under cover. She had scrambled out of the cockpit, grabbed a line draped over the bow, and managed to wrap it around a piling. She saw John stagger out and deftly tie off the stern to a broken cleat on the dock. He shut the engine off and sat heavily on the deck. She smiled now, thinking of how his face had been broken by a ragged grin as he looked up at her and said in a raspy voice, "Good job, sailor." She had jumped back into the boat, knelt beside him, and listened while he gave her instructions. She did not want to leave him, but knew she had no choice.

He had given her the name of a small hotel, and of the man who ran it. The place was only a few blocks away, off an alley behind a fish house. He told her how to find it, and she had made her way, pulling her soaked jacket close around her trembling body. No one else was out on that hellish night, and she was grateful. After making two wrong turns, she found the entrance to the hotel and banged on the locked door until a man's voice yelled angrily at her in Italian. She kept pounding until she saw a dark, slanted face peering at her along the edge of a paper shade. She shouted, "Bright Red Edsel!" and waited as Jameson had instructed her, but the face just stared at her. She shouted it again, then again, and after the third time, the door was unlocked and swung open. A small, thin man with a twelve-o'clock shadow on his rough jaw, dressed in pink silk pajamas, stood there. He smiled rakishly and said, "Well, why didn't you say so? Where is he?"

A short while later, after the man had hurriedly dressed and shoved a small glass of amber liquid into her hands, they parked near the dock in his battered sedan. Before either of them could get out, Jameson had opened one of the back doors, thrown in a large gym bag, and struggled into the seat behind them. The small man turned, stared at Jameson a long moment, shook his head, and said, "Well, well, if it isn't the long-lost James Sampson, gentleman and spy." He grimaced. "Sometimes I wondered if I'd ever see you again." He added as an aside to Cat: "Sorry I didn't get the identifier the first time you bellowed, miss. It took me a minute to remember what it meant."

"Guido," interrupted Jameson, "I need to get to Mamma Steffie's place. Remember it?"

"No problem, James," replied Guido, "I gotta tell ya, though—you look terrible. Who's the girl?"

"My mother."

"Thy mother."

"Thine, spaghetti-bender."

"Thine, English pig."

They both laughed. Cat just listened. She still held the glass Guido had given her.

"You picked some night to be out and about, James," said Guido as he drove the car away from the dock area. He looked at Cat, nodded at the glass, and said, "You should drink that, miss, and give some to our hero back there, too."

"Guido," said Jameson, his voice weakening, "You'll need to—"

"The boat," replied the man as he nodded his head, driving the car through the darkened streets, heading north. "Make the boat disappear for you. What? You think this is the first time I done some little thing for you guys?"

But Jameson didn't answer.

Cat stood now, and stretched. She glanced at her watch. She knew "Mamma Steffie" would be along soon, bringing them hot meals as she had three times every day for the past four days. She looked at her laptop sitting on a small desk and thought of the story she was almost ready to send to her boss, Simon Blake, in Paris. A donkey brayed nearby, and her thoughts went back yet again to the night they had arrived at the house, Guido helping tumble Jameson into bed, giving her a smile, and leaving without another word. She wondered where John found these people, and how many he had stashed out there, waiting for the "identifier" that would set them in motion. She looked at John again and wondered what Simon Blake would do if he learned where she was, and whom she was with.

She was an experienced international journalist covering world events, and she was hiding out in a secret safe house. After millions had disappeared in a silent, instant ripple of universal energy; after much of the world had been torn by the total warfare waged by the Muslim mujahideen forces led by the wickedly evil Izbek Noir; after burning hail, decimated crops, seas of blood, apparitions of color scratching at the ashen skies—many said the end of the world had come. The civilizations of man had been plunged into chaos, fear, and spiritual confusion. Many returned to their Bibles—and many to the gun—for answers. In this fearsome darkness and devastation, one light seemed to shine the brightest, bringing reason, order, and hope. One man who might unite the convulsed nations of the world against the rampaging mujahideen, one man who might save mankind and his world. She sighed. She was in the safe house, caring for the man who had attempted to assassinate Minister Azul Dante, leader of the new free world.

CHAPTER TWO⊕

The young girl knew she needed a new look, better clothes that were nonmilitary. Her close-cropped, ragged, self-cut hair would work for now. Her lean face, slim, angular body—these would do also, as they had for several months. But she needed new clothes and some money—preferably U.S. dollars. Or the new ECs, not the old Euro-dollar, but the currency representative of the European Coalition pulled together since the day of the disappearances. The Israeli money was strong, but she never had felt comfortable with it. Clothes, cash, and a new identity. These she searched for as she walked away from the place of her execution.

She had made her way carefully through the rear lines in northern Saudi Arabia, each step taking her farther from the battlefront, where the mechanized armies of the mujahideen led by Izbek Noir clashed with Iraqi forces streaming from the north. The Saudi armies had already fled or been smashed, the sun-seared fields of battle strewn with the burnt-out carcasses of tanks, armored personnel carriers, and attack helicopters. Scattered across these same defiled sands lay the twisted and burst remains of thousands of soldiers, of several armies, almost all of them followers of Muhammad. Near places that had once been towns or cities lay the many civilian dead, men and women. The children of Earth had been spared the horrors of this latest war when they had all been "taken" on the day of disappearances. Izbek Noir had illustrated early on his contempt for the niceties, rules, or *ethics* of war. His was total, global warfare, his Muslim mujahideen bent against the civilizations of man. He had no respect for race, culture, religion, or society, and his fighters had seen by his own example that their enemies could expect no quarter. Old men were killed outright. Soldiers who fought hard, and lived, had a choice: join the mujahideen unconditionally and immediately, or die. What women the mujahideen fighters came upon were viewed as objects to be used, tortured, then killed offhand. In war, man became the beast up on his hind legs, rapaciously cruel, savage, and merciless.

She needed a new look, a new identity, and she found these among the dead. She carried only a small kit bag with some water, meager rations, and a first-aid pouch. She did not want to travel without a weapon, but decided not to carry one of the many assault rifles left among the clumps of dead soldiers she passed. She found a pistol and kept that tucked into her waistband under her shirt. On the outskirts of one small village she found several burkas—

the full robe of the pious Muslim woman. This would cover her from the top of her hair to her feet, with only her eyes barely visible through the fabric. But the bodies in the burkas were bloodied and flyblown, and she could not bring herself to touch them. Traveling as a woman, alone, was not a good thing in these times anyway. This she knew from her own experience.

Not long after the global disappearances, when chaos and anarchy ruled before some rudimentary order was restored, she had been out searching for food for her parents. Three men chased her down, trapped her in an alley, and forced her to submit to them. After they left her, she struggled back to her home, only to find her parents murdered, the small house ransacked for what few possessions they had. She had fallen to her knees sobbing, crying out in anger, pain, and fear. That night she had buried her parents, alone. She went back to her home, bathed in hot water for a long time, and cut off her hair with her mother's scissors. Her older brother had been conscripted into the Saudi Army, and they had not heard from him since the war began. She took some of his clothing, a few personal things. When she walked away from what had been her life, it was as a slight and angular young man with fine pale skin, lips almost too sensuous, and dark, angry, disdainful eyes that challenged anyone who looked into them an instant too long.

She had tried to slip away in the confusion and terror that gripped the Saudis upon the approach of the seemingly unstoppable mujahideen armies, but had been spotted and forcibly conscripted into the infantry. She had been given a uniform, an assault rifle, a few minutes of hurried instruction on the weapon's use, and shoved in with a group of frightened and equally ill-trained young men. Her new squad leader had looked her over, spat, shook his head, and groused to the others that his new guy looked like a skinny girl, and he figured the little wimp would run away after the first shot. His new guy had kicked him squarely in the crotch, his dark eyes fierce, and after that the squad leader had left him alone. Not a week later she watched her unit get completely destroyed by the tanks and infantry of the mujahideen, who fought and died with a terrible, unrelenting fanaticism. They rushed forward screaming, these soldiers of Islam, running right into the combined fires that the Saudis threw at them, apparently unburdened by the fear of death. Many of them died, but many came on, and the frightened ranks of the Saudis crumbled as they threw down their weapons and tried to flee. She had fought on grimly, firing her rifle, using all her ammunition, and taking more from the dead. Finally their position was swarmed by the mujahideen, and calling out for the mercy of Allah, the Saudis surrendered. That was when she saw with her own eyes the mujahideen leader, General Izbek Noir.

General Noir, the Saudis discovered, was in the flesh more evil than his chilling reputation made him out to be. She stood within the huddled group of defeated, suppliant, Saudi soldiers, and with covert glances, saw how the general's face twisted each time another man was made to kneel before him. She saw how Noir's eyes brightened, and his tongue licked his lips at the moment a bullet was sent crashing into the prisoner's upturned face, how he seemed to become aroused at the horrific spectacle of death. Finally she had been singled out—perceived even by the mujahideen as a skinny young man—and given over for execution to a tall, powerful, dark Muslim fighter with sad eyes. But the big dark man had walked her away from the spot where the rest were being murdered one by one—fifty yards away, where the ground was uneven and mottled by clumps of sparse grass and scrub. She guessed he somehow knew she was female, and intended to use her as he wished away from the others before killing her.

But he had not used her, and he had made her place of execution a place of resurrection for her. She had not believed him at first, but when she looked into his eyes, she saw his heart, and there she saw he was giving her a new life while he pretended to take her old. She knew he placed himself at deadly risk by doing so, and she realized at that moment, without knowing how, that the dark mujahideen was not a Muslim. He had hurriedly told her what to do, that he was leaving his small bag with some provisions and water lying nearby, and then he shot her. He had fired his Kalashnikov assault rifle at the left side of her neck, under her ear, and the bullet burned as it grazed her skin. She had screamed and collapsed without faking it, and lay in the hot sand holding her breath. The dark soldier was gone, and after a few minutes she heard no more shooting. Then she heard the sounds of the mujahideen moving out, and soon she was left lying near the dead. When night fell, she began her journey away from those killing fields and toward a new life.

The first steps she took were heavy, hesitant, and aimless. In her heart she knew it made no difference—her old life, her new life. The world had become a place she did not want it to be: a sad, terrible charnel house, where man fed on man, hope was a fugitive, and love was carried off by the winds of hatred. But within the first hours, two things began to drive her, to give her purpose and strength. One was like an acid, eating at her sanity, her reason. There was no voice, but *something* told her she had a job to do. Even though her enemies had so far been Muslim even as she was Muslim, the *real* enemy of them all was the one who formed the European and Christian nations against the followers of Allah. The acid dripped onto her tongue, and the words burned there told her the greatest enemy was the greatest infidel, and that she must destroy him. She felt lost to the acid, lost to this sinister power that had somehow entered her. She could not fight it, she feared. There was a dark place within her mind, her heart, and she could not go there. She had to submit, obey, act, as if she were experiencing an out-of-body awareness while still *in* her body. She could observe her own actions, and she could question them, but she was not sure she could resist or change them.

The second thing that drove her, that kept her alive, that gave her a fragment of hope even as she fought her own demons in a hopeless world, was the dark soldier who had returned her life. She was a child of Allah, but in her life all her suffering had been so far caused by those equally faithful. Her brother, her parents, her chastity— these had all been forcibly taken from her by Muslims. But the dark soldier had given her life. He had looked into her eyes, had seen her as a young girl, as a fellow human being, and had called her a child of God. That he was a Christian among the Muslim mujahideen she could neither understand nor dispute, but she knew it with an immediate and unarguable clarity. *John* was the name he had told her, John. Against the war-scape of her life, against the demonic force that drove her, stood John—and because he stood, she would continue to fight the battles within, and continue to live until she found reason and peace.

She drank sparingly from a water bottle now and looked at the sad and bloody tableau spread before her. She was somewhere north of Al Jawf, west of where most of the fighting with the mujahideen had been. She was near the outer fences of some kind of trash dump, near a small town where spires of black smoke reached lazily for the somber skies. Sprawled along the edge of a black-topped road and in the ditch beside it were hundreds of bodies. The people, men and women in mostly civilian garb, had apparently been lined up and gunned down, their bodies left where they fell. She did not remember approaching them, but now she stood among the dead. She glanced down at her boots and saw near her right one the waxen skin and bluish fingers of a hand. The hand was on an outstretched arm of a thin-faced, slight young man with curly black hair, the beginnings of a wispy beard, and opaque, staring eyes. In the hand was a passport. She bent slowly, tugged at the passport until the dead fingers released it, and examined it. Not only was it current, but the document was French, as well, and in the name of Piet Dardon. She leafed through it and saw that before his death, the young man had traveled to Algeria, back to France, then to Jordan, which was the last entry stamp. She took a breath, hesitated, and then looked at the attached photo. A slim, pale, dark-eyed young face stared at her, the black hair short, the lips full. *Perhaps he had been kidded about being "girlish" or a "wimp,"* she thought. The photo was close enough, she knew. She made herself look down at the young man's dead face once more and said thank you as she turned to get away from his empty stare.

So she who had for twenty years been the girl, Faseem, from As Sulayyil, Saudi Arabia, became the young man, Piet Dardon, from Paris, France. She chewed her lip as she pulled open and rummaged through various scattered pieces of luggage, backpacks, and bags lying along the road. She had a new name; she was working on a new look. *Now*, she thought grimly, *all I need is a new life*.

+   +   +

It was all so normal. Life was going on around him, and on this morning he found himself suddenly *angry* about that. *Fools!* he wanted to shout. *Don't you understand what is happening to us?* But he didn't shout. He grudgingly admitted it was in fact a lovely morning, and he was in a lovely place, surrounded by people going about the business of living. Shops were open, cars purred along in the narrow streets, people stood shoulder to shoulder as they waited for the traffic light to change before crossing. Sometimes the muted hubbub was punctuated by a short burst of laughter, or of someone calling to another. He saw news-papers being sold, heard music coming from a corner café, watched as an old man scattered crumbs for a jostling flock of pigeons near a park. At first glance he might be taken for one of the young university students in the town. He was in his early twenties, tall and gangly, wearing washed-out jeans, work boots, a long-sleeved shirt with the sleeves rolled to his elbows, and a baseball cap. Cinched around his waist was a leather belt with a large silver buckle with the letter *T* emblazoned on it. On his back rode a beat-up backpack with a jacket strapped across the top. Closer in-spection would show more. He was lean and sunburned, and the skin of his hands was rough and scarred. He had deep crow's-feet etched into the corners of his clear green eyes, and a shade of rusty beard on his jaw. He was watch-ful and wary, and he moved with relaxed physical confi-dence, a controlled economy of energy. He was Tommy Church, son of Thomas Church, lately of the far ranch-lands of west Texas, USA.

Normal, he thought, *Here we are—man—the inhabiters of the planet Earth, which, if anyone took a moment to notice, appears to be in its final days, and what do we do? We live.* He stopped on the sidewalk in front of a small deli or bakery where a line of locals, college students and working stiffs, waited. He joined the queue, and after fumbling a bit with the language and the new currency, managed to walk out with a cup of coffee and a warm muffin. The rangy Amer-ican appeared not to notice the open or shy glances several of the young women in the place gave him as he moved through the small tables. He found a spot across the street and sat on a low wall while he ate his breakfast and watched the goings-on around him. He decided the coffee—rich, aromatic, hot—was probably the best coffee he had ever tasted. Lyrics from a tune ran through his head, something about life continuing even after the thrill was gone. But it wasn't the *thrill* of living, he realized. It was the *necessity* of it.

Really, he argued in his silent debate, *what choice does man have? We could all kill ourselves, take ourselves out en masse. The millions of us left on earth could line up and march like lemmings into the sea and be done with it.* He shook his head. Although he had heard reports of group suicides here and there, those had been rare enough to become news. There were probably many personal, individual cases also, he acknowledged, but for most people it was apparently still the desperate and unattractive choice it had always been in times of extreme stress, pain, sorrow, or fear. Besides, suicide was against God's law, and even if there were many varied opinions on the subject, and a full-scale war over it, God's laws still had some dominion over this world.

He took a bite of the moist and crumbly muffin and sipped the coffee. There was *food*, and man still availed himself of it, to sustain, to nurture. He had read somewhere that eating was an act of self-love, the care and maintenance of the body God had given one. He savored the taste of his breakfast and said, "Oh yeah! Must be lovin' myself this fine morning." The old man feeding the pigeons turned the see if Tommy were addressing him, and a young woman hurrying past smiled, shook her head, and said something in her own language. Tommy held the cup an inch from his lips and watched her as she strode down the sidewalk. He did not understand her words, but the shake of her head said no, while her smile said yes. He sighed. *Life*.

He was Tommy Church, son of Thomas Church, originally from Long Island, New York. He had tried college, bolted, and after knocking about for a while, found work he truly loved in Texas. He became a cowboy employed by a medium-size spread as a ranch hand, paid little, fed well, and promised nothing but a sound horse and plenty of open range to ride. His married sister lived in Virginia, his parents had divorced, and he was on his own for a time. There was a girl, too, a girl in his eyes unique and lovely, rare and beautiful. Maria. She had come across the border from Mexico, worked on the ranch at the great house, and was coveted by several of the other hands. But her smile, her warmth, her young woman's innocent touch was only for Tommy. For a time life for him was simple and clear. He had his work, he had Maria, and the future could only be good.

Then came the day of the disappearances, when millions of souls were literally lifted up, out of this life and away from this world. There were massive, global earthquakes; societies fell into chaos and anarchy; the order and structure of civilizations crumbled in man's fear and panic; and a howling darkness covered the earth. Those who knew Scripture asserted without hesitation that the Biblical end times had in fact arrived. All one had to do was take a glance at Revelation, and there it was. Others blamed it on aliens, some cosmic fluke, or a secret weapon directed against Christians by Muslims. Many not taken in the lifting up were devastated by the fact that they had *not* been taken, when others had, and they stumbled through the days in wanton fear, disappointment, and confusion. Since that day there had been other signs or occurrences Biblical scholars pointed to as confirmation. Large areas of the seas had turned bloodred. There had been burning rain, the ruination of crops worldwide, famine, disease, great loss of life. War had come, of course, as man fell right back into the global power struggles that had always been part of his history. This time it came in the form of a continent-storming Muslim uprising. The mujahideen forces of General lzbek Noir gutted Africa, pummeled the Middle East, and were poised to turn toward Europe. The fighting was horrific, the amount of human suffering unprecedented. None of that meant much to Tommy, at first. In the chaotic, vicious, panicked turmoil that followed the disappearances, his Maria was taken—not by the hand of God, but by the hand of man. He had been unable to get to her in time, and she was killed as she fought off her attackers. Tommy's heart had been blackened by the searing fires of anger, guilt, and revenge, and during those dark hours he willingly descended to the animal level as he avenged her. For a while his mind snapped, then became numb, and he wandered among the dead on the sprawling ranch, wounded and maddened by anger and loss. Finally, on the edge of death, he had been reunited with his father, who had left New York in search of his son.

He took the last bite of muffin, chewed it, and sighed. Since then, he had continued to do what most people did—live life. He was no Bible scholar, by any means, but at the insistence of his dad he had begun to study, with special attention paid to Revelation. All the signs were there, he acknowledged, and if that's the way it was going to be, he figured the next couple of years ought to be interesting indeed. But—and this was the point that seemed to be ringing in him this morning—after a sense-challenging seven years or so, there should be another *thousand* years of life on the still-great planet Earth. What was man to do? Man was to *keep on.* The way he saw it, if the Bible was in fact being validated right before the eyes of the masses, and man was still the child of God, then it was time to cast aside doubt and fear. It was time to embrace faith and approach the coming days in respectful wonder and a willingness to hear the Word and be true to it. He wished he were with his dad, so they could talk. His dad, Thomas Church, had gone from being a sort of apathetic, affable, agreeable agnostic to a full-fledged believer. He was still hesitant to say he was "born again." Tommy knew his father well enough to guess his dad's reticence came from his deep respect for the reality of faith, his refusal to prematurely claim something that he had not fully earned. But his dad told him he believed in the Bible, plain and simple, that God had a plan, and man had a clear responsibility: Have faith, and live the plan.

He stood, walked across the sidewalk, and threw his trash into a municipal can. *See?* He mused, *Here in Lyon, France, the bureaucracy still functions. The electrical power is on, hospitals and colleges are open, and the trash is being picked up on schedule. Even when he seems hopelessly confused, at war, and on the edge of complete panic, man does what must be done to* keep on. Tommy thought of his dad again, back home.

He thought it was such a cool thing that his dad had driven all the way out to west Idaho, met with his mom, and talked her into joining him for another try. That was love, sure as could be. He thought of Maria and wondered for a moment if he'd get another shot at love. He remembered visiting the New Christian Cathedral in Alabama, a church headed by that impressive black preacher, Henderson Smith. Nice people there, people who believed they were the children of God even amidst all the pain, loss, and confusion. He frowned as he remembered his last visit. There was that weird storm of sulfuric, burning rain coming down, the wind buffeting, fires starting on the roofs of houses. Totally scary. He arrived at the cathedral as the storm raged, in time to see some crazy guy shoot at the preacher and hit a woman instead. The guy had tried to run away after the shooting, but Tommy had tackled him, whacked him a couple of times until he dropped the gun, and held him for the police. The last he heard the woman, Ivy something, was in the hospital, and the crazy guy was in jail. There was another woman he and his dad had met there, too. Shannon Carpenter. Good people. His dad had told him he was sure—it was in his heart, in his head—that he and some of the others there made up *seven*, and the seven had been drawn together for a specific purpose by God, or through God, something like that.

Tommy passed a sidewalk kiosk and glanced at the newspapers stacked there. He couldn't read the French words, but he recognized the face. A large photograph of Minister Azul Dante, head of the European Coalition, smiled reassuringly at him. He had heard there had been

an attempt on Dante's life recently, and there was a huge
flap about it, various intelligence agencies all pointing the
finger at one another for failing to protect the official. In
Liverpool a couple of days ago, while waiting to sail down-
coast and cross the channel, Tommy had read an article
that said the shooter—he was part of a group of Arab
terrorists—had been found and killed along with four or
five of his companions a short distance from where a bullet had narrowly missed Dante. Dante's personal valet was
killed instead. *Par for the course*, he mused, *the poor schmoe
standing next to the king takes the hit.* The Reverend Henderson Smith had spoken of Azul Dante in glowing terms,
Tommy remembered. Something about the New Christian Cathedral, and others like it scattered around the
United States and maybe other parts of the world, teach-
ing the *new Biblical* message. And the nation-bonding political workings of Azul Dante tied into all of this. *Sounds
good to me*, he thought. His dad had some vague, undefined
misgivings about Dante, Tommy knew, but so far the guy
seemed to be helping the world pull it together. Not to
mention the whole Muslim mujahideen war machine
blasting its way across half the free world. They were led
by that demonic Izbek Noir, and according to a lot of believers, Azul Dante was the man who could put a coalition
force together to stop them.

He rubbed his face and shrugged to ease his shoulders.
All this deep thinking was giving him a headache. It was a
beautiful day, he was in a beautiful city on his way to adventure, and why should he bruise his brain thinking about

things he couldn't control anyway? He *was* on an adventure, just living in this world in these times, he thought. He had cowered with a huddle of terrified strangers in Savannah the night the skies turned to lead and then were streaked with the colors of the apocalypse. That was the night of the crushing rogue waves that inundated coastlines around the world after a huge fireball of burning ash fell from the heavens. He had seen with his own eyes the areas devastated by the earthquakes that followed, the lines of bodies pulled from the rubble. He had said a simple prayer asking for the safety of his loved ones—Sissy and Mitch, his mom and dad—felt in his heart they were okay, and kept moving. He gave his pickup truck to an old farmer, but kept the worn Bible he had found in it. He was turned away a couple of times, and finally talked his way onto a rust-streaked freighter of questionable lineage headed for the partially flooded north coast of Venezuela, then on down to Rio. He took some ribbing from that first rough crew about being a lost cowboy, but it hadn't taken long for him to learn the ropes. From Rio he had signed on to a German ship for the crossing to England. His cowboy hat just didn't work onboard, nor did his well-worn boots. He had given the hat to a Filipino cook who took a fancy to it, and the boots were in his backpack on the off chance he found himself around horses again. He had seen enough of the ocean, bloodred, metallic green, or purple blue, to last him all the rest of his days, but he was glad he had done it.

He had been in England only a week or so. It was sort of like home, he discovered, but the people spoke English funny. From there over to France, where he had hitch-hiked inland from Brest. Because he had no real destination and took his rides without care of direction, he had found himself in Lyon. He could head south into Italy, or backtrack if he wanted to visit Paris. Seeing Azul Dante was one of the reasons he was on this trip, he admitted to himself, and he figured Paris would eventually be the best city to get a chance. He hoped to hear Dante speak, sort of see and hear him in the flesh, see what the guy was all about. In the meantime, he had a few bucks in his pocket, a valid passport, and no strings.

He watched as an old woman shuffled toward him, pushing a cart loaded with rags. *We still have homeless people*, he thought, *even in enlightened France.* He took a closer look as he passed her, and wondered if she were a gypsy rather than homeless, or was that the same? The rags turned out to be clothing she might be collecting or selling; the cart was a baby carriage without a baby. He stopped and looked all around him at the morning hustle-bustle in Lyon. No babies, no children. The greatest horror, the greatest cause of pain on the day of disappearances, came with the unimaginable taking of the world's children. This, in his mind, negated the Muslim-secret-weapon argument, because all Earth's Muslim children were taken in the same blink of an eye. The mother's cry in Sri Lanka sounded exactly the same as her cry in Medina, in Tehran, in Chicago, Santa Fe, Tokyo, and Lima. Gone, just like that, the children of God's children were gone, and the pain was beyond measure. His own sister, Sissy, married to Mitch the college professor over in Virginia—her baby had been in her womb and then not. When he and his dad had visited them, Sissy told them about it, and he remembered her words. "Where my baby was, is empty. I am empty, and only new life can fill me again." She had been terrified of the Biblical implications of the disappearances, not because it heralded the end of the world, but because it meant she would never have a chance to give birth to a child. Their father had done his best to convince her that all of it was part of God's plan, and if man was meant to live on, even in the end times, then new life would indeed happen again. They had left her filled with hope and resolve.

Tommy crossed the street. He had no particular place to go, but always felt better on the move. He wanted to let go of his cluttered thoughts for a while, be a simple tourist, and just observe the small chunk of the world he currently inhabited. He turned and bumped shoulders with a young woman who came out of a sidewalk shop, causing a small stack of files and magazines she carried to slide away from her grasp. He managed to grab them in his big hands before they fell. He stood close in front of her, taking in her beauty as she gathered her materials neatly in her arms. She had an oval face, big eyes with full brows, long light-brown hair parted in the middle and brushed out to her shoulders, and pale skin. She had a small nose, a wide mouth, and a tongue that pushed against her lower lip in concentration. She wore a white long-sleeved pullover, a beige skirt to her ankles, a thin black belt, and shiny black low-heeled shoes. She was lovely, smelled clean and fresh, and the smile she finally gave him was enough to instantly clear his mind of anything he had been thinking. *"Merci beaucoup,"* she said in a soft voice, and walked away. He stood watching her, a lopsided grin his mute response, and was rewarded with a glance over her shoulder before she disappeared around a nearby corner. *Yep,* he thought, *Even if the world is ending, that was a girl, and I am a guy—and I'll bet life will indeed go on.*

CHAPTER THREE

Hiram Sarco studied himself in the full-length mirror in one corner of the bedroom suite in his luxury New York penthouse. He liked the image reflected back at him. The whole look said *power,* baby, and power was what Hiram Sarco was all about. He used the manicured fingers of his right hand to flick a stray hair behind one ear, and he pursed his lips. To be honest, he remonstrated with himself, he was all about wealth, but power and wealth. They were the same, you know? Came from the same table, held hands, drank the *good stuff.* He mentally fondled an old favorite. *Heard the expression "money talks"? Well, money doesn't talk. Money jumps up on the table, kicks everything off, rips open its shirt, beats its chest, screams for anything it wants—and* gets *it.* Thus, money was power, yes? He ran his fingers lightly through the hair on top of his large round head. It was a toupee. *But not some crummy rug, baby—this was a coupla thou worth of weave, and it looked good, looked real.* He looked over his shoulder in the mirror at the two cell phones lying on the dresser near the room phone, almost willing them to ring. He waited for the word, and when the word came, he would be launched. He would be back in action.

He frowned. Even with the messed-up communications everyone put up with nowadays, dumb satellites on the fritz half the time, he *still* gets a call this morning from his second ex's hysterical sister. How she tracked him down, he had no idea. She's in tears on the phone, wanting him to know his second ex was apparently one of the many dead in Hilton Head. Seems her overpriced condo, that *he* had to pay for, collapsed during that night of the earthquakes, tidal waves, and hurricane winds. They were having a common service for everyone feared lost, cried the sister of his second ex, and shouldn't he attend? *Yeah, right*, he thought. He had told her he'd try. It was a gimme, he figured. No more dumb hassles from the ex, and when he needed it, he could use her loss in the sympathy angle.

He turned, studied his form, and sucked in his gut a little. Right at this moment, he knew, at this point in his life, he did not need sympathy. He admired the tailored charcoal suit he wore like a suit of armor, the crisp shirt, discreetly patterned silver tie, gleaming black shoes. It all said *power*. He turned, walked across the room to the breakfast table, and sipped the rich coffee in the fine china cup. He nibbled a croissant and gazed out across the sturdy, still-standing Manhattan skyline. He felt composed, confident, as if he could stand right there in that room, suspended in the reality of who and what he was, while he waited for *the* phone call. His confidence, well earned and validated every day, allowed him to revel in the moment, to drink in the possibilities . . . the *potential*, baby. He envisioned the lovely, hungry, starstruck face of that young female interviewer from the other day while he put on a professorial air and thought of a few of his favorite words.

Kingmaker, he was called. He had taken the time to see if there was an actual definition of his job title, and found "One who wields powerful influence in the enthronement of a king." The words *powerful influence* resonated within his formidable ego. The verb he liked also, as it pointed back to the one who acted, the one who *made it happen*, as in "to king, to *place* on a throne, to *make* a king of, to *elevate* to a kingdom." He was Hiram Sarco, maker of kings. He glanced at the phones, then at the concrete-and-steel skyline once more. *If I stand beside the king I have "elevated," or "made," does that make me a king also? Like a lesser king of some kind?* The word *lesser* bothered him. No, better to be the man standing at the elbow of the king, recognized for his power and influence by all who mattered.

One of his cell phones buzzed, and he skipped across the room with surprising agility to pick it up. He saw by the displayed number it wasn't *the* call, and answered briskly, "Sarco."

"Mr. Sarco? This is Bennie. Sorry to call so early, but we've got a problem, like a *major* problem."

"And what on earth could that be?" responded Sarco. Benjamin Tasson was head of one of the most powerful and prestigious publicity firms in the world, owned by Sarcom, of course, and he was one of the few who had a direct line to Hiram Sarco.

"That luncheon press conference for Chat Silver on the East Side today. Now she says she can't do it unless Kendall is there. So you told me Kendall is in town, I call his people, they say no way he'll come, because last time we sent your limo and he got carsick because it's too big. I said we'd get a smaller limo, they said forget it 'cause he's tired of limos anyway. I said we'd send your helicopter, but they said he'd get airsick. It's like he just don't wanna go, you know? And if I don't have Kendall, then I don't have Chat, and the whole thing goes down the tubes."

I'm waiting for a call from the new most powerful man in the world, and I gotta deal with the multiple and over-the-top egos of a hip-hop diva and her movie-star boyfriend? mused Sarco. He took a breath and reminded himself that handling this nonsense was what *made* him, and to be fair, he still *liked* being the one who got it done. When he was profiled, as he often was, as an amazing success story, his "hands on" work ethic was lauded. He had been known to personally deliver contracts, help a valet fix a flat on a limo, refill paper towel dispensers in office bathrooms, and escort various female luminaries who found themselves unattended for some gala. That he did these things only when it worked for him didn't seem to matter. Ben Tasson knew Hiram Sarco insisted on having the final say in these matters, even if they seemed trivial. That these stupid ego-crises events still went on, even in the midst of what many said were the end times—and even if these *weren't* the end times, these were certainly weird, frightening, uncertain, and tumultuous times—amazed and amused him. He reviewed a conversation he had been part of a couple of days ago about this very thing. Some publicity flack from one of the major houses wondered why the entertainment business was still *in* business, what with this being the end of the world and all. He had reminded the guy of how millions of people who were still *here* began to return to their churches, or *any* churches after the disappearances. The steeple people flew back to the pew, he had opined, because they searched for answers and reassurances. The other side of that search, of course, was denial. When times were hard, like these times, people wanted to be entertained, to be *taken away* from their troubles for a while. Glamour, style, film, music. Show biz, baby. It still mattered, it was still important, and it still made money.

He was a born skeptic, of course, and a self-taught cynic, but admitted he could still be surprised by how *small* people were. Take these two schmucks, Chat Silver and Kendall Kraft. Silver could move her body better than she could sing, barely wrapped it in tiny diaphanous outfits, and had one current hit called "No Tomorrows." Kraft was young, had a fine, chiseled face, blue eyes, and pouty lips, big money behind him, and one blockbuster film during which, in Hiram Sarco's opinion, he showed how he could use the same expression to denote lust, anger, glee, confusion, and resolve. But these were the people Hiram Sarco, through his media and entertainment superconglomerate, Sarcom, *made*. And it all added up to money. He indirectly put movie stars into roles, and put singers on

tour and in prime-time interviews. He arranged endorse-
ments for superstar athletes, placed CEOs in international
corporations, and did PR for ex-politicos, ex-dictators, and
ex-madams. He felt he had a direct effect on national elec-
tions, with presidential candidates from every party woo-
ing him. He did it all with communications. *"You can knock
over the biggest tree in the whole forest,"* he liked to say, *"but if
no one hears it, baby, do you make a sound? You can be a movie
star on home video, or Sarcom can show your face to the world."*
He was print media, he was television, he was cable, and he
was satellite. He was Sarcom, and now he was one phone
call away from the absolute *top table*, baby.

"Bennie," he said patiently, "Kendall doesn't want to
look like he's being chauffeured in for Chat, okay? Sure,
he wants to *be* there, but it has to be on his terms. Call Sid,
tell him to get a couple of his baddest motorcycles down to
Kendall's hotel. Tell Kendall's guy—Pauli—tell Pauli to
remind Kendall that Chat digs that whole biker thing, you
know? He can ride across town in his famous leather
jacket, stomp into the press conference like a big deal,
Chat will kiss him till his lips bruise, and it will be swell.
Yeah?"

"Yeah, Mr. Sarco, double yeah. They'll *both* like it! You
are a genius!"

"I thought you knew that, Bennie," replied Sarco, subconsciously puffing his chest out. "Now you get it done."
He disconnected and said, "Putz."

He glanced at the *Times* lying on the table with his
breakfast. The lead stories had to do with the war. The

mujahideen forces of Izbek Noir had unaccountably paused after chewing up the new Iraqi army all along the Kuwait–Saudi–Iraq border. Observers had expected Noir to perhaps turn east into Iran, rather than have an enemy at his back when he turned toward Turkey and beyond. There were reports of an accord of some kind between Noir and the Muslim leaders of Iran, which frightened everyone, but there had been no formal announcement. Either way, when the mujahideen turned west, they would for the first time encounter large, mostly Christian, European Coalition forces pulled together by Azul Dante, led by the British general, Reginald Urquhart, a former NATO commander. Coaliton forces had battled the mujahideen armies in North Africa, slowly pushing the Muslims back across sands already bloodied, but at great cost and with nebulous results. Land won back was devastated, whole countries and populations laid to waste, and the "victors" accomplished nothing more than pushing the Muslim hordes out of ruined places of death and desolation. In other places around the world, there were smaller versions of the same horror. Africa was gutted. South America was at war within; the far eastern governments tried to deal with fiery Muslim uprisings all over; Japan, Korea, and China eyed one another nervously; and almost nowhere on Earth was immune from sporadic, small, searing acts of terror wrought by the fanatical followers of Izbek Noir. Even the United States had seen terrorism. So far it had been only against fuel-related targets—huge truck convoys, tank farms, port facilities. But one airliner had recently been downed by a heat-seeking missile as it lifted off from Chicago, and President Clara Reese had advised the American people to remain vigilant.

All of this was quickly acquired and stored in his head. He acknowledged world events as important in minute-by-minute increments, each piece in one way or another related globally, each segment having the potential to be used to his advantage. He had found it especially amusing through the years to serve those on both sides of a conflict at the same time, and to profit from both. Like the companion article he read—there was good stuff, rich with possibilities. Ten leaders of the "free" world were scheduled to meet to discuss the viability, the possibility, of naming one man, one new leader, as supreme. This was, even in these unbelievably chaotic times, a hard sell. Even in the face of an army that might just destroy the world, leaders of various countries still clung desperately to their own little seats, loath to hand over control. The one man was Azul Dante, of course, and everyone knew it. Dante was *already* running things, as Sarco saw it. But his position as big dog had to be formalized, recognized.

And that's where Hiram Sarco came in.

His corporation, and it surely, undisputedly *was* his, Sarcom, spoke to the masses. It was the voice, the music, the images of information that people around the world relied on to keep up with what was happening in their lives. It could be in the form of a broadcast television morning news show, an afternoon gab fest hosted by an ex-sitcom "personality," 24-7 cable news feeds, late-night ruminations by a panel of experts, or a satire-laced "comedy hour." All over the globe, people tuned in to see the familiar, reassuring faces of commentators telling them the way it was. Radio stations? Sarcom was hundreds, and the format varied from suavely intellectual to savagely political, from wholesome to coarse and raw. Music? Any and all you could imagine, some of it with real lyrics. Sarcom was on-line, of course, *the* Internet news source, and in print under a hundred banners in twenty languages. Sarcom was *the word* for many, so huge, so pervasive, that most people of the world had no time to consider words like *biased*, *slanted*, *manipulative*, or *monopoly*—let alone *Orwellian*, or *Big Brother*. Hiram Sarco, thinking about it, smirked. Sarcom even owned various religious media outlets, television and radio stations dedicated to spreading the message of what many were calling the New Christian Organizations. He puffed up his chest again, confident, infused with a reckless feeling of omnipotence. *You want to hear the voice from on high?* he thought. *Listen to Sarcom, baby.*

The phone buzzed. A European exchange.

"Hiram Sarco."

"Mr. Sarco, this is Azul Dante."

"Yes, Minister Dante."

"Thank you for taking my call so early."

"I'm honored to speak with you at any hour, sir," said Sarco.

"Well, thank you for that kindness. Listen, I have, as you know, been casting about for someone who might help me solidify, or perhaps clarify is a better word, my status in the eyes of the world's leaders, yes?" Pause. "My personal aide was tragically taken from me recently, as you know, and I need help."

"Yes, sir. I was saddened to hear about that senseless attempt on your life by those animals."

"Yes. Well, I'm calling to say I've studied Sarcom, and you as its head, of course, the success you've had, the vision you've shown. I have decided I'd like to have you stand beside me in this dark hour, perhaps help me, if you see my cause as just, as . . . important. I am but one man trying to be heard in these stormy and unpredictable times. You, through your amazing Sarcom, can give my voice power, can help me send my message to all corners of the earth. Do you think you could be in Paris soon?"

"Tomorrow, sir." *You have that little Gulfstream G-V, on loan from the Brits, Dante,* mused Sarco, I've *got my own private 767, baby, with more high-tech communications goodies than* Air Force One. *Prettier flight attendants. Better food.*

"Excellent. Have your secretary contact my assistant, Sophia Ghent, at the Château Elise. I'll look forward to seeing you."

The call was disconnected, and Hiram Sarco felt a swelling in his chest as a big grin stretched his lips. "Yeah, baby," he said.

+　　+　　+

Shannon Carpenter looked at her hands, which were being held in the warm, strong grip of Ted Glenn. He had big hands, hands he had used all his life to build things, just as her husband, Billy, had. But Billy Carpenter and her three children were gone, all taken—lifted up—on *that day*. Billy had left his old Bible for her to find, and through it, and the passages he had marked for her, she had come to know Jesus Christ even as her broken heart seemed beyond ever feeling again. She had made her way to the New Christian Cathedral in Selma, Alabama, from her empty home in Ohio. Billy had left a note in the Bible mentioning the Reverend Henderson Smith and the Cathedral, and Shannon had felt drawn to it. She met Smith, Ivy Sloan-Underwood, and her husband, Ron. She had also met Thomas Church when he passed through briefly with his son, Tommy. She had come to know, along with Smith, Church, Ivy, and Ron, that they were somehow part of *seven*. Their coming together was part of God's plan, and they had a mission of some kind. It was spiritual, this being part of seven, it was inside the heart, it unnerved her, and frightened her . . . it was so very real.

This man who sat with her now, in the shade of a reaching tree in the small parklike area behind the Cathedral, he was real also, as were his feelings for her. It was late morning; the skies were clear but for a few lazy, puffy clouds low on the horizon. A slight breeze pulled at the branches and leaves of the tree, and a couple of mockingbirds competed from opposite sides of the green expanse. They had spread a blanket, sipped cold iced tea, ate sliced apples, and read passages from the Bible to each other for a half hour or so. It had become one of her favorite things, sharing time with this big, gentle, considerate, and unpretentious man. He had caught her off guard this morning, though. She knew as she sat reading that his eyes were not on the Bible in his lap, but on her. She had looked up a couple of times to find him gazing at her with a funny smile, and when she asked him once, "What?" he looked away and said sheepishly, "It's the light in your hair, the sun against the skin of your face, your eyes. It's just that you're, you know, you're lovely." She had always thought of herself as plain, and the closest Billy had ever come to talking about her like that was to say she was "the pick of the litter." Being here now, with her new spiritual self, with this man, was like another life, a new life, and the things he said to her seemed like they came from a poem, and they made her feel like a young girl.

She scolded herself for being surprised at what he asked as he gently pulled her Bible from her grasp and took her hands in his. She should have seen it, should have guessed from the way he had been with her.

"Marry you, Ted?" she repeated, "Oh . . ."

"Shannon," he said as he leaned a bit closer to her, "I know you had Billy, and you loved him and he was a good husband, and you had your kids, and you guys were a family and had a life and that was the only life you ever wanted or needed. And you know I had my Rhonda, and our daughter, and I swear I loved them as much as a man can, and was thankful for the life we had. But they were lifted up, and Billy and your kids were, too, and you and me, we became like the others we call Christians Not Taken—we became people stuck here in this world that seems like it's comin' to its end."

"But, Ted—"

"Since that hard day we've both—you and me—we've

found Jesus, and we've found each other. You know I'm a simple man, and I've got less now than when I had somethin', and even then I didn't have much. I don't have college, but I've worked hard, honest work all my life, and I can take care of you, of us. I can keep us goin', and I . . . I can love you." He stopped, took a breath, held her eyes with his, and added, "I *do* love you."

"But *marriage*, Ted?" she managed, her pulse beating.

"Yep, marriage, *the* partnership, husband and wife. That's what I'm talkin' about." He shrugged and looked at their hands. "Oh, I know somebody could argue, you know, 'Hey, Ted, you big dummy, it's the end of the world, man, getting married now won't mean anything.' But I think they'd be wrong." He looked up at the reaching tree, at the skies beyond. "The children of the world—yours, Shannon, mine, all of them—taken in the blink of an eye. But millions of men and women around the world are still here and still part of God's plan." He pointed to her Bible, "It's in the Scripture, I don't have to tell you, even though Revelation *is* a hard read, and to be honest I'm not sure I understand every bit of it, it talks about *time*. Time through which the life of this world plays out, and living men and women are here and we *also* must play it out. I'm still a man, and you are still a woman. We are mere human beings and the children of God, and we still have souls, hearts, minds, bodies. We are physical, we are spiritual, and we are *alive*."

Shannon felt a fullness in her heart as she listened. This was a man of few words, she knew, and she guessed he had been going over this discussion in his head for some time now.

"Listen," said Ted. He wiped his face with one big hand and licked his lips before charging on with the things he was determined to say. "Man has always needed woman. Man is *incomplete* without woman, and man alone cannot possibly succeed in carrying out God's plan. God lifted up millions, and He lifted up the children, but He left millions of men and women to carry on, and we will, we *are*. So, Shannon, I'm a man, and I'm incomplete in this ongoing world. I need a partner, a woman, a wife . . . and I choose you." He sat back, folded his arms across his big chest, and watched her like a man who has said his piece and hoped he said it right.

She looked at him, watching his eyes. She saw in them sincerity, honesty, and love. She smiled.

"But, Ted," she said quietly, and heard him sigh. "You are right, of course, all of your arguments, your reasoning. You are right."

"But . . . ," he said as quietly.

"But," she replied, "but it's such a—a *serious* thing, marriage, Ted. It's a promise, a covenant, a very real giving over of oneself to another in total commitment. Ted, I just lost the man I had committed to, and now I've given my heart over to Jesus. How can you know I can live up to what you see in us, when I still don't know what my life is, what my commitment is, what my life promises?"

He shrugged. "Because of you, Shannon, who you are."

"Ted." She held his gaze, then felt her cheeks flush, and looked down at her hands as he reached out to take them in his once more. "Ted, we've hugged, we've held hands, we've kissed, and"—she looked up into his eyes again—"and I've liked it, especially the kissing."

He grinned, but turned his face.

"But a marriage is between a man and a woman, Ted," she went on, "and we are, as you said, physical, and our joining—if we understand God's plan—is designed so children will come of the union. And in each child would be a soul, and a spark of God. Yes, we'd be partners, and you are a good man, and I know you'd stand by me and take care of me and we could be there for each other in these times." She felt awkward, uncertain. She ran the fingers of both hands up through her hair, then shook it out. "Since we're being totally honest, I'll tell you this, Ted. There's a part of me, and I can't deny it, that feels, um, excited about—you know—I no longer have a husband, I'm with a new man, a good man whom I am attracted to, and I sort of—imagine us, you know, um . . ." She straightened and smiled. "It's like I don't know if that would be *right*. I mean, now, in these times when we have important work to do, God's work, and it might be selfish, simple. You've heard the discussions we've had with Reverend Smith. I mean, it comes up all the time, about whether creating children in these end times is part of God's plan, if there will be more children. Are we to bring children into a world that's in its last days? Children will become the people who populate God's earth to live, to learn the difference between right and wrong, good and evil, to learn about Jesus and His sacrifice? It's like no one really knows. If there will *not* be more children, then what purpose would there be for a man and woman, um, other than the *feelings*, you know, to—" She let her hands fall into her lap and shrugged. "I don't know."

He said nothing, but his silence was warm and embracing.

After a moment, she spoke again. "Now we have determined there are seven of us, Ted. I've told you it's as real as a thing can be in my head, in my heart. Ivy feels it, her husband, Ron, Reverend Smith, that Thomas Church who was here—and that news reporter, um, Cat Early, and a man named Jameson, someplace. We are going to act on those feelings, and you know we've decided our part of the plan is missionary. To get out there as messengers for the God we have always had, the God who gave us the Scriptures and His son and His love. You know what manner of beasts are described in Revelation, Ted, what terrible things happen during these times. Man might be completely lost, might fall away from the Word, be led away, might be turned into the damned. But if we keep the Word out there, get into the world with the message just like missionaries have done for thousands of years, maybe some will be saved, and maybe we will have done our part. I'm going, Ted. We'll all scatter to different points, different countries, where we can spread the good gospel that's always been there if people would just listen—"

"And I'll go with you, Shannon," said Ted, his eyes bright, "I don't care where, I don't care how, I don't care what manner of man, beast, or trouble we find along the way. Where you stand, I will stand, where you spread the Good Word, I'll mark the page, where you fight the fight, I'll fight alongside." He paused, and his eyes became wet. "I'll stand with you as companion, Shannon, partner, friend, or husband. I'll stand with you."

Her eyes filled with tears, she leaned into his arms, and they hugged tightly. "I know, Ted," she said, "I know . . . and I thank God for you."

CHAPTER FOUR

Azul Dante, Prime Minister of the European Coalition, new leader of the free world, best hope for mankind, felt confined. He was impatient, eager to bust out, to spread his wings, to unleash all the volcanic energy and power he knew simmered inside his form. But he could not do so; it was not yet time. Sure, the world, what was left of it, and man—what was left of him—was ripe for the picking, his for the taking. But certain small steps still must be taken, little pieces of the mosaic still had to fall into place, and until then, he could only bide his time. He shook himself, and a rash of goose bumps rippled the skin of his face. It was an odd sensation, walking with infantile metronomic steps along the primitive digits of linear time, when he was actually not a creature of time or of space. Odd. Confining.

He stood at the windows of his hotel, looking out over the far landscape around Chartres, France. Nice town, he thought, nice church, filled with nice people all disillusioned, frightened, and hungry for a leader who would once more set their world right. He was tall, with an athletic body, and he had a handsome and craggy face topped with salt-and-pepper hair cut in a schoolboy style. A carefully maintained wayward shock of the hair hung over one eye, so he could casually sweep it back in place with his hand in the manner of a well-loved past U.S. president. Nothing by chance, nothing accidental. His suit, of the finest quality, was impeccably tailored, his shirt was custom made, his tie perfectly knotted, his shoes gleamed. He understood *appearance*, studied it seriously, and maintained his own to full effect. He felt a thread of heat warp through him and smiled at his physical self. The heat, he knew, came from an abstract thought regarding his attractiveness. Not only men saw in him what they respected, but women did also. Mankind was almost a slave to physical desire between the sexes, he mused, and his base form was not immune. His appraisal was substantiated daily by women who told him, in one way or another, that they were his for the taking. He knew there was something about the human heart that made his being a widower even more appealing. His personal history, dutifully reported as he made his first appearances on the world stage, included the sad fact that he had lost a young wife and child to a Muslim suicide bomber in Croatia, years ago. The young woman and the child had been cynically contrived, of course, but the world did not know it. *Talk about your sacrificial lambs*, he mused. Perhaps it was because women saw in that loss his commitment, that he was a man capable of keeping a promise. Whatever it was, women constantly signaled they wanted to *really know* him. His eyes narrowed, his lips thinned out, and he chuckled. The sound was like that of ice cubes rattling in a metal cup. *Oh, no, you don't*, he thought.

He was anxious on this day, unsettled. He had been worrying of late, nagged by sophomoric feelings of jealousy. He glanced to his left, at the Bible lying on the coffee table. He found it a loathsome and troubling book, misleading, inaccurate, and small. He made it a point to carry one with him, though, as part of his *things*. The "people of the book" found it reassuring to see him with it, and he occasionally referred to it in his speeches, for their approval and his entertainment. Of course, at the moment of his *becoming*, as a created being, he was aware of every written word of man, every verse, every record, every history, every "revelation." But he found the act of reading to be pleasant. The whole symbiotic relationship between the inked symbols on the page taken in through the eyes to the brain, processed, and understood was, for the most part, a pleasant and elementary pastime. But this *Scripture*, this *Word*—he felt it was condescending and diminishing in its superior assumption of complete and unalterable accuracy. *How accurate could it be*, he thought, *the supposed Word of God transcribed by the brutish, primitive, and ignorant hand of man?*

He crossed the room, picked up the Bible, and felt the same bothersome lash of static electricity he felt each time he touched one. He watched the pages fall open to 2 Thessalonians, 2:9. He read, "The coming of the lawless one will be in accordance with the work of Satan displayed in all kinds of counterfeit miracles, signs, and wonders." He frowned and stroked his chin. The pages fell again, this time to Revelation 13 words he had stared at before. "The dragon gave the beast his power," he read, "and his throne and great authority." He scanned the part about the head wound, smiled as he remembered the assassin's crude and slow bullet, the energy curve he had transmitted with the blink of an eye, the exploding of Drazic's head. That had been perfect. The attempt on his life made him more valid and valuable to the observing world, and the immediate killing of the Muslim "suspects" in the attempt solidified the face of the common enemy. He knew who had sent the real assassin, and as that thought came to him, the number *seven* ricocheted through him like a wasp. He blinked, cursed, and dismissed it. He did not want to be distracted, and returned his mind to what was really bothering him. He needed no *God;* he needed no one to *give him* his power, his authority, his throne; he was not here in accordance with the work of that other being of like substance. No, he *was*, he had *become*, he *is*, and *he had no equal.* Besides, he argued, if the dragon (clumsy metaphor for what was in fact a beautiful entity) gave the beast his power and his throne, blah, blah, blah, then it was now *his.* The dragon, according to the way he read these fine words, had *given it up*, and was thus diminished. Certainly less than he. He nodded and spoke to the empty room. "It's simply a desire to know one's *place*."

He set the Bible on a desk, blew on his fingertips to cool them, and smirked. He had sent out another installment of his message, *willed* it actually, in the darkness just before dawn. There were all those churches out there, all across the globe, the *New* Christian churches. In the fear and confusion of those first terrifying days after the disappearances, millions cried out for help, for answers, for explanations. Many crying out were not part of any religion or set of beliefs, people who lived their lives of free will, not wishing to spend a lot of time worrying about the big picture, or about *meaning*. Many of these people turned to the churches they had shunned all their lives when their world convulsed. Millions of *Christians*, those who considered themselves believers, made a beeline back to the nearest pew after weird things began happening to Earth that seemed to match events described in Revelation. The strongest catalyst for these so-called Christians Not Taken, he knew, was their confusion over *why* they weren't "lifted up" like the others. All these "people of the book" hurried back to church, looking for guidance, reassurance, and answers. A poisonous smile twisted his face. They wanted answers, and the preachers—those trusted voices of the Word—would give it to them, especially in the *New* Christian Cathedrals and churches. They would hear the Word, but within the old stories would be a new truth.

He heard a discreet knock on the door. "Please come in, Sophia," he called pleasantly.

Sophia Ghent was a tall, full-bodied young woman with an almost translucent complexion, big eyes behind big glasses, a lovely face, and brown hair pulled into a tight bun on the top of her head. She wore one of her business-look navy skirt-and-jacket combinations, a white blouse with narrow collar, and navy low-heeled shoes.

"Hiram Sarco, from New York, Mr. Dante. He has arrived, and his secretary has contacted me. He seems anxious to meet you."

"And why wouldn't he be, Sophia?" kidded Dante, forcing himself into a better mood, "I'm about to be the best thing that ever happened to him."

"Yes, sir."

He sensed the reticence in her, the hesitation. He knew it was about that young man, an American "diplomat" she met a few weeks ago, here in Paris. James Devane was the man's name—athletic, unlettered, and plain, in Dante's estimation. Of course Devane was not a *real* diplomat, but a member of one of the American security agencies. All these agencies had initials identifying them, he knew, and he felt they should all be called RRD—Rough, Ready, and Dumb. But. But Devane was *American*, and like it or not, the United States of America was a big and extremely important part of this world. Since the president and first lady had been among those taken on *that* day, the country had been capably led by Clara Reese, who had been the vice president in the former administration. America had a sturdy infrastructure, was financially strong, had the best communications and logistics found anywhere, and it had weathered the chaos and upheaval that ravaged most of the world after the disappearances. It was a strange country, he mused, where religion was woven into the very fabric of it, but a place where *freedom* allowed all manner of dissention, disagreement, and discourse. In America, a minority of opinion was given due respect by the majority. It was a democratic republic based on capitalism, formed in pursuit of God, while great debates raged within about the *reality* of God. He shook his head. Still, America had proved to the world through its brief history that provoking its people was a mistake. Nobody made war like America, even though they sent their young men and women to war hampered by self-imposed *rules*, which he found ludicrous in the extreme. But America had wealth, power, and status, and his message would find great voice there, and thus the world. He looked at Sophia's expectant expression and knew it was time to tighten her loyalty to him.

"Sophia," he said casually, "Do you remember that young American, Mr. Devane? Supposed to be part of their diplomatic staff, but we now know he's a bit more than that, isn't he?" He almost laughed out loud at how her expression changed. He had already done a deep self-examination regarding his feelings about Sophia and James Devane. It *bothered* him that she was attracted to the American. He experienced a sort of juvenile jealousy, actually struggled with it. He found his feelings, his reaction, odd and entertaining. The feelings were real, though, and he had acted harshly at first, using his pull to have the young man sent off on other assignments, away from Sophia. He knew he could not have a relationship with Sophia—or with any woman, for that matter—but he liked having her on his arm. She was an attractive and intelligent companion, and the powerful and worldly men with whom he worked *expected* him to have one like her at his disposal.

"Yes, Azul," Sophia replied cautiously. "We saw him recently on that terrible day in Nice, when those maniacs tried to kill you, and we . . . we lost Drazic."

"Good," said Azul with a smile. "And young James Devane was not only there, he *acted*, took immediate action in our behalf, exposed himself to danger, and I—well, I was impressed. He was the first one to spot and return fire at the assassins."

"I remember," said Sophia quietly. Her mind's eye replayed those horrible, terrifying moments when the stillness of a sulky gray morning was shattered by the punch of a rifle shot, people screaming and shoving, Drazic sitting slowly, a dark hole between his eyes, a smear of blood behind his head. Then there had been another burst of fire. That had been James shooting at one of the assassins on a nearby roof. Then there was more shooting a minute or so later, and it was over, the Muslim hit men killed in their apartment by the combined security forces. "I remember," she said again.

"I have asked that Devane be assigned as part of my security detail, now that things seem to be getting nasty," said Dante.

"Here? With you, with . . . us?"

"Yes, Sophia, with us, and I hope you'll do your best to integrate him into the team, make him feel welcome, all that. Okay?"

"Yes," she answered, her face beaming even as she visibly willed herself to remain impassive. "Of course, Azul."

"Good," he said, laughing inside. How transparent she was. Besides, he would rather have Devane close, where he could keep an eye on him, and on Sophia. It would amuse him to watch Sophia attempt to surreptitiously pursue the crude object of her misdirected and ignorant desires.

Lastly, he was sure that given time, Sophia would see the difference between the superficial Devane and the worldly, infinitely attractive Dante. "And what else?"

"Excuse me?" she responded. Then her eyes widened. "Oh, I'm sorry, sir. Hiram Sarco is waiting for my call, and so far we have seven of the ten leaders lined up for your conference. We expect to have the other three locked in today."

"Excellent work, Sophia," he said in dismissal.

She smiled, nodded, and closed the door behind her.

He took a breath. He thought about *seven*, then he thought about kingmakers and kings, and lastly he thought about the Mosque of Omar, the Temple, and a pig.

+ + +

"Ivy," said Ron Underwood carefully, "I . . . I thought it had been agreed, we all agreed."

"Well, go then, Ron," replied his wife, Ivy Sloan-Underwood, as she fought to keep the edge of bitterness from her voice. "Go with the others, spread the good word, save a few souls along the way."

"Oh, Ivy," Ron responded wearily, "How can you still be so angry, so . . . cynical?" He was tall and lanky, with a mop of black hair, pale skin, and black-rimmed glasses. He wore loafers, slacks, a buttoned shirt, and a sweater vest, which gave him the look of the college professor he had been before the day the world changed forever. They were in Ivy's room on the second floor of the dormitory-style apartments provided by the cathedral for staff and visitors. Ivy, though seemingly reconciled with Ron, still refused to room with him, and their newly developing relationship suffered under the tension. Ivy sat on the edge of the bed; Ron straddled a straight-backed chair.

Ivy shrugged. She was a woman who made men turn their heads to stare, with an attractive body, long dark hair, and a face that was sensual in its model-like severity. On this day she wore sandals, white shorts, and a sleeveless coral blouse. All her adult female life, she had been aware of her effect on men, and even while her marriage to Ron was solid, she was constantly seeking their attention. She had given Ron one son, Ronnie, who had been born severely disabled, a "special needs," wheelchair-bound child. She had loved Ronnie with a fierce determination, was a good mother, but railed against the injustice of having a child who demanded constant attention yet had very little potential for realizing what she perceived to be a full life. Her anger and frustration had poisoned her heart. When a dark entity came to her, one who called himself Thad Knight, a tempter who saw right into her desires and weaknesses, she did not turn away. Her tempter held her vulnerability in his cunning hands and offered her a deal. She took it, knowing she stood on the edge of the abyss. When Ronnie was "taken" on the day of disappearances and she realized Thad Knight's promise came from the tongue of a serpent, she became lost. The voice of Reverend Henderson Smith on the radio had filtered through her black emptiness, and she had traveled across the country during those first chaotic days to the New Christian Cathedral, seeking answers. She shrugged again, and stared at her husband.

"Ivy," tried Ron again patiently, "you've sat there with me and the others, you've been a part of the discussions. *You* are the reason I came here and heard the truth. You are the reason I have Jesus in my heart." He had not come there for Jesus. He had come there to kill Henderson Smith. After Ronnie was taken, after Ivy left their home following the reverend's voice, a heartbroken, confused, and irrational Ron decided Smith was the reason for his loss. He had been a believer in God, a believer in Scripture, before the disappearances, and these subjects had been a source of contention between him and Ivy. But in Reverend Smith's message, in his agonized state, Ron heard lies, and he had decided to act. He had tried to shoot Smith on the day the enraged skies streaked overhead and burning sulfuric rain fell with a hiss. Ivy had thrown herself in front of Smith, took the bullet, and nearly died. Ron went to jail. While Ivy lay recovering from her wound in a hospital, the truncated and dismembered judicial system tried to figure out what to do with Ron Underwood, attempted murderer.

Ivy looked at her husband, the man she had fallen in love with those years ago, the man who had throughout their marriage tried to be a good and loving husband for her, a good father for their child. "You have Jesus in your heart, Ron. You can go out there and *tell* people about Him and be honest and sincere about it because you *believe*, Ron, as do the others. I'm not sure I can do that. Can't you see? I understand how important this is to you, to the others—perhaps to the world—but I *don't know if I can do it*. I'm afraid people will hear doubt in my voice, see it in my eyes. Then where will the message be?" She folded her arms across her chest and turned her face from him.

Ron stood and began pacing the room: five steps one way, five steps back. "Ivy," he said in the tone she recognized as the professor about to expound on today's lesson, "you told us about Thad Knight—clearly not a man, clearly not, uh, *good*. It took some doing, but Nateesha Folks finally told us about the specter that seems to be tormenting Reverend Smith. That Andrew Nuit thing, she said it was like a 'burning man.'" He counted on his fingers. "There's two."

"Two what?" she asked listlessly, having already heard this thesis discussed by the others.

"Two at least *otherworldly*, uh . . . things, or beings."

"Demons, Ron."

"Yes," he agreed. "Exactly. Demons. And what do they prove? If there are negative beings, entities not of this world, and these creatures are known to us from Scripture, then they are real. If they are real, then *Scripture* is real, and it can be *trusted*. Yes? Yes?"

"Yes, Ron."

"To add to that, you, along with the others, you saw Stan, or Ayak, that wonderful being who visited me in my jail cell, who helped me get out of there and back to you. You saw him. And what did we decide ol' Stan or Ayak really was, Ivy?"

"He was an angel," answered Ivy, waiting him out.

"Good. Yes. An angel here on earth, helping us. More validation of Scripture, of God's work—as if any were needed."

"Good, Ron," she said. "Now we know the Bible is real,

and God is real, because we've seen demons, we've seen angels, we've seen millions—including the children—lifted up, we've seen all the extreme meteorological weirdness described in Revelation. But you know Ron, you *know* this still doesn't help me, it doesn't answer *my one single question*, does it?"

It was his turn to wait, frightened for her.

She stood now and faced him, her hands on her hips. "You want me to go with you and the others, to share the gospel with those not taken, the masses of people out there on the brink of darkness, to *save* them. And while I'm out there selling myself, selling the evangelical message about God's love, about God's plan, *I still want to know* why. Why was Ronnie born to us so helpless, so twisted, so unable to live his life like a normal child? Why did God in His mercy do that to us, Ron?" Her face reddened, and she began to cry. She balled her hands into tight fists and held them against her heart as she stared at him with a trembling chin. "Why did He make me so weak and hungry, I jumped at the chance that creepy Thad Knight offered? Why did He let me shame myself in Ronnie's name when all I really wanted was *my own* freedom, Ron? Why did He do that to me? To us?"

"So we could know love, Ivy," replied Ron simply. "So we could know love."

She stared at him, sobbed, and straightened. She turned, got a tissue from the nightstand beside the bed, and blew her nose. She looked at him again, saw his uncluttered, straightforward honesty, and shook her head. "I don't think I can do it, Ron. I don't think I can do it."

"Don't forget the *seven*, Ivy," urged Ron. "You saw how

the names spelled it out, you admitted knowing without doubt you are part of seven, as am I, and we as seven are part of God's plan. How can you *not* be part of it?"

"Maybe there will be six, Ron," she said as she tilted her head. She remembered what she saw in Henderson Smith's eyes, the fear, and thought, *Maybe it will only be five.*

Ron looked into his wife's eyes. *I know you, Lord*, he silently prayed. *I love you and I love Ivy, and I loved Ronnie and will always love him. Please, Lord, answer Ivy. Answer her.*

"I don't think I can do it, Ron," whispered Ivy.

+   +   +

Tommy Church smelled it first, and it made his heart skip a beat, made him smile. *Horse.* He smelled horse, or horses, the earthy, rich, aromatic mix of fresh hay, manure, sweat, dirt, and grass that filled his nose and swelled his chest. He was somewhere between Lyon and Paris, on a long country road lined with small, straight trees and fields of low yellow-flowered plants. His last ride had let him out at a nearby crossroads, and drove off with a wave and a *"Bonne chance."* He had swung his backpack over his shoulders and lit out down the road on the shoe-leather express. A few minutes later, he began to enjoy the immediately familiar smells and was surprised at the intensity of his feelings. He had grown to love being a cowboy out there in West Texas, where his dad had found him, to love the rough, honest work, the mostly good people, the open spaces, and horses. He had become a solid and knowledgeable horseman the hard way—by getting up with the sun, pulling on his boots, and heading for the barn. He had fed,

he had watered, and he had mucked the stalls. He had finally begun riding on an ornery mare that knew the tricks.
He got himself rubbed against fences, knocked off by low-
hanging tree branches, and slung off when he zigged as the
horse zagged. He had learned what happened when the
girth you thought was cinched tight enough wasn't, about
getting a horse to take the bit, and about the things a horse
would tell you if you'd just listen. He had tacked western-
style for the work, of course, but had the good fortune to
learn a bit about English tack through the ranch owner's
wife, who showed a beautiful gelding in equitation classes.

He heard it next, the commotion, the fear, and thought,
Uh-oh. He had seen white wooden fencing on one side of
the road for several miles, and now saw a gated entrance
with beautiful landscaping and two guard houses. He
crossed the road and climbed up on the fence to get a better view of what he could tell by the sounds would not be a
pretty picture. It wasn't. The *horse* was pretty, an Arabian,
pale gray white, with an ash mane and tail. It was a big
horse for the breed—sixteen hands, easy—sleek, powerful,
and agile. He could tell it was agile by the way it was dancing and weaving all around the man trying to control it.
The man was heavy, swarthy, dressed in street clothes, and
wearing rubber boots and a scowl. Tommy could hear him
grunting and yelling in a language Tommy did not understand. He was pretty sure it wasn't French. It didn't matter,
because as any fool could plainly see, the horse wasn't listening to the man anyway. The horse reared up then, flailing his hoofs, and the lead rope on the halter slid through
the man's hands as he tried to hold the animal. The man

flinched and cursed the pain as the rope burned the skin on his palms, then he grabbed the rope harder and jerked. This did not help, but caused the horse to jump, his head down, his ears flat back against his skull, his eyes rolling white. Tommy saw the problem and wondered at the man's decision. The lead rope had a chain on the horse end, which the man had threaded through the halter across the horse's face, in the hard bony distance between nose and eyes. Each time the lead rope was jerked, it caused the chain to tighten down painfully. Tommy understood it was used to keep a spirited animal under control, but he instinctively knew it wasn't necessary here. The horse pulled back again and dug its front hoofs into the dirt of the ring, snorted with an angry, injured sound, and Tommy could not stop himself.

He shrugged out of his backpack, let it fall, and jumped into the ring. Out of the corner of his eye, he saw several other people along a far fence; they were yelling at him or gesturing, but he ignored them. The swarthy man fell back from the wild hoofs, dropped the lead rope, and scurried on his bottom across the dirt. The horse trotted in a circle, the lead rope bouncing behind him, and stopped in the center of the ring. Tommy wished he had the time to take his boots out of his pack, so the horse could smell them, but he walked forward, one hand outstretched, and said, "Whoa, there, big fella. Stop all that dancin' around." The horse eyed him, but did not move. His ears were up now, not flattened, but they were constantly moving. Tommy took a couple of steps closer, then a couple more, saying softly, "Yeah, big fella, I can see what's got you all riled up.

Look at you, actin' like such a wild thing when you should be standin' proud."

When Tommy was close, the horse danced a bit in place, shied, then stopped again, and Tommy reached out slowly, talking in that same low tone the whole time. Finally he was able to put one hand on the horse's neck, the other on the halter. He patted the horse gently, talked to him, and using one hand, unfastened the lead rope and chain and slipped them off. He could see the cruel mark the chain left, and he gentled the horse with his touch and voice. When he saw the animal calming, saw the great chest begin to take easier breaths, saw the big black eye watching him patiently, he sighed. "Well, ain't you the pretty thing," he said. He moved to the other side of the horse, one hand always on the animal, looked across the ring at the four people standing there, and asked, "Uh . . . tell me where you want this boy, and I'll walk him over for you."

The swarthy man, standing now, waved and shouted at Tommy. The horse shied at the harsh voice, and Tommy calmed him again. He didn't know the words, but understood the man wanted him to *get out of there*. Two of the group on the other side of the fence began to climb over. Their angry expressions matched that of the swarthy one, and they wore combat boots, jeans, and bomber jackets. They look big, fit, tough—and angry. *Uh-oh*, thought Tommy. Then another man spoke, and they all froze. Tommy looked at the man, who was older than the others, had thick black wet hair combed back and a trimmed black mustache. He wore a lightweight, white jogging outfit and white jogging shoes smudged with mud. Even from across the ring Tommy, could see the flash of a gold watch and a big ring on one finger of the man's right hand. The man spoke again. The two on the fence jumped down lightly, and the swarthy one backed away and climbed out of the ring. None of them looked happy about it. "We were trying to move him from here, up the road, to the barn. He has been out here for days, and the, um, the farrier has come to check him." He hesitated, saw the way the horse stood waiting, and added, "I would be grateful if you could help us with that. Perhaps you could walk him, lead him?"

"No problem," said Tommy. He looped the lead rope through the bottom strap of the halter, patted the horse, and walked him toward the gate. When he got close, the older man opened it and stood aside, beaming.

"Wonderful, wonderful," he said, "What is your name, young man? Are you American?"

"Yep," replied Tommy, "I am. Name's Tommy. Tommy Church, and mister, this is a fine animal you got here."

The man nodded, studied the horse appreciatively, and responded, "A wondrous creation, no? He is called Sultan, which in my language means 'commander.'"

Tommy said nothing. He walked beside the horse, the older man beside him. The three unhappy guys in bomber jackets kept back a respectful distance. He could see what he guessed was "the barn" a quarter-mile down the road. It was a big, fancy structure where several vehicles were parked. Beyond it was what had to be the house. It dwarfed the barn. A fenced side pasture stretched away from the barn, and he could see three more Arabians and what appeared to be three jet-black Firesians, judging by their long manes and tails. Tommy let out a low whistle. "This your place, mister?" he asked.

The man smiled, shrugged, and said, "It is one of my places, yes." He turned to look for the other person who had been at the fence beside him and added, "I am Khalid . . . a Saudi." He saw Tommy's expression and smiled ruefully, "I know, not a great time to be a Saudi—or a Muslim, for that matter. But as luck would have it, I'm wealthy. And in France, as anywhere, a man's wealth has a way of helping him find acceptance."

Tommy saw no reason to disagree with that.

"I'll send one of my men back for your bag, Tommy Church," said the man. He grimaced. "They are security types, really, not horsemen—as you could see. All of my best people—it was an international group—were part of those strange disappearances. So I'm frantically trying to get in a new staff that knows horses and how to run *this place*, as you called it."

The horse leaned a bit so his shoulder pushed against Tommy as they walked, and Tommy leaned back and said in a low voice, "Yeah, big fella . . . I'm still here."

"Are you looking for work?" asked Khalid.

It was then Tommy noticed the other person who had been at the fence with the older man. He was a pale and thin young man with big, searching eyes, ragged hair, and long fingers. He wore boots, jeans, and a rain jacket over a turtleneck shirt. Tommy looked at the young man and was bothered by the way the guy stared at him. The face bothered him also, and after worrying about it a moment, he figured out why. The young man had a face that was almost too pretty.

CHAPTER FIVE

"My sweet brothers and sisters," said the Reverend Henderson Smith in a rich, melodious voice. "Welcome to our cathedral on this fine day, and may God bless you." He heard the answering murmur lift up from the watching faces of his congregants, aware of the collective *hope* in the sound. He stood in the high, jutting pulpit of beautifully carved wood, the center stage and second pulpit to his left, the choir arranged behind him. The light that filled the nave of the church this morning was soft gold, streaked with beams of light from the tall, encompassing windows. The pews were almost entirely full, as they had been for every service since the disappearances, and he knew many of those sitting there waiting to hear the Good Word had made pilgrimages from all over the country. His sermons were broadcast live on several television channels and on broadcast radio, and recorded for later dissemination. He took in the moment.

Tall and lanky, with big, working man's hands, broad

shoulders, a square face with small ears tight against the short black hair on his skull, Smith bore humble looks that revealed his beginnings. He wore a black suit on this day, with a pale blue shirt and tie emblazoned with a gold cross. He was the Reverend Henderson Smith, a black preacher from Selma, Alabama, a self-made, hardworking family man who had lost a good wife and kids on the day they were lifted up. He had not been taken, felt the initial fear, loss, and confusion, but soon learned he remained in this world for a reason. He stood now, the man of the moment, the man who knew the Word, the man who would pour light onto the darkened souls of the lost, the man who would explain the unexplainable, the man who might *save* them. *Even if he himself is lost,* he thought.

"Dare I say to you, good people, 'pride goeth before the fall'?" he asked with a humble smile.

A smattering of sympathetic laughter rippled back at him, but the sound was supportive, as he knew it would be. He knew they knew, everyone knew, of his personal failure of faith and collapse on the day Ron Underwood tried to kill him. He had seen death, up close, personal, and one heartbeat away, and it frightened him to the bone. A normal reaction when one stares into the barrel of a gun, the trigger finger of a madman pulling tight—but not for a man of God who believed and taught his whole life that death meant victory for those who believed in Jesus Christ. "Christ showed us the way," he had preached for so many years. "With Jesus in your heart, you can walk without fear, knowing death will bring life." But in his moment, he had failed. He had been reduced to a blubbering, helpless, dysfunctional baby, unable to care for himself, unable to *go on*. Only a very close few knew of his vulnerability before that day, knew of the tempter who had burned his old church down and tormented him. Even those few did not know the tempter's offer that Smith could not turn away from, or the attendant price. A cold shudder clenched his back muscles as he stared at the Bible on the pulpit before him, but he shrugged it off, thinking, *The show must go on.*

"So you all know I was prideful, and yes, I fell." He rubbed his chin. "Do you all remember for a while when preachers in various churches around the land used to play a sort of 'Can you top this?' What I mean is, using the theme of redemption as their bedrock, some of these preachers used to shout loud and proud about their sordid pasts, like, 'I was a bum, a drunk, a prideful slacker who spent time in jail, kicked puppies, lied, cheated, stole and all that.' Once established before their flock as total losers, these preachers would then tell how they found Jesus, *were forgiven*, and He turned their lives around. They became living examples for their common followers—if they could be saved, why, almost *anybody* could." He stopped and smiled. A few tentative *amens* floated up to him. "Then," he continued, "the preacher down the road, seeing the other's success, came up with his *own* sad story. 'Why, that's nothing,' he'd say, '*I* stole the puppy's food before I kicked it, and I lied to *my mother*, and I *broke out* of jail! *Then* I found Jesus, and look at me now.' Then another preacher would hear this and say, 'Oh, *yeah* . . . well, *I . . .*'" He held up his hands, grinned, and said, "Anyway, you get

what I'm saying. I'm standin' here as the worst preacher,
the smallest man, and the best example of why the love of
God is so important on this beautiful day. Can I hear an
amen to that, brothers and sisters?" And it came back to
him, the voices reaffirming his righteousness, protesting
his own harsh self-evaluation, loving him and his message.

"Amen, Reverend."

"Tell, it, brother."

"No, preacher, you're still good, still good."

"Stand up, Reverend, we hear you."

"But enough about me," he said, and heard the laughter. "Let's talk about God, about His plan, about this apparently lost world, these crazed times we're livin' in. Let's
talk about the *Word*, about *truth*. He raised his eyebrows.
"I know, let's go to the Bible, sweet book, sweet message.
Let's go to, uh, *Kings*." He lifted his worn Bible, the pages
falling open to the spot. "In Kings we find many stories
about many kings, but I want to talk about that one called
Solomon." He used a long bony finger to tap the side of
his tilted head. "Now that boy was *smart*, are we all
agreed?" He paused while they responded, then continued, "And ol' Solomon has a very famous story to illustrate
just how smart he was, doesn't he? Oh, yeah, now here
come these two women—it's the Old Testament, so we're
told they were prostitutes. Given the social mores of the
day, who are we to decide what unmarried women who
lived apart from men but had relations with them should
be called? Anyway, seems they both had babies at the same
time. One died during the night, one woman switched the
dead child with the live one while the other slept, and the

other saw through the sad ruse when she awoke. You guys know the story. The one mom protests, the other holds tight, and they take the matter before Solomon. Each of the women swear the living baby is her child, and it looks like a stalemate until Solomon orders the infant cut in two with a sword so *both* mothers can have equal parts." He looked around the nave at all the upturned faces. "But he knew, didn't he, ol' wise Solomon. He took a mighty big gamble, but in his heart he knew that *love* would identify *truth*. Love would rip the heart out of the real mother of the child, but that love would make her recant, make her say, 'No, the child is hers. Give the child to the other woman so the child will *live*.' It was a hard act, a harsh act, an act of love committed by the mother to save her child. *She would give up her baby rather than see it destroyed.*" He took a clean white handkerchief out of his breast pocket and wiped his brow. When he was done, he carefully folded it and put it back. The church was silent, expectant.

"So where am I goin' with this amazin' story about love?" he asked. He sipped cold water from a heavy crystal glass at his elbow, took a breath, and stared at the high ceiling. He felt, as he always did while giving one of these *new* sermons, as if he tottered precariously on the edge of a sharp precipice, a foul darkness beneath him. "I'll tell you, brothers and sisters, I'm goin' back to the truth. You have heard me talk before about the Bible, how through man's history it has been there, the Word has been there, guiding us, showing us His way, His plan. We all studied it, tried to understand its nuances or simplicities, searching each word for hope, inspiration, and explanation. We all knew, and know, that *life* has no certainties, no guarantees, no simple explanations. We are born, we live our days mostly scrambling to hang on, to keep up, scrambling to make some sense of it all. So there was the Bible, the Word, and we could go to it and *have* gone to it. Now"—he held up one finger—"now we've seen what many identify as the end times fallin' down on us. We can look into Revelation, never an easy task, and see the signs, see the words that describe much of what has happened. Sure, I know I might sound a little too bold, a little too adventurous, when I say this, but *it's possible we have outlived the Word as it has been given to us.*"

He saw them shifting uncomfortably in their seats, their squirming bodies manifesting their mental discomfort. He even heard one female voice—it might have been Nateesha's, from the choir loft—"Careful, Reverend."

He held up both hands, palms out. "Easy, I know what I want to say, stay with me now. I am in no way saying the Bible no longer has meaning, or that the words there aren't the Word of God. I'm saying if we are living in the end times, we were not taken, then we are still part of God's plan and it might be God's *evolving* plan, and if the plan is evolving perhaps the *message evolves, too.* Scripture ends, chronologically, at Revelation. If the world, *life,* doesn't end at Revelation, then either God will send *more* words, or *we must see the existing words differently, look at them with today's eyes, find the meanings in them that relate to today's truths.*" He paused again, his heart pounding, his very fiber rebelling against what came from his mouth. "Go back to the story of Solomon and the two mothers, one baby," he said breathlessly. "Have we awakened in these times to find an old interpretation of Scripture that is a dead child? The living baby is the new truth, today's truth and reality, a new truth found within the words of God. The old truth is valid only if we look backwards at it, and we know there must be a new truth because this is a *new world*. We can destroy our new truth as easily as that sword would have destroyed the baby, we can do that by *denying* it. Or we can be wise, like Solomon, and loving, like the real birth mother, and *share it*."

He wiped his brow with his handkerchief again, took another sip of water, and looked out over the faces. *Easy now*, he thought. "Friends, you know I've been tellin' you all it's almost time to begin hittin' the streets, the neighborhoods, knockin' on doors with the new gospel. With my sermon today, I'm tryin' to prepare you, to give you confidence in your message. We all know how hard it is— we used to do it—how hard it is to stand at someone's doorstep and try to explain the Good Word, right? How many of you brothers and sisters have experienced it?" He watched as many hands reached up, many heads nodded in agreement. "Good. So now we're preparing to get out there again, in *these* times, with this *new* message, and it will not be an easy task, no. Many people will refuse to hear you or to even take a moment or the courtesy to try to understand what message you bring. They want God's help and salvation, but they don't want to *work* for it—by that, I mean study, listen, learn, commit." He paused, gathering his thoughts. "Now you have heard me speak of the man, Azul Dante, in the past. I have been circumspect in my discussions about him because of the sensitive nature of his mission, his vision. Finally the mainstream media have gone beyond the fact that he is a world leader without peer, a diplomat, a reformer, a man who can reach out across borders and fences and heal old wounds, bring men, ideologies, and countries together in a common fight for a better world. His recognition by other world leaders, including our own President Reese, and Israeli Prime Minister Pearl, as head of the European Coaliton—which might be more accurately called the World Coalition—confirms his importance on the world's stage. But am I talkin' *politics* here, in this New Christian Cathedral? Politics? No sir, no ma'am. I'm talkin' good, old-time, Bible-thumpin', Lord-praisin' *religion*. You might say, how is that, Reverend? I'll say how Azul Dante signaled he was all about religion before he took his first step as world leader. He did it by his quiet, unheralded, largely ignored formation, creation, of the Prodigal Project. His Prodigal Project, as you know, is the foundation for this fine New Christian Cathedral, and other churches equally enlightened all over the land. Azul Dante is a man—I'm not hesitant to say he might be as wise as ol' Solomon—who put religion *first* when he began his plan. He started out with the gospel, with the Word, and used his own resources, energy, and commitment to build the many churches and cathedrals I'm talkin' about. Places where people like you could come to hear *the Word*."

The Reverend's flock sat silently, many leaning forward slightly, intent on hearing and understanding his every utterance.

Henderson Smith looked out over the faces and took a

breath. "I want you to think of this New Christian Cathedral, of the Prodigal Project and all of its good work in preserving and spreading the gospel in this dark world, and of Azul Dante, a wise man who leads us, the man who might very well be *the one* who will lead us out of the darkness."

Seven rows from the front of the nave, roughly in the center, Ron Underwood sat beside his wife, Ivy. He stood now, awkwardly, pushed his black-framed glasses up on his nose, looked around at the faces staring at him, and said in a loud voice, "Excuse me, Reverend Smith."

Smith gazed down upon him a moment and, with a small smile, responded. "Yes . . . Ron?"

Everyone in the church held their breath. This was the man who had tried to kill the good reverend.

"Well, Reverend," said Ron. "I love your sermons, your message, and the way you give them. And I am grateful for you. But I struggle sometimes with the message. I don't know. Like it's not always clear to me what you've tried to get across."

"Then I have failed as a preacher, Ron."

Several gasps came from the congregants, and a few said quietly, "No, no."

"It's me, Reverend Smith, not you," said Underwood. "Maybe I'm too thick." Ivy sat beside him, watching his face carefully. She had not been prepared for this.

Smith shook his head and smiled, "C'mon, Ron. You're a college professor." He put on finger against his chin and added, "Tell you what, Ron. Give me an example, something you're not getting."

"This whole concept of looking at the gospel, at

Scripture in a new way, with new eyes, a new heart," responded Underwood. Then he shrugged, and waited.

Smith nodded. He was glad Ron had remembered to say "with a new heart."

"Ron Underwood," he said loudly, "let's see. . . ." He turned the pages of his Bible, pretending to search for something. "Ah." He read for a moment, flipped from one section to another all the way in the back, and began. "Let's use Kings again, as example, and I sure hope you all will be able to follow me here, Ron. Look at First Kings Ten, fourteen, 'The weight of the gold that Solomon received yearly was six hundred sixty-six talents.' How's that for a number, Ron? Strike a chord? Yep, me, too. So then we go up here to Revelation Thirteen, eighteen and we see the words 'This calls for wisdom.' Now wait, friends. Didn't we see that same word associated with Solomon—wisdom? When we read this in Revelation, is it telling us we need the wisdom of Solomon, or we can *relate* to Solomon? Then a bit further we see, 'for it is *man's* number. His number is six-six-six.' *Man's* number is six-six-six. Ron, do you read that, hear that?"

"Yes. Yes I do, Reverend Smith," answered Ron.

"And ol' Solomon the wise," continued Smith, "how many talents a year did he receive, Ron?"

"Six-six-six, uh, six hundred and sixty-six."

"Yes, he received that number of talents, and Solomon was only a *man*, a *good* king, a *good* example for us, and that number was used casually, matter-of-factly." He tapped his nose again. "Maybe this is a clumsy example, but I'm using it because that number is such an edgy buzzword for us and always has been. I'm trying to illustrate a new way of looking at Scripture, a new association of the words found in this old book that will help us to put this *new world* into perspective. That number, as we read it, is associated with man, with *us*, and perhaps"—his mouth went dry; his tongue ran ineffectively around the rough edges—"perhaps we can read these words in our new light and take the evil connotation *away* from it."

There was a hesitation, a collective pause. Then Ron asked tentatively, "So you're saying six-six-six is not necessarily the mark of the beast, Reverend?"

"I'm saying this, Ron," replied Smith as he looked out over the listeners, "Every word of Scripture comes from God. Of that, there is no argument. But there is an Old Testament from the ancients, a New Testament from those who had a new story to tell, and each was written and applied truths valid during those times until these. Now there is a fresh perspective, a *new way of interpreting the very words God gave us*. That's what I'm saying. That's what I'm hoping you'll understand."

Ron stood silently, his part done.

Smith sighed. "Ron, come up here. No. Now, c'mon up here a moment."

There was a moment of shuffling, people turning their legs so Ron could make his way out of the center row, then across the carpeted expanse before the pulpit, then up the wide carpeted steps to the main stage. As he did so, Reverend Henderson Smith descended from the high pulpit and stood to meet him. When Ron came before him, Smith smiled, reached out with his right arm, and they shook hands. There was not a sound in the cathedral. Then, still holding Ron's hand, Smith pulled him close, hugged him, and patted him on his back. Ron Underwood began to cry, and soon many in the audience joined him. In another moment, the entire congregation burst into a round of thunderous applause, getting to their feet, laughing, praising the Lord, and enjoying this overt and loving act of forgiveness by Henderson Smith.

Over the tumult, Smith cried out, his amplified voice booming in the nave, "Now stand with me, Ron Underwood, while our wonderful choir sings loudly the praises of the Lord, and of our faith. Let us listen to their song and feel blessed. Then we—you, me, all of us here—we will *pray*. We will pray for the understanding we'll need to *survive* in this world, to flourish, and to *spread the new gospel as it is shown to us*." He leaned his face close to Ron Underwood's right ear, his left hand on Underwood's left shoulder. The congregation felt the warmth as they saw him whisper something, probably an encouraging, loving word, in Underwood's ear. "Thank you for helping me today, Ron," he whispered. "You were perfect."

Underwood said nothing. He was filled with emotion, filled with the spirit, grateful and humble that he could play some small part in getting the Reverend's message out there. He looked out across the faces of the crowd until he found Ivy's. He smiled shyly at her, wondered how she'd feel if she knew he spoke up today because the Reverend had secretly asked him to, and he saw a curious, troubled expression on her face.

The choir, taking its cue, launched into a rousing old gospel, and before long the New Christian Cathedral was rocked to its foundation with released spiritual joy and wonder.

CHAPTER SIX

Thomas Church was convinced it was the most beautiful morning he had seen in a very long time. The colors had a new vibrancy, the light was amazing, the breeze gentle, the sounds crisp. He took a deep breath and smiled. He was in his early forties, of medium height, with a stocky build that for many years was pudgy. He had slimmed down some lately, even though he still carried what he described as a well-earned gut. He had a full head of brown hair going to gray; a gray-flecked, trimmed beard; and dark eyes bright with intelligence and wonder. He wore frayed jeans, hiking boots, and a light blue long-sleeved work shirt. He looked at his wife, Rebecca, as she stood beside him in line to shake hands or share a moment with Reverend Henderson Smith. He was pretty sure she felt the same way; he *hoped* she felt the same way. It was like he was young again, a college know-it-all who finally gets the girl of his dreams and can't believe it even as it actually happens. It had been several weeks since he had found her living in a commune in western Utah and talked her into joining him once more. She had changed her name since the divorce, and her appearance somewhat, but that didn't matter to him. She was a bit taller than he, long-limbed and graceful, with curly rust-colored hair that fell past her shoulders and was parted in the middle. She had hazel eyes flecked with green, pale skin, and full lips needing no artificial color. Today she wore a long-sleeved white T-shirt, soft corduroy jeans, jogging shoes, and a glow on her cheeks. She had traveled east with him, first to visit their daughter, Sissy, and her husband, Mitch, on the campus of the University of Virginia. Then south, toward Alabama, because he wanted her to see and hear Reverend Smith, his sermons, and perhaps meet a few of the others. He wanted to confirm his role as one of *seven*.

They had arrived the night before and managed to find a room in one of the bigger chain motels still operating. They had not been together as man and wife since she climbed into his Bronco in Utah, and he was content to simply be with her. He did not want her to feel crowded or pressured, and he made a conscious effort to give her space even while he ached to hold her again. Their renewed relationship, he knew, was a fragile thing, and he had decided to strengthen it through a shared faith. This was a new thing for him also this faith. Sissy and Tommy knew he had become a student of the Bible since the disappearances, and had both joined in lengthy, emotional discussions about it with him. He told them he was convinced Scripture was *truth*, and even when the world was being torn apart, strength, answers, and love could be found within it. His kids grew up knowing him as a disinterested bystander at best when it came to matters spiritual, at worst a dark and aggressive agnostic. Now he seemed swept up in it, excited about his new awareness, eager to share his beliefs and anxious to see his loved ones accept them for their salvation. He stopped short of saying he was born again. He felt a deep-down, very intimate, and personal reserve, and until it was resolved, he would not openly identify himself that way. But he felt it, and he enjoyed knowing it was there, simmering, waiting for release.

He had been pleased and grateful to see how open and willing Rebecca was regarding the message of Scripture. She had embraced a New Age lifestyle after their separation, a student of this and that mystical "revelation," the whole "Relax, we're all children of the universe" thing. He was sure she would resist his efforts to study the Bible with her, and was caught pleasantly off guard when she readily joined in. Her approach was quieter, more reserved, than his, but he was content to let her accept at her own pace. The last earth-racking happening they shared had been while heading south on I-95. It was the night of howling winds, leaden skies, and earthquakes, the night those skies were streaked with the colors of Revelation. To him it was as it is written, plain and simple. She agreed everything that had happened to the world since the disappearances *might* be as foretold in Revelation, but hedged a bit by suggesting there were *symbolic* similarities between Scripture and world events. He found his faith deepening in his heart, and he desperately wanted her to experience the same fullness.

But last night. There was a room available at the motel,

and it had two double beds. After dinner, after their show-
ers, he had changed into his T-shirt and pajama pants like
he always slept in, climbed into one of the beds, and read
his Bible for a few minutes. Rebecca came out of the bath-
room in the oversize football jersey she slept in, came to
him, and kissed him lightly on the forehead. She got into
the other bed, a few feet and several lifetimes away, said
good night, and turned out the light. He grew sleepy, put
his Bible on the nightstand, turned out his light, and tried
to get comfortable with the miniature pillows. It was in the
soft darkness of deep night that she came to him, sliding
under the covers, holding him tightly.

"Mr. Church? Mr. Church?" said Henderson Smith.

"Thomas," said Rebecca gently.

Thomas Church grinned sheepishly, shook hands with
Smith, and introduced Rebecca. "Great sermon, Reverend," he said. "Very, uh, thought provoking, very interesting."

"Thank you, Mr. Church. How is your boy, Tommy? I
met him the first time you two came here to the cathedral.
And you have a daughter in Virginia, right?"

"Yes, we do, and she's fine, thanks, Reverend Smith,"
replied Church as he held Rebecca's warm hand. "Thanks
for asking. Tommy has taken off to Europe. Told me he's
got to go see for himself what's happening out there in the
world. Said he'd like to somehow get to hear Azul Dante
speak. Don't know if he'll be able to pull *that* off."

Smith pursed his lips and said, "Well, we know the
Lord works in mysterious ways." He turned and gestured

to another couple standing nearby. "Thomas Church, Rebecca, this is Ivy—and her husband, Ron Underwood."

They all shook hands, smiled, and nodded, and Ivy said, "Welcome to the *New* Christian Cathedral."

"Everything is new, Ivy," said Smith in a gently reproving tone.

Ivy did not reply. Ron stared at her.

"Tommy and I met you the first time we were here, Ivy," said Church, "You and Shannon. Shannon Carpenter."

"Yes," said Ivy. Then she added, "Why don't we find her and Ted later, and we'll visit."

"Sounds good to me," Church responded. He squeezed Rebecca's hand, took a deep breath, looked all around them, and said, "Isn't this a grand day, a great day, a *wonderful* day?"

They all looked at him except Rebecca, who stared at the toes of her shoes, her cheeks red.

Ivy watched him, then her, with a bemused smile.

"Amen, brother," said Smith quietly.

A few minutes later, Church and Rebecca sat under a shade tree a short distance away from the front steps of the cathedral. They held hands.

"Thomas," said Rebecca. She shook her head as she looked at him. "Will you wipe that silly grin off your face?"

"I might just wear this silly grin for the rest of my days," he replied.

She looked at their hands shyly. "I mean, it wasn't some special thing, last night. It was just . . . us."

He leaned forward and kissed her on the corner of her right eye, his lips barely touching the soft skin there. "You are special, Rebecca," he said as he sat back and looked at her. "You are special, and I am special when we are together. You are a gift, simple as that. Last night was a gift, and every minute of every day and night I am *with* you is a gift."

She looked at him and saw a man who loved her. She smiled.

They sat quietly for a few minutes. The breeze shifted direction, lifting her hair from her shoulders.

"Thomas," she said as she gathered her hair behind her neck.

"That's me, silly Thomas."

"No. Listen, I want to say something."

He sat up.

"The sermon," she said. "Reverend Smith's talk today. What did you think about it?"

He shrugged, "It was interesting, like I told him. Made me think."

"It made me think, yes," she said, "It made me think something was just a little . . . off."

"Off."

"Off, Thomas." She let go of her hair and took his hands. "The one thing that makes Scripture so, so . . . *sure*, the one thing that makes it stand up to all the fancy intellectual arguments and dissections, is the fact that it has *always been*. I've watched you study it, listened while you read it to me, Thomas. You believe, and you want me to believe, that the words are divinely inspired, written by man as the

message from God. It is *the Word*. I understand perception
and interpretation come into play with any written message, and we both respect a good, serious debate between
respectful students. But the Bible. Thomas, there's only
one truth, one *spiritual* truth, and the Bible is the key to
that truth given to us by God, and illuminated by the life
of Jesus. Isn't that what you've been telling me?"

"Yes," he answered, consumed by her.

"Yes. Then tell me what the good Reverend Smith was
selling today, Thomas."

He sat back on his heels. He thought a moment,
frowned, and replied, "It's a new world, Rebecca, might be
the end. So he was challenging us to take a new look at
Scripture, to find new . . . truths."

"New truths, Thomas?"

"Well, yeah." He didn't like the sound of that either.

After a moment, Rebecca went on, "You said there are
seven of you. That Ron Underwood is one, and his wife,
Ivy. I liked her, Thomas, but she for sure has an edge, like
she is one angry woman. Shannon Carpenter you told me
about. There are two more, but not here. I'm just saying
what I feel, Thomas, okay?"

"Okay."

"You told me the seven had a purpose, some mission.
You are somehow part of God's plan during these times.
It's got something to do with the Prodigal Project, right?"

"Yes, Rebecca," he answered, perplexed.

"Maybe your part of the plan is to remind everyone
that the truth can be found right where it's always been.
Maybe you and the other six are to spread the Word not to

worry about *new*, but concentrate on what is given." She leaned forward and brushed her fingertips lightly across his brow. "Thomas, I've seen how you've changed. Faith is in you, in your heart, and it is *real*. I've watched as you've read from the Scripture, and in my mind I'm walking right along beside you. I know I'm not one of the seven, and maybe I don't have a handle on what I'm trying to say, but I know this. Reverend Smith was trying real hard to make his point today, but it was off."

He turned his eyes from hers, looked all around him, then up into the clear skies above them. He nodded. "My intellectual self, which I admit is attached directly to my ego, enjoyed the possibilities Smith suggested," he said. "And I'm aware that sometimes thinking *too much* can get in the way of a simple truth. And you're right, Rebecca, Smith *was* trying hard in there today." He stopped, took a deep breath, and added, "But Henderson Smith is one of the *seven*. He knows it, we know it. He's one of us. So how does that figure?"

It was her turn to look away. "I don't know, Thomas," she said, "I don't know."

+   +   +

In the city of Jerusalem, the ground shuddered. It was a deep, thudding vibration that many who walked the ancient pathways or newly paved roads felt in the soles of their feet. It was enough to give pause to the bustle of diverse peoples going about their various tasks or pursuits. Many held their breath, thinking momentarily that a *really big* car bomb had been exploded some distance away. But

there was no smoke, no screaming, no convergence of
sirens. With a wary and fatalistic resolve, perhaps disquieted by the occurrence, the people resumed their activities. In the Mosque of Omar, an imam stopped his
harangue of an assistant and frowned. For a tilting moment, he had experienced a slight disorientation, as if
there had been a shift, a bending of some kind, in his surroundings. He forced himself to look down at his feet,
which stood firm on bricks that had been in place for thousands of years. The bricks, worn smooth by those who
trod on them, remained impassive and immobile. Or not.
He looked again.

A fissure separated a section of floor. It was but a crack,
really, hardly a thumbnail wide. But it had not been there
an hour ago, of that he was certain. He reluctantly let his
eyes follow the path of the crack, and saw that it ran in a
jagged line across the floor to a far corner. His eyes narrowed in the soft light, first refusing to see, then making
out the pattern of reaching cracks that spiderwebbed the
wall. His mind spasmodically considered the possibility
that the Israelis were crashing their heavily armored tanks
against the mosque as they did when they wanted to push
down some "suspected" Hezbollah or Hamas dwelling
over in Gaza. He shook his head to clear it. Not even the
Jews, he told himself, could be that insane. He reminded
himself the building was indeed ancient, and that buildings
did shift from time to time. He decided the cracks, inconsequential, hardly worrisome, were purely cosmetic. He
would inform the lazy maintenance man to do something
about it. He looked around him and sighed. Nothing

should mar the beauty of this holy place, he knew, and it would stand solid as the faith for a thousand years.

+   +   +

General Izbek Noir smiled. His black eyes brightened in intensity, flecked with embers of red, and his tongue leached around his lips. He was impressed. Although many miles from Israel, and only a few from the Iraq–Turk border, he had been aware of the shudder beneath Jerusalem even as it happened. There could be only one explanation, and it pleased him. The weakening of the firmament beneath that foul city had a certain inevitability, a symmetry he found exciting. *This will set those fools afire*, he thought. When the next step occurred, as it surely would now that the sequence had been initiated, the Palestinians would be unable to contain themselves. They would rise in a terrible, tormented convulsion and hurl themselves against the Israelis. This time there would be no constraints, no parry and thrust, no limited response. All bets would be off, and so would the gloves. Israel would once and for always solve the "Palestinian problem" by finally unleashing its forces with orders to destroy the enemy. The result would be wholesale slaughter. Slaughter always pleased him. Within what he guessed would be a fairly short time, the Israelis would secure the area. Then, before the smell of cordite and burning flesh was blown away by the wind, they would begin to build—having waited more than a thousand years for the chance. He put his head back, and his neck muscles bunched and stretched as he laughed. His laughter had the sound of splintering bones, and those around him who heard it felt a spasm of chilling fear.

He sat on a log within the perimeter of the headquarters unit of his vast mujahideen army, dressed in an unadorned desert camouflage uniform and dusty combat boots. He wore a black beret with a flame-red star. His was the form of a large, rugged, weathered soldier, dark, with a brooding brow, a cruel cut for a mouth, and piercing eyes. He had big hands, the backs covered with coarse black hair, long fingers with pointed nails. Under the beret he had soot-black hair, short and spiky. He carried a .45 automatic pistol in a leather holster on a wide webbed belt around his waist, a wicked curved killing knife in a sheath on the opposite side. His personal Kalashnikov assault rifle was always near at hand. He was surrounded by armored communications vehicles and armed soldiers of Allah. They were loggered down, dug in. It was a time for rest, reorganization. His logistics convoys had been left behind in the tearing dash his troops had made across the desert. His tanks and other vehicles needed fuel; his guns, ammo; his soldiers, food. It was all right. His mobile radar units were on-line, his perimeter security attack helicopters on patrol. He had ordered a temporary halt to the barrage of ground-to-ground "dumb" missiles his troops had been indiscriminately firing toward populated areas behind the front.

This was a time of waiting, a pause as the earth spun on its axis, and the life of man spun in the hot desert winds. His armies had been fighting for months now, all across the globe, and it had been horrific and beautiful. Africa had been gutted, as well as the interior of South America, most of the Pacific nations, the rim of the Far East, pockets of vast Russia. Recently the so-called European Coalition forces had landed in North Africa, and his armies had fought ruthlessly for every yard of burned and defiled ground they gave up. It had been a hard lesson for his mujahideen soldiers. They learned at great cost that soldiers from other nations and other beliefs could fight just as well as they, and just as ruthlessly. The British general that Azul Dante had appointed to lead the forces was a hard-driving tactician, moving his units to positions of best advantage while the mujahideen fanatics simply came at them . . . and came at them. No matter—it was all a delaying game for now. He loved war, truly relished it, drank it in like a rich and aromatic brandy, rolling the stench and ruination of it on his tongue to prolong the pleasure. But now he paused. Everyone knew his next move would be west into Europe, even as everyone knew Dante's European Coalition Forces would be there to stop him. His heartbeat quickened as he thought of the fighting that would come, the chaos, the exquisite loss of life.

He looked around at the panorama of an army at rest. *But today*, he mused, *today in Jerusalem something has begun that is really* rich. He admitted he was impressed because he had not been the one to initiate the act, so of course it had to be his "adversary." The one who would eventually save man from himself—Azul Dante. He shook his head. Clearly Dante's plan was to remain faithful to the sequence of events as described in *that book* as it suited his needs. What splendid irony, what—he thought of a word that had always tickled him—*chutzpah*. He frowned. Dante had, of course, survived the attempt on his life by that dark Muslim from the west who would have us know him as Jo-

hann Rommel. He had given Rommel the mission because
he grew impatient and wanted to heat things up a bit, and
Rommel had made his way to France and attempted the
hit. He would have bet "Rommel" would simply have van-
ished after leaving the mujahideen camps, but the man actually tried to carry out the orders. Like a creature with
brittle legs, the number 7 crawled across his thoughts, and
he shook his head angrily to make it go away. He wondered if Rommel would try to make his way back to the
mujahideen army as instructed. Izbek Noir shook his head
again, stood, and stretched. He looked to the southwest, in
the direction of Jerusalem and the Mosque of Omar. He
thought of Azul Dante, of the events so primitively described in *that book*, of the consequences of this latest
wrinkle. *I wish I'd thought of that*, he mused. *Got to give the
devil his due, as they say*, and his laughter fell like the edge of
a razor against rime ice.

CHAPTER SEVEN

"John Jameson might still be alive," said Benjamin Carter, "and actively pursuing a goal within his own agenda." Carter was the head of the CIA, a career politician, more bureaucrat than spy.

Mike Tsakis said nothing. He was a veteran Agency field agent, brought inside Langley to act as supervisor. Both men wore gray business suits and ties, but Tsakis had the knot of his tie loosened. They sat in Carter's spacious office. Taskis, stocky and muscular, with a fighter's face and scarred hands, sat in a straight-backed chair. Carter, tall, slim, with smooth skin and a schoolboy haircut, sat square-shouldered behind his desk. The office door was closed. Tsakis did not know if the hidden mikes in the room were hot, and he figured it would depend on the conversation.

"Surprised, Mike?"

Tsakis shrugged. He knew without doubt that a dangerous game was being played. At least one man's life, one of *his* men, hung in the balance, and each misspoken word or misstep could have immediate and dire consequences. He wished he could answer, like any veteran, that he was no longer surprised by anything he saw or heard. But that was not so. John Jameson was one of his guys, and also one of the Agency's guys. Jameson was a man who had lost his wife and kids to the disappearances, a man who then returned to the Agency to take on an impossible, suicidal assignment. He had, posing as a Muslim mercenary with a Dutch passport in the name of Johann Rommel, actually penetrated the structure of the mujahideen armies. His fighting skills won him respect and eventually he had been assigned to the elite personal guard of General Izbek Noir himself. This put him in position to direct an attack on Noir's headquarters vehicle, which was destroyed by a missile. Noir had escaped death, something he had apparently managed before, and Jameson grimly held on, focused on his mission for the agency despite his precarious position.

Tsakis, in answer to Carter's question, shrugged and waited.

Benjamin Carter looked at the impassive face of the rugged agent sitting on the other side of his desk, and sighed. These Agency veterans just didn't get it, he knew. These were times that rewrote the book, times when old loyalties, missions, and guidelines became nothing more than nostalgic nonsense. Carter knew this particular mission—an attempt to assassinate Izbek Noir—came down from the president herself, but it didn't really faze him. He had been around the political block, so he acted with appropriate caution when he decided to circumvent, then undermine the mission. If Agent John Jameson was lost in the fallout, so what? There was the *really* big picture to consider, and it was forming right where anyone with a discerning eye could see it. And he had a discerning eye.

He knew Hiram Sarco, head of Sarcom, had flown into Paris just when Azul Dante prepared to meet with ten world leaders, including President Clara Reese. Sarco's presence there meant only one thing. Dante was going to use Sarcom's global communications capabilities to spread the Good Word, the *new* Word. These were exciting times, the world was in total upheaval, and a new world with a *new power structure* was emerging. He intended to be a member of that new power, and he didn't need some clumsy Agency plot, championed by this has-been, Mike Tsakis, to muck things up. Izbek Noir? He was confident Azul Dante had a plan to deal with that crazed Muslim. It would play out as intended, without the help of the CIA. The plot was spearheaded by this old-school guy, Jameson, and Carter had already secretly implemented a plan to take him out of the picture. He thought Jameson *was* out, until that bloody little event in Nice, France.

"That attempt on Dante's life, in Nice," Carter said, by way of answering the question for Tsakis, "The result was skewed, but the operation had all the earmarks of a pro."

"The French security troops took out the shooters— four, five young Arabs hiding out in an apartment in the building," said Tsakis for argument's sake.

"C'mon, Mike," replied Carter, leaning back in his chair. He made a steeple of his fingers and held them in front of his face. "Those guys were a bunch of clowns.

They had some C-Four some AKs, and an autographed poster of the late, lamented Osama bin Laden. They were laying around, cooking goat guts, when the French posse kicked in the door and shredded them. You know they found the weapon on the roof, Mike. An old Mauser bolt-action with a pretty good sight. Good enough for the job."

Tsakis nodded. He revisited the attempted hit in his head. Jameson had been dispatched by Izbek Noir himself, and he and Tsakis had communicated while he was en route to France with that American combat photographer, Slim Piedmont, at his side. On the road to Baghdad, they had been ambushed. Jameson had killed the attackers, but knew the encounter wasn't coincidence. Taskis had agreed, and from that point on, Jameson was out in the cold. *Still* Jameson made the bogus attempted hit on Dante, even though he knew he was a marked man.

"I'm trying to stay with you, sir," said Tsakis politely.

Carter's cheeks flushed, he pursed his lips, and said, "Keep up. There's more. I know you saw the same report I did about the boat. What do you guys call them? The *paper cup* boat—use it once, then throw it away. But this one was used more than once, Mike. It showed up in Nice. Then, during that night of the crazy weather, the night of the storms, the tidal waves, the whole apocalyptic thing, the boat travels from Nice to Portofino, Italy. Odd, no? A couple of days later one of the locals, guy named Guido, tries to sell the boat, which is apparently not pretty, but sound. I believe Guido was a part-timer, buried deep for a rainy day. One of those non-agency-sanctioned freelancers you field agents like to keep on a long string and use when necessary. There is no record of it, but I believe he was one of Jameson's. He was questioned, and his answers pointed to a safe house not far from the coast. The house is empty now, but the villagers say a man and woman stayed there. The man was apparently injured."

Tsakis kept his face impassive. "Who questioned Guido?" he asked after a moment.

"My people," replied Carter.

Tsakis did not miss the significance of *my*. "If it was a safe house, there was a caretaker. What did your people learn from him or her?" He knew Mamma Steffie—he had put her in place years ago.

"She seems to have disappeared," sniffed Benjamin Carter. "Locals say she went off to visit a sick relative or something."

"What else did this Guido have to say?" asked Tsakis, already dreading the answer.

Carter shrugged, "He seems to have died while discussing it." He kept his gaze steady as he looked at Tsakis and added, "Heart—or something."

Tsakis forced himself to shrug, a cold place hard in his belly. He decided the hidden microphones were *not* recording this little session.

Carter leaned forward in his seat, his expression tense. "Look, Tsakis," he said quietly, "Jameson went in on an approved mission. He *failed*. Then he's apparently turned by Noir, cuts all *sanctioned* communications with us, and takes a bead on Azul Dante, for cryin' out loud. Jameson is rogue, Tsakis, *rogue*. Apparently he did *not* die in Iraq, and he's out there untethered, uncontrolled, and dangerously unpredictable. He must be found and stopped, and I've already given directives to that effect. I'm meeting with *you*, Mike, so you'll understand. If you have any info on Jameson or if you are contacted by him in any manner, you are to report to me *immediately*." He paused, turned his chair so he could look out of one of the large windows in his office, and added, "I know Jameson is an old-school agent like you, Mike, out there doing what he thinks is *right*. But I think you are savvy enough to understand that kind of thinking is so, so . . . *passé* . . . you know? It's a new world, Mike, changing fast, and in the end there will only be the quick and the dead. You need to choose sides, Mike."

Tsakis stood and nodded. He glanced at the American flag furled on a stand against the wall behind Benjamin Carter's right shoulder. He thought of the old Bible in the top drawer of his desk, the Bible he had been studying with intensity at the suggestion of his friend, John Jameson. "Don't worry, sir," he said easily. "I chose sides a long time ago."

+   +   +

Vatican City, like all major spiritual focal points around the world, was teeming with pilgrims. They came from everywhere, seeking answers, comfort, and reassurances. The new tourist was a serious one, there not to simply enjoy the pageantry, artwork, and history, but for more. Most went home emboldened, heartened by the journey, filled with a renewed desire to *know God*. Some would not leave, afraid to step away from such an established place of worship, a place rich in symbols given strength by the sheer numbers of seekers. These people had flooded the hotels, rental apartments, youth hostels, and private homes with rooms to let. Many simply camped out, sleeping in parks or alleys, taking what meals they could from the Red Cross, the International YMCA, and mission organizations of different faiths. Rome itself was a city bursting at the seams, crowded with the infusion of a numberless, jostling, anxious, multiethnic horde of people. Many, of course, were *not* there for reasons of faith, but simply for survival. The larger cities around the globe still offered the best chance for food, shelter, medical care, communications—the best chance for some semblance of order in a world gone crazy.

All of this worked for Cat Early and John Jameson.

She had been quietly impressed with Jameson's ability to tap into a network she realized had taken years to put in place. She had gone into his bedroom in Mamma Steffie's safe house one morning to find him standing at the sink in his shorts, examining himself in the mirror. He had already shaved and had removed the dressing she had covered his left eye with, replacing it with a couple of Band-Aids. "You, Cat Early," he had said with a grin, "look incredible this morning. How do I know? Because I can see you with both eyes, that's how. You can now add *doctor* to your credentials."

"But how does the rest of you feel?" she had asked, pleased to see him up, but still worried about the nature of his head wounds.

"I'm weak, I'm shaky, and I've got a dull headache," he answered matter-of-factly. "I think I suffered a slight concussion, but no brain injury. My eye was bruised and bloodied by bursting vessels, but I don't think there's lasting damage. The blood loss weakened me, and the concussion caused the rest, but I'm on the mend."

"Good," she had replied. She saw the way his stomach muscles tightened as he leaned over the sink, watched his wide shoulders, his strong legs, and was suddenly aware she wore only her thin night robe. They had shared the intimacies of nurse and patient, of course. She had cleaned his wounds, had held his head as she spooned soup into his mouth, held the bucket as he vomited, and held his hand as he slept fitfully. Once when she had leaned over him to straighten his pillow in the middle of a particularly rough night, he, in the throes of delirium, had wrapped his arms around her, pulled her to his chest, and hugged her gently as he mumbled soft words in the darkness. She had pulled away only after his arms slipped to his sides as he slept again. "Another few days of rest," she had added, "and you'll—"

"We must leave now, Cat," he had said as he crossed the room, found his folded clothes, and began dressing. She hesitated, and he told her, "Cat. Listen. I thank God you found me in Nice, and I know I would have never made it out of there without you by my side. But I also wish you had been somewhere else, with Slim, maybe, covering the Azul Dante story, going on with your life. You were there, you helped me, and now you're hooked up with a broken-down, has-been espionage agent on the run." He had given her another grin. "I'm pretty sure I'm not welcome in any camp right now. I doubt if my mujahideen buddies are gonna take me back, and my own team seems to be gunning for me, too. Running with me is probably not a healthy enterprise, Cat, and I wish you were not part of this."

"But I *am* part of it," she had countered, her chin trembling, her fists clenched.

"Yeah," he agreed. "And you are a sight for a sore eye standing there in this lovely morning light wearing that nightgown—but get dressed, Cat, we're outta here."

They had walked down the hill from the tiny house in the small village carrying the bundle of warm pastries and thermos of coffee Mamma Steffie had given them. They both had backpacks slung over their shoulders, and wore jackets and hats with their jeans and long-sleeved shirts. Jameson had spoken in Italian to Mamma Steffie for a moment, and there were tears in the old woman's eyes as she hugged Cat good-bye. Mamma Steffie would be leaving the village for a while, Jameson had explained, and the villagers would turn a deaf ear to any inquiries about her. A few minutes later, a dusty van carrying a farmer, his wife, and a small pig stopped at a crossroad. Jameson opened the side door, and he and Cat climbed in. There was very little conversation as they traveled south, and the pig only ate *some* of the pastries.

The trip down the long peninsula was tiring, but without mishap. It was as they traveled that Cat came to appreciate Jameson's well-placed, nondescript network. They rarely rode in one vehicle for more than three or four hours. They avoided public transportation entirely, and it seemed to her that a new ride would be waiting only a couple of minutes from where they left the old one. Once Jameson stopped her from getting into a small SUV. The driver was someone he did not recognize, and it was only after a terse exchange that he nodded and they climbed in. He explained to her that the driver was the son of the man he expected, but said no more. Finally, when they approached the outskirts of Rome, they stood at a shady bus stop, waited with a group of old women who stared at them and whispered among themselves, and climbed aboard a rumbling and hissing bus headed downtown.

She had followed Jameson as he walked along the uneven cobbled streets shaded by leaning buildings and sun-faded awnings, until he turned into a dark entranceway. He checked the five empty mailboxes on the wall, listened for a moment, then went up a narrow stairway to the second floor. He loosened a tile on a flowered ledge, brandished a dull brass key with a flourish, and unlocked the door. She looked around at the rooms and decided the decorating style would fall under the label of early Mediterranean spy. Spartan but clean, with a bedroom, bath, and small kitchen separated from the living room by a low partition. There were plants in pots here and there, a television and phone, and a current newspaper on a mahogany coffee table, fresh bread on the kitchen counter. She put her pack on the wooden floor, stretched her arms, and listened. It was quiet, even though she knew they were less than a mile from the Vatican City and the boisterous hustle-bustle of one of the oldest cities in the world. Jameson had found a place where they could stay lost in the midst of it all. She had watched him as he looked in the small refrigerator and a couple of cabinets, turned to her, grinned, and said, "You can take a bath first if you want, Cat, then you have a choice for dinner: pasta, bread, wine, and salad—or salad, wine, bread, and pasta."

She had grinned back, glad to be off the road. "I'll have wine, bread, wine, salad, wine, pasta, and wine," she said.

+ + +

"Did you, um, *intend* to kill that man who was Azul Dante's aide, or valet? That Drazic?" Cat asked as they sat at the small wooden table sipping coffee, the dinner finished. "Or did you just *miss?*"

Jameson stared into his coffee cup a moment, then lifted his eyes to hers. His professional self was put off by the suggestion he could have muffed the shot, but he understood that's how it might appear to someone who didn't see what he had seen. He took a deep breath, hesitated, and replied, "I intended to kill no one, Cat."

She heard the strain in his voice. "I didn't mean—"

"Izbek Noir gave me the mission: Kill Dante," said Jameson. "That left me few options. Believe me, I was glad to get away from him and his mujahideen headquarters, and was doubly glad to have that young guy, Slim, with me. Truth be told, I didn't think I'd leave there alive." He paused, lifted his cup to his lips, and sipped. "Problem was, I *already* had a mission, as you know. If I wanted another shot at Noir, I had to appear to be following his orders. I don't know—maybe I'll never be able to infiltrate the mujahideen forces again anyway." He shrugged. "It all looks fairly simple on the face of it. Azul Dante represents the forces of good; Noir, the forces of evil. Dante has his Prodigal Project, the hope of mankind, but—"

"But," she said for him, "we are part of *seven*, you and me, and there is that little book at the end of the Bible, Revelation, and if we read Revelation in correlation with what has been happening to our world, it can only mean one thing—"

"Azul Dante cannot be the savior of mankind," said Jameson as he rubbed his face with one hand. "And his Prodigal Project is going to be somehow used to further his plans—whatever they are."

"So did you intend to shoot him, or Drazic?" she asked. It was *important* to her. She wanted to know about this man, his values, his limits.

"It was to be a ploy," he answered after a moment. "My boss at home agreed I needed to act, so I did. Izbek Noir would learn of the attempted hit and know I had tried to follow his orders. I would be validated, which might make it possible for me to get close to Noir again. No one would get hurt, there would be a flurry of excitement, and my guys could use the situation as reason to bring maybe one or two more of our people close to Dante. The Muslims, Noir's mujahideen, would be immediately suspected, and my boss would be given more time to figure out why I'm on the hit list." He stretched his arms over his head, then rested his big fists on the table. "Cat," he said quietly, "I had a scope-mounted bolt-action rifle. I'm a marksman. The crosshairs rested on Dante's face, and I moved them a bit to the side so the bullet would snap past his shoulder and impact the trunk of a potted palm behind him. It would be loud enough and close enough to frighten every-one, including him. But Cat"—he paused—"Cat . . . I watched Dante's face through that scope, and he was look-ing right into my eyes as I squeezed the trigger. *He knew.* I saw him blink—he *blinked*—and the trajectory of the bul-let curved. It took Drazic right between the eyes. Then one of the security people on the street below with *really quick* reaction time blasted my position on the edge of the roof, and that was all the time I had."

Cat remained silent for a long moment, trying to come to terms with what he described. Finally she asked, "Are you saying Dante can bend the path of a bullet, and *he* did it to his own man?"

"You saw Izbek Noir, Cat," responded Jameson as he leaned forward over the table and stared at Cat intently. "You were one of the first journalists to take note of him when he was a rising star, one of the first to question whether he could be killed. Slim told me all about it—"

"Yes," she agreed, remembering the time a young girl tried to kill Noir with a grenade. After the explosion, Noir was bloodied and blackened, but still standing—and laughing.

"Go back to Revelation, then," he pressed on. "If Rev-elation is real, then certain, uh, otherworldly personalities are real."

Cat felt cold, and involuntarily shuddered. She wanted to change the subject.

"I really must contact my boss, Simon Blake," she said as she rubbed her fingers through her short brown hair. "He's head of our European bureau. He hasn't heard from me in too long, and probably thinks I've fallen for some big mysterious hunk of a man and we're hiding out in a cozy love nest in Rome."

He looked at her, then down at his hands.

"I need to call or e-mail him, John," she went on. She had managed to scan a few headlines over the last couple of days and knew about the planned summit meeting, and about Hiram Sarco and Sarcom. Sarcom, of course, was the parent company of the media group she and Blake were part of. "But I'm afraid it will be traced or something. I don't want to compromise your situation. I can carry my laptop into town, to one of the big hotels. I can use their business center there."

"Use the phone here," he said. "Or the jack for your laptop." He stood, walked over to the television sitting on a wooden cabinet, and turned it slightly. Using a small tool, he quickly opened a panel on the back of the set, and she saw a small black box with blinking red and green lights. "Cable and phone satellite rerouting," he explained. "Anything going out of here seems to originate from Singapore, Seattle, or someplace else." He paused. "My home team electronic whizzes might eventually determine that this location was active, but not the specifics."

"I'm impressed," she said.

"Good." He grinned. He felt tired, but almost fit, thanked God for his life and the chance to *keep fighting*, and was becoming very aware of *her*. "Now tell me more about this, uh . . . love nest you mentioned."

They each watched the other's eyes for a long moment. She saw in him, and felt about him, something she had never known, and doubted she ever would. He saw in her, and felt about her, something he had once known, cherished, lost, and did not think he would ever know again.

"You'll be heading for Paris, then," he said quietly.

"Yes," she said, "probably in the morning." She looked away, then into his eyes again. "And you, John?"

"Not sure. I might stay here long enough to contact my boss, discuss future . . . action. Perhaps I'll head toward the front again. Looks like the Turk–Iraq border will be the next line."

"Are we part of seven, John?" she asked. "Is our being together part of a plan, part of some design, some *reason?*"

"Yes, Cat," he answered. He knew it in his heart. They were part of seven, and still part of the *fight*.

"But tomorrow we go in different directions."

"You'll be here," he said as he tapped his heart with one finger.

"And you." She looked at him, took a deep breath, and said, "Tomorrow is tomorrow. We have tonight, and we haven't finished the wine."

CHAPTER EIGHT

Clara Reese, president of the United States, sat at the right elbow of Azul Dante. For her, the decision expected to be reached at the conclusion of this momentous meeting was a no-brainer. She knew, of course, her agreement to it was historically unprecedented, and it would reap skepticism and outrage from her own Senate and House, and from American citizens—voters—in general. America had signed pacts, partnerships, treaties, and agreements with other countries throughout her more than two hundred years, usually to the good, always with what were perceived as just and prudent reasons. Often these pacts with other countries came as a result of trade, or war. This time, in these *times*, she knew, it was all of that and more. Still, this would be the first time in history the United States agreed to be part of a worldwide coalition under the control and supervision of another leader. Sure, there had been NATO, the OAS, and the inept and embarrassing United Nations, but this was different. Azul

Dante was clearly emerging as the most powerful figure in the world, and America was going to stand with him, defend him, and follow his ... directives. She, a black woman, was sitting as president because the man who had made her his vice president was taken on the day of disappearances, along with his wife. They were, and then they were not, and Clara Reese set aside her questions and fears about why *she* had not been taken and confidently grabbed the reins of political power.

There were twelve at the large polished-wood oblong table. Behind each of the twelve sat another, their aides. They were the leaders of the most powerful and influential countries or regions in the world. Great Britain was represented, and France, as host, Germany, Brazil, Japan, Russia, Australia, Israel, and South Africa. In some cases, like Canada and Mexico, the Far East, or the gutted African states, their larger neighbor represented them. None of the Muslim countries were present, even though many had hoped Iran would come, and China remained aloof, with Korea on her knee. The table was in a paneled and mirrored conference room in the stately and newly refurbished Château Brozek. Reese saw how the reflections in the mirrors appeared to multiply the number of people in the room, then these were reflected, almost ad infinitum, as if all the world's people these leaders represented were there, too. Many could be seen glancing at themselves now and then, but Reese used the reflections to watch the expressions of those on her side of the table. She thought about the nice, private discussion she had with Azul Dante a day earlier.

* * *

Dante had told her unequivocally he could not make the coalition work without her, without America. The United States had the strength and structure to survive after the first horrible days that followed the disappearances, to help hold a defense, then mount an offense against the rampaging mujahideen armies of Izbek Noir. Food, fuel, and medical supplies were still available, banks and schools were open, and the American penchant for sports and entertainment was still being nurtured. People actually went to football games, the movies, and concerts, he had admired, and he had seen a recent article about the renewed efforts of the publishing industry. But more important, he had continued, America had communications capabilities—Sarcom, of course, being the largest and most comprehensive—and she had churches. America was, in the majority, faith based. This meant a large network of people already in place who *believed*, who studied or were at least familiar with the Scriptures, and who would be receptive to an unashamedly faith-based leader . . . like himself. His Prodigal Project was already a viable entity throughout the U.S., and it was helping get the Good Word out about the coalition, about the new world, and the future of mankind. Hand in hand with all that, Dante had continued, America was partners with Israel, and Israel was an important and integral part of the world, like it or not. If the president of the United States publicly agreed to a partnership with the coalition, naming and accepting Azul Dante as its head and his Prodigal Project as facilitator, the world would take note. From that moment, he felt, the handwriting would be on the wall, and any leader that desired freedom, peace, and prosperity for his or her people would climb aboard.

President Reese had listened politely. She found no flaw in his reasoning, and agreed with it in substance. She understood she would have to be politically adroit back home, as this pact would be a volatile issue on two fronts. The first would be subjugating America to foreign leadership; the second would be the religious aspect, that old "separation of church and state" argument. Even in these times, which to her personal self appeared Biblical, many still resisted discussion that advocated a spiritual-theological explanation—let alone solution. She would have to sell Azul Dante's strengths, sell the organizational power and reach of his Prodigal Project, sell them with the theme of making America safe, keeping her strong, and giving Americans the chance to live their lives in peace. Hiram Sarco being in concert with Dante, she knew, meant Sarcom's great multimedia reach would be employed to help in the sell. The world was on fire, she would argue, the Muslim hordes were a very real physical threat, and she as a leader was charged with making a decision for the good of the people. America had to choose sides, and Dante and his Prodigal Project were on the side of right.

Another part of her reasoning she held close, and did not share with Dante. America *was* strong, and almost totally self-sufficient. Geographically, traditionally, and historically, the United States was removed from other parts of the globe, and liked it that way. Americans, even in these strange and worrisome times, were fiercely independent, beholden to none, and not afraid to go it alone if necessary. The very minute, she knew, Azul Dante appeared to be getting too big for his britches, or began implementing strategies that countered the will of the American people, she would advise Congress and resign the U.S. from the coalition. That she would suffer the fall-out from such a decision, that it would be political suicide, did not faze her. She made her decisions from the heart, based on what she thought was the right thing to do for her country. If she sacrificed her political career to pull the United States *out* of a bad pact, so be it. For now, all things considered, Dante and his widespread and respected Prodigal Project was best for America. They had shaken hands at the end of the meeting.

On this day, in the mirrored conference room, President Reese and the other leaders listened as Azul Dante opened the session.

"This is a solemn and momentous occasion," said Dante as he glanced at the faces at the table. "And I am humbled to sit in this place of honor among you. It is not necessary for me to make introductions, as you know each other and what you represent. I thank you for having the courage, vision, and heart to be here on behalf of your people, in behalf of peace for this world."

Behind Dante sat his aide, Sophia Ghent, a glow on her cheeks, excitement in her eyes. At his left elbow sat Hiram Sarco. Sophia glanced at the American multibillionaire. She chastised herself for already deciding she did not like the man. He seemed like a puffed-up martinet to her, accepting the admiration and ministrations of his retinue as if it were his due. He traveled with a squad of aides and secretaries in his entourage, and had his own security types who seemed a little too eager to keep the great, unwashed masses away from him. Her thoughts of security made her think of an American more to her liking, James Devane, recently assigned as part of Dante's detail. She had actually spoken to Devane this morning, just for a moment. Both of them were pleased with his new job. His being there gave them a *chance*. She forced herself to pay attention.

Dante turned to his left, smiled, and Hiram Sarco smiled back. "My friends," said Dante, "I'm sure all of you here know Hiram Sarco, and of the capabilities of his wondrous Sarcom."

Several heads nodded. Of course they knew Sarcom. The media megaconglomerate was a major part of the communications structure for almost all the countries present, and a growing part of the rest. No one denied the power Hiram Sarco brought to Dante, and they were impressed with Dante's ability to bring him onto his team.

"Hiram stands with me now," continued Dante, "and with the Prodigal Project, and with you. With his voice, with President Clara Reese of the United States at my right hand, and with all of you standing with us, we can— we will—prevail." He paused and watched them intently. He perceived their doubts, understood their motivations, heard the echoes of their self-serving desires in their minds. They gazed back at him, and their expressions ranged from neutral to encouraging. He knew each of them silently asked, *What's in it for me?*

"So," he went on, "The formal proposal is in the documents on the table in front of you." There was the bustle and shuffle of papers, aides leaning forward to whisper busily. President Reese opened the folder, but did not look at it. She knew it by heart, and listened as Dante added, "Of course your staffs have already dissected each of the hard points in excruciating detail, so we'll just skim through it to make sure nothing jumps out at us. Okay for now?" It was.

The meeting proceeded.

Outside of the double doors to the conference room stood the American security agent, James Devane. He was officially a junior diplomat on the ambassador's staff, but it was thin cover indeed. He was armed, physically ready, determined, committed, and briefed. He personally did not care for or trust Azul Dante, but he was a team player. He had witnessed the attempt on Dante's life in Nice and had managed to get a quick burst of fire off at the shooter on the roof of a nearby building. He had also seen what was left of the young Muslims found in an apartment in that building and killed by the French security troops. The dead Muslims had been identified as the assassins by the French, and there had been a lot of congratulatory back-slapping after the action. Devane still didn't buy it. It was all too pat, too simple.

So he kept a wary eye, not comfortable with what he now saw as simply *too* much security, too many agencies from too many countries. Everywhere he turned there were serious people in severe suits, wearing scowls and dark sunglasses. Every other person he saw, man or woman, had a wire running out of the back of a jacket to an earpiece, and many people seemed to stand near doors and other exits mumbling sotto voce into their hands. It was getting so an agent needed a scorecard to tell the players, he mused. He stopped musing when he thought of ol' General Izbek Noir, out there in the battlefield wreckage with his crazies by his side. For some reason, the mujahideen had ceased launching medium- and short-range missiles at targets throughout the Middle East and Europe. It was high-tech terrorism, in his view, and he was glad for the respite. He winced at the thought of one of those babies finding its way into this gilded hotel on the Seine River and taking out all the important leaders of the free world. He knew the techno-whizzes from the CIA and other agencies had satellites monitoring the mujahideen forces, and knew several air forces, including the best, had their jet-jockey flyboys up in the skies over Paris, but he still didn't like this gathering. He admitted to himself he *was* okay with his knew assignment, though. He thought of Sophia, and his mind drifted for a moment, wondering how she would look in more *relaxed* attire. He remembered a discussion he had been part of recently, about whether these were the end times as described in Revelation. The lifting-up of the souls had occurred, it was said, and all the children of the world gone in the blink of an eye. Where did that leave *man?* Would man continue? Would there be more children? When *he* went back and studied those passages in Scripture, it seemed to him— even if it all took place *literally*—there were many years of life ahead. In order for humankind to continue, he reasoned, humans would have to, well, *continue*. He was no scholar, but he figured this meant man and woman . . . continuing. He thought of Sophia, of her fine, unblemished complexion, of her delicate hands, her soft hair. He straightened and continued his rounds.

+   +   +

Tommy Church was tired, dirty, smelled of horse manure, had mud on his boots and straw in his hair, and was happy. He had been with the wealthy Saudi for a couple of days, and had worked from sunup to sundown getting the stables and horses squared away. Some of the locals had signed on to help, glad to find work with the economy skewed as it was, and Tommy found himself learning bits of French and Farsi in order to communicate. It was all horse to him, and even if the tack looked different and the farrier, a temperamental Spaniard, seemed to do things the hard way, it was all to the good. He had been given a small but neat loft apartment, took his meals with the other workers at the employee quarters, and had pretty much free rein regarding the boss's stable. The glowering security guards were a constant presence, but he ignored them. He knew he could not really settle in, as he still had places to go, things to do. But, he figured, if one had to linger anyplace, this spread wasn't too bad. He had even managed a telephone connection back to Virginia, to Sissy's place. His sister had been excited to hear from him, and amazed at his good fortune. She told him she had heard from their parents, who were safe at the New Christian Cathedral in

Selma, and she would tell them about his call the next time they spoke. He told her he didn't think he'd stay put long, still determined to get to Paris in time to hear Azul Dante speak, if he could.

So, he had a job, three hots-and-a-cot, and a new friend. Actually he mused, he had a new shadow—the slight and quiet young guy he saw the first day, Piet. The wealthy Saudi, Khalid, told Tommy that Piet was a Jordanian who had recently lost his family as the mujahideen swept through the Saudi–Jordan border. He had taken Tommy aside, placed one hand on the lanky American's shoulder, and leaned close as he spoke softly. He explained it was his opinion that the recent traumatic events in the young Jordanian's life had made Piet so withdrawn, so awkwardly shy. The young man usually communicated with a nod or shake of his head, and if he spoke, it was in barely audible monosyllabic tones. Tommy determined the wealthy Saudi to be a basically decent man, genuinely concerned for the welfare of those around him, including this Piet Dardon waif. Didn't matter to Tommy much either way, as long as the guy kept from underfoot. He had learned that the young guy was not afraid of hard work, seemed to have a natural way with the horses—which went a long way in Tommy's book—and was a quick learner. The way the guy stared at Tommy was a bit disconcerting. Piet would follow Tommy all day, do what he was told, then be right there again, watching. At the dinner table, Piet always managed to sit next to or across from Tommy, his big brown eyes on him only. Once or twice the other men there tried to kid with the shy young man, but his reaction was so politely muted, his feelings so carefully masked, that they stopped.

* * *

It was late afternoon, and Tommy was in the large, well-appointed barn. He had brought two of the black Fresians in from a near pasture and was getting ready to turn out Sultan, the Arabian. He was not surprised to find Piet standing hear him, but was caught off guard when the young guy asked quietly, "Will you go to Paris, then, Tommy?"

"Yep."

"Will you see Azul Dante?"

Tommy shrugged. "Gonna try."

"Perhaps I could go with you?" asked Piet, his face turned to the side. Piet wore, as was his habit, a hooded sweatshirt, sunglasses, and a ball cap over his short black hair. He had smudges of dirt on his jaw and one cheek.

Tommy did not answer, concentrating instead on the big horse shying nervously in the stall. He stood quietly, the halter in his right hand, and waited for the animal to take his scent and attitude. In a moment the big gray, his ears up and forward, his breathing easy, took a couple of steps toward Tommy and stood with his head up but relaxed. Tommy slipped the halter over the horse's face, checked to make sure the stall door was open all the way, and led the animal out. Piet followed, a half-step behind Tommy.

They were out of the barn, and on a gravel walkway, when Piet asked again, "Perhaps I could go with you, Tommy? To see . . . Azul Dante?"

Tommy was surprised by Piet's question because the young man was such a loner, even sleeping on a cot in one of the tack rooms rather than the well-appointed bunk-house with all the other hired hands. "No offense, Piet," said Tommy with a grin as he walked the horse, "but with you bein' a Jordanian and all, I mean, I figured you to be a Muslim, like the owner here, Khalid. Dante is the man puttin' together the forces that will try to defeat that General Izbek Noir, and all those mujahidden Muslims of his. Why would you want to see him?"

For the girl, Faseem, masquerading as the young man Piet Dardon, this was an unfortunate and frightening question right then. She felt at a loss, emotionally and mentally, as if her life were not her own to live. That she was *driven* she understood, but it was the *why* that eluded her, the motive. Ever since her life had been spared on that far blackened battlefield by the tall dark westerner, she felt both free and enslaved at the same time. She was free because she had been given a life, an identity, even some modest funds to travel with—these she had taken from the dead. But she was enslaved by her past, by heredity, customs, mores, and history. She was also enslaved by an unseen, powerful, insidious force, a *persuasion* of sorts, which had penetrated her heart and mind. She felt pulled along by it, her very footsteps guided as if preordained. That's how she came to be on this beautiful horse farm in the lush lands of central France. She had read about Sheik Khalid through the years, of course, about his many holdings around the world. The moment she began to travel across the scarred Saudi Arabian landscape a few weeks ago, she knew she followed a path set for her, and was powerless to turn away from it. The path took her, with Piet Dardon's French passport, into Khalid's house. She had been wel-

comed there, as Piet, perhaps because even the wealthy
and powerful Sheik Khalid saw some potential good use in
the dual Jordanian-French citizenship of the quiet and
troubled young vagabond. She knew the path would also
take her to whatever place Azul Dante was.

Still unable to answer Tommy's question, she watched
as he unlatched a gate, hipped it open, swung it to her to
hold wide, and led the Arabian into the pasture. The big
horse pranced a bit, impatient, and Tommy deftly slipped
off the halter, made a clicking noise with his tongue, and
smacked the animal on the left flank with the open palm of
his right hand. The horse jumped and spun, ran a circle
around the lanky American with his mane and tail flying,
then took off prancing and dancing across the cool green
grass of the pasture. She envied his simple, uncluttered
joy. For Faseem, nothing was at that moment simple, and
joy was an emotion she guessed might still exist within her,
but buried very, very deep. She waited while Tommy
watched the horse run. He walked out of the pasture, and
she closed the gate behind him. She watched as he hung
the halter and lead on a fence post, his hands tough and
sure, his body lean. He was her other problem, she knew.
The first moment she saw him, she was rocked by a heated
and unrelenting rush of emotion and excitement. He was
like no man she had ever known: quiet, self-assured, good-
natured, and good-hearted. He was a man who didn't mind
making fun of himself, or even having others do it. He had
those pale eyes he used to *look* at you when he spoke to you,
that easy grin, his unruly straw-colored hair. He actually
walked around chewing a stalk of grass, and she knew

absolutely she had never seen a man whose blue jeans fit him like his did. She had seen, once or twice, other men stomping around in cowboy boots, pretending to be like someone from one of the forbidden American movies. Tommy wore his boots like the very real horseman he was and the same went for the large silver buckle on his leather belt. Her close examination of him told her something else: Tommy was young and easygoing, but he possessed an inner toughness hinted at in his eyes, his . . . *awareness*. There was serious depth there, she was sure, and Faseem wished she had the courage to ask him about the small scars on his hands and forearms where it looked as if he had been burned and cut.

He was a problem for her because she wanted desperately to drop the stupid sunglasses, shrug off the hooded sweatshirt, throw away the hat, run her fingers through her hair, and stand before him as Faseem, a girl. This thought made her even more unsure, because she guessed he was a man who had . . . known . . . more than a few women in his life. American women. On rare occasions she had thumbed through magazines from Europe and America and had looked at the photographs of the women on the pages with alarm. They were all so perfect, so groomed, so . . . *healthy*. They were curvaceous and bold, unafraid of their bodies, unafraid of the stares of men. She unconsciously glanced down the front of the sweatshirt at her slim torso, her long legs in her boy jeans. She placed her right hand, fingers splayed, over her chest, and doubted a man like Tommy would give her a knowing look even if he *knew*.

"Piet?" said Tommy, "Hey, ol' buddy, you okay? I didn't mean to pry, or nothin'—about the Muslim thing, you know. Just wonderin'." He began to walk toward the barn, and he grinned at her. "C'mon, we got more work to do before they serve up another one of these fancy dinners they give us workers at this spread."

"Stop," she replied as she lightly put her left hand on his right forearm. "I'm sorry, Tommy. Your question raised more questions in me, um, within me. Sometimes I have difficulty—"

"What? Your English?" interrupted Tommy, "Well, Piet, your English is a lot better than my Jordanian, follow? You don't talk much, but when you do, I understand you fine. Don't worry about it."

It wasn't her English, of course. Once again she was awed by her mother's strength and foresight. In a culture where most girls are allowed only a minimum of formal education, where women are considered unworthy of higher learning, her mother had insisted Faseem go to school. Her mother had arranged an English-language tutor for her, explaining and validating it for her father and their local imam by telling them the influence of the West was unavoidable, and it would be better to have one of their own know and read the infidel language so it could be monitored and controlled. Faseem had hated it at first, but when it gave her access to various books and the magazines, she came to look at it as a gift . . . as she surely did now.

She wanted to turn her face and look at Tommy, but she stared at the ground as she responded, "You asked why I wanted to see and hear Azul Dante. I—*must*, that is all I can tell you." *And I must travel with you, Tommy Church*, she said to herself. *I must remain by your side.*

He nodded absently, pulled the chewed stalk of grass from between his teeth, "Yeah, I guess that would be my answer, too. I mean, this is our world, these are our times—weird and unsettled as they are—and I want to be part of it, you know? This Azul Dante is clearly a man who will make a difference in the world, and I feel pulled to him, to what he stands for, his energy." His first choice would be to travel alone. He was used to it, it was simpler, and when it was just you, you didn't have to worry about anybody else missing a meal, getting tired, or whining. Whining grated on him. But there was something about this Piet that made him want to, like, *look out* for the guy. "Tell you what, Piet. I think ol' Khalid might be headin' up to Paris for some business in the next day or so. . . . That's what he told me, anyway. Maybe we can ride along. Don't seem like he ever leaves this place without at least three cars in caravan anyway, what with his security dummies, and all his bags and stuff. Hear me, though." He waited until she lifted her eyes to his, her hand still on his arm, "I travel light and fast. If you come with me, you got to keep up, understand?"

She fought the urge to move closer to him, and forced herself to pull her eyes away from his gaze. "I understand, Tommy," she said softly.

+   +   +

In the old Kurdistan region of Iraq, north of the town of Mosul, fighters who called themselves "soldiers of the

dirt" felt the ground tremble. They were in front-line positions facing south, toward what was left of Baghdad and
the entrenched mujahideen forces. An observer of the area
would appreciate the name the fighters had given themselves, as the dreary landscape of dirt, rocks, and mud,
overhung by a clinging wet mist showed no sign of battle
units at ready. Closer inspection by a trained eye would re-
veal cleverly camouflaged bunkers, armored vehicles dug
in and covered with dirt, and muddied armed men embracing the very earth they were prepared to die for. The
ground trembled, and for many, that tremble resonated
within the walls of their hearts. The tremble came not
from the heaving earth's crust, but from tons of armor-
plated, steel-tracked tanks. Faintly rattling the mists in the
distance came a metallic clattering, as if a flock of steel
birds was beating its way into the wet air. Attack helicopters. All the Kurds tightened the grip on their weapons,
their eyes squinting into the mists, their breathing shallow,
mouths suddenly dry. They waited for the bellowing roar
of the beast, the artillery fires that would surely be unleashed within seconds.

One of the older combat veterans heard a young man
near his left elbow moan softly, and he glanced at the man.
He saw the young man's white-knuckled grip on his assault
rifle, saw his lower lip quivering, the wide, fearful eyes
blinking and staring.

"Do you feel the earth beneath you, soldier?" he asked
the youngster, his voice urgent.

"Yes," the man muttered.

"Do you feel the richness, the smell of it . . . the dirt

that covers you, the soil that runs through your very veins?" asked the veteran.

The young soldier did not respond.

"Out there," said the veteran as he jutted his jaw toward the south, "are the foul mujahideen. Hear them as they awaken? They come today, *now*. They come at us, to crush us as they move through our lands. Back there"—he shrugged his jaw against his right shoulder, toward the north—"back there wait the Turks." He spat. "They will sit back and let the mujahideen scum weaken themselves attacking us. So."

"So?" responded the young soldier, his eyes never leaving the mists in front of him.

"So, we are Kurds, we are *soldiers of the dirt*, and it is *our dirt*. We have the Muslims to our front, the Turks to our rear, good weapons in our hands, and the very earth we live and die for beneath us. Look around us, boy."

Reluctantly the young soldier pulled his eyes from the front and scanned the area to his flanks.

"Look at the wonderful tools of war we possess now," said the veteran. "Not like the old days, no. Now we have the finest, provided by the Americans. Yes, we are soldiers of the dirt, but those who come at us will find there are stones in this dirt, and it is not easily plowed."

"Yes," agreed the young soldier. He took a deep breath and settled.

It was not the roar of artillery that came first, but a deep-throated, howling, primitive, and guttural moan that grew steadily in volume all across the front until it washed against the Kurd lines with a palpable force, bringing with it the hot winds of anger and terror. The mujahideen battle cry rose until it became a leaning wall, and as it crescendoed, the first tearing rockets and punching mortar rounds began to fall.

"Now, child," said the veteran, "they come. Kill as many as you are able—then teach them how a Kurd dies."

It was raw and total war unleashed, condensed into a small area of valley, ridgeline, and low red mountain. A burning red sun threw its metallic glare across the battlefield, baking off the mists, illuminating scenes of brutal, merciless carnage. The mujahideen attack helicopters wolfed among the Kurd bunkers and armored vehicles, firing their armor-piercing missiles, machine-gunning the Kurd infantry. Mujahideen tanks rumbled forward, crushing with their treads those fortifications they had not already blasted with their guns. Behind came the hordes of Muslim foot soldiers, screaming, running, firing, falling. They fell as they lunged forward, their legs still kicking, their mouths open, eyes staring, fingers locked on the triggers of their weapons.

They fell because the soldiers of the dirt lay down a withering sheet of fire from their positions that scythed through mujahideen ranks, rending and piercing vulnerable flesh armored only by anger and hatred. The waves of Muslim attackers washed against the Kurd positions, here overwhelming a line, there falling back in bloodied and torn retreat. The deafening storm of war came from the belly of the beast, and with it came tearing explosions and punching machine-gun fire, which ruptured and ripped the screaming soldiers of both sides. In sheer weight of numbers, the mujahideen outgunned the Kurds. But they fought over Kurdish soil and learned—as had many before them—the price of dirt.

One of the Muslim attack helicopters took a shoulder-fired missile in the turbine engines, and it spiraled down wildly, burning as it fell with a crunching crash just behind the Kurd lines. The rotor blades splintered and flailed away from the wreck upon impact, killing several nearby Kurdish soldiers. The Kurds looked over their shoulders at the wreckage a few yards away and saw that all the Muslims in the chopper had been killed outright except the copilot, sitting on the front left side, behind the cracked windshield. They could see him writhing and fighting as he tried to extricate himself from the twisted wreckage before the licking flames came to him. They saw he was pinned and would not escape. Many turned away, back to the fighting. The young soldier beside the veteran, his face blackened by gunpowder, his eyes white and wide with adrenaline, saw the Muslim copilot trying to beat away the oily orange flames that ate at him. The copilot's face was stretched, his mouth a wide black hole as he put his head back and screamed as he flailed and burned. The young Kurdish soldier turned a bit in his trench and pointed his assault rifle at the copilot. He would shoot the Muslim, and end it.

"No," spat the veteran as he pulled the barrel of the young soldier's rifle down toward the dirt, "don't waste a bullet on a dying Muslim—let him burn—"

"But . . . but . . . ," gasped the younger man as he stared at the veteran, "no one should have such a death."

"Let him burn," repeated the older man over the screams of the dying Muslim copilot, which cut through the rumble and spit of battle around them.

The young soldier squeezed his eyes shut, a tear ran down his left cheek, and he turned back toward the oncoming attackers. He grunted, stiffened, and fell facedown into the Kurd soil as a bullet punched into his face, right between his eyes.

The veteran saw the young soldier die at his elbow, ripped off a long burst from his weapon at the charging mujahideen, and screamed, *That's how a soldier of the dirt dies, my child!*"

Less than a mile behind the thunder and fire of the front lines, standing alone on the hood of a utility vehicle, was General Izbek Noir, Supreme Commander of the Mujahideen Armies. He felt a ripple of seductive energy course through his body, and he fought the desire to give himself over to it. These were the most difficult times for him to maintain the rigid self-discipline required to remain in this brutish, limited form. He stood as a man, dark, angular, strong, with a beak nose, hawklike eyes of blackened embers, a cruel purple-blue cut of a mouth, and long, pointed fingers. He stood as a spiky, black-haired man dressed in a plain soldier's drab uniform, the only thing identifying him as a general the blazing red star with a black border pinned to his collars and hat. He stood as a man, and his sinewy, obscene tongue licked his stretched lips as he caught the first scent of burnt human flesh. These were the moments of reward for him in this complex game of power and destiny, moments too few, in his estimation—too few and too long as he chafed at the contrived delays in this absurd theater of man. War, that was the reward, war and all that it spawned, the hate, the fear, the suffering, the waves of death—the repeated cessation of life, the *ending* of man, over and over again.

Several of his staff officers called out to him status reports of the battle as it raged. He acknowledged them offhandedly. He didn't care. He already knew the outcome anyway, and he was more interested in the immediate *effect* on the soldiers of both sides. There was no finesse here, just a bloody full-frontal assault by his mujahideen against those entrenched and incredibly tough Kurds. Didn't matter, he reflected, Kurd, Muslim, or what-all. When the hot steel came tearing through the flesh, when the skin was seared, when the blood bubbled, spat, and vomited out, the dying was the same, the crying was the same. *Why do so many men cry out for their* mother *when death comes for them?* he wondered. *Their mother*, he mused, *woman, the weak and defiled vessel, suckler of man as infant.* Woman was a bag of fluid and tissue, duplicitous in nature, desirable, repulsive, inconsequential in his eyes. *Why don't they cry out for their* father? He wondered, *Supposedly* the *father of us all?* His skin tingled and began to redden around his eyes. He forced himself to take a couple of deep breaths, to let his mind relax.

One of the staff officers called to him that a few prisoners were being brought to his headquarters. This pleased him. His forces had an overall policy of taking no prisoners, of course. But he always gave orders to a few of his special units to capture some of the enemy soldiers alive, if possible. They were to bring the prisoners to headquarters, ostensibly so these enemy survivors might be questioned by his intelligence officers. He could give a fig for the intelligence gleaned from this rabble. His real desire, known by his staff, but never acknowledged, was to watch as they were executed, often taking part in the killings. Depending on the numbers of defeated and captured enemy, he might get creative, devising interesting ways for them to die. He enjoyed watching the eyes of the condemned man, seeing through them and into the puny soul. The sickly sweet and poisonous stench of fear was a tonic to him, and he found intense pleasure in seeing the moment of death as it came, seeing the last moment of recognition and screaming disbelief in the rabbit eyes of man.

He was filled with anticipation and accomplishment as he waited for the prisoners, his eyes on the close horizon now cut by thick, roiling columns of heavy smoke. Burst and burned tanks and armored vehicles burned like that, he knew, and in them lay the twisted, charred, and ruptured shells of men. He filled his lungs and smirked. Azul Dante should thank him for this little rumble in the war between good and evil, he thought. Got to keep the pressure on. He turned to his left suddenly, cocked his head, and became very still. *There* . . . there it was again. His senses had picked up movement in the firmament of the earth, a shifting, a pulsing warp of energy that caused *change*. He knew the movement would be undetectable to any of the men around him, but to him it was as real as the pressure of his skin against his inner substance. He stared south, and west, in the direction of the shift, the direction of Israel, of Jerusalem, of the southeastern quadrant of the old city—of the Temple Mount.

"Ah, Azul," he said quietly, his voice thick with jealous admiration, "you are truly an artist."

CHAPTER NINE

"Minister Dante! Minister Dante!" cried one of the reporters jammed into a small lobby near a set of elevators in the Château Brozek. Dante, Hiram Sarco, Sophia Ghent, and three or four others had stepped out of an elevator into the din of questions being shouted at them. The American, James Devane, and several other security agents from various countries were there, too, as were members of the hotel staff. Dante turned his head slightly. "Minister Dante," cried the same reporter once more. "You will know by now that the mujahideen forces have renewed their advance—in the northern regions, the Kurd regions, of Iraq. Turkey will be next, sir, then— then—" Other reporters began shouting, clamoring to be heard, each one with the *most* important question. But the first would not be denied. "Minister Dante! Isn't it true the bulk of the Coalition Forces are in North Africa? Aren't they really chasing the tail of the dog, sir? Everyone knows there is nothing left of those areas anyway. Why is

Turkey left undefended? Are the meetings here designed to address these apparent *weaknesses* in your overall strategy, sir?"

Dante stopped. He stood tall and poised while the questions rattled around him, and finally stuttered to an expectant halt. Only when it was quiet and every eye was on him did he smile and respond. "My good man. First—yes, of course, I'm aware of General Noir's assault on the peaceful Kurd people. As for the Coalition Forces, they are being brilliantly led by General Reginald Urquhart, of the famed British Combined Forces. I selected him because he is a respected and experienced military leader, and he knows what he is doing. Perhaps he has seen a dog turn on its *own* tail when threatened. But hear me, the last thing a military man needs when waging a righteous war is some know-it-all politician like me telling him how to go about things." He paused, in total command of everyone in the room. "As for your reference to weakness, my friend, that is precisely why I asked for these meetings with so many of our greatest world leaders at this time. I cannot stand alone against Izbek Noir, nor can anyone. But *together* we can defeat him and his lawless followers. I don't have to tell you who is assembled here—you know already. We have scheduled a full press conference for this evening, followed by cocktails and mingling, as it were. At the press conference, you will hear from President Clara Reese of the United States, Prime Minster Daniel Pearlman of Israel, and other leaders who have joined me in this struggle for world freedom." His smile widened as he glanced at Hiram Sarco, and he added, "The word will go out, believe me, my friend. The word will go out to Izbek Noir and any who will hear it. The word will be *strength*, because that's what this new agreement between world leaders represents. The tribes of man are bonding, melding. Even though the tribes of man speak in many tongues since the Tower of Babel incident, the *desire* of man embedded in his heart speaks with one voice. The energies of man will no longer be scattered like dust motes on the winds of individual self-preservation, but focused like a beam of light, brought together by a globally common desire for peace, for direction. Yes, this war seems unrelenting, but it is no more unrelenting than man's desire for *oneness*."

Someone in the room began applauding, and soon everyone was caught up in the good feeling. It felt *right*. Dante mused as he basked in it, *And I am the one*.

The security agents began opening a corridor through the crowd so Dante and others could make their way out of the lobby. Hiram Sarco turned quickly to one of his aides and whispered to her, "Find out who that was." The young woman nodded. She knew Sarco meant the reporter who shouted the questions at Azul Dante, and she guessed the reporter would be getting a new assignment shortly— if the poor sod still had a job. She had been around Sarco long enough to know another thing about that little session next to the elevators. In the evening papers, and on the news channels across the world, the readers and viewers would learn Minister Azul Dante was questioned about the renewed mujahideen assault, and they would be given the best parts of Dante's response, and the enthusiastic reaction of the journalist audience. No more, no less. The crowd in the lobby dispersed.

* * *

As the various participants in the conference began to go their own way in the hotel, Dante and his group walked out of the lobby toward a private banquet room for an early lunch. Sarco walked next to Dante, Sophia and Sarco's aide tailed them, and the hovering security agents were everywhere. Suddenly Dante stopped, his smile tight, his eyes brittle. "So *there* you are, Cat Early."

"Minister Dante," replied Cat. Her smile was cautious, and she held her pen and notebook by her side.

Dante had known she was in the hotel the moment she arrived, of course, but he said, "Didn't know you'd be here for this diplomatic stuff, Miss Early. Thought you preferred the battlefields."

At least on the battlefield you usually know who your enemy is, thought Cat. Her boss and head of the Paris Bureau, Simon Blake, had already told her Dante had asked about her, and told him she was welcome to attend even the press conferences limited to the *select* journalists. "I just go where I'm pointed, Minister Dante," she said, strangely emboldened, "and right now I'm pointed at you."

Dante's mind replayed the image of the high-powered rifle pointed at him from the rooftop, that dark soldier of Izbek Noir's looking at him through the scope, the bullet deliberately aimed to miss him. The number *seven* rang in his head. "Yes," he said evenly. He paused, and for a moment it was as if no one else were there. "So," he continued in a lighter tone, "been on sabbatical, Cat? We haven't seen you around."

She shrugged.

"No matter," said Dante. He turned to his left. "Hiram

Sarco, Cat Early. I believe this impertinent young whelp of a reporter is one of *yours*, sir."

Sarco grunted and laughed. He shook Cat's hand and said, "Keep up the good work, kid. Looks like you've got him on the run."

Sarco's aide laughed louder than the others, and Cat said simply, "Yes, sir, it's a pleasure to meet you." She knew the newspapers she wrote for, and the news channels she occasionally filmed a piece for, were but small parts of Sarcom. Still, Hiram Sarco was her ultimate boss.

"Sophia will see you have a pass for this evening's affair, Cat," said Dante dismissively. He and the others turned away.

Sarco walked a few steps with Dante before saying quietly, "That one, that Cat Early—I believe she had a sister that worked for one of our groups—Caroline Early. The sister was killed in Africa, I believe, maybe a year ago. Only reason I'm mentioning the sister is it seems I remember she was sort of a troublemaker, too." He sniffed. "All you have to do is say the word, Azul, and this one, this *Cat*, she will *be gone*."

Odd way to put it, thought Dante, but he said easily, "No, no, Hiram. The young lady is just doing her job. Besides, with the aggressive ones like her, I think it's better to keep them close. Easier to control that way."

"I bow to your wishes, learned one," said Sarco.

You, and soon the whole world, pig, thought Dante.

Cat watched them go, then turned and gave Sophia a quick hug. The two women studied each other a moment, and Sophia said, "Cat, guess who's here?"

"Hmm," responded Cat as she put one finger against her temple and scrunched up her face in concentration, "could it be a certain American diplomat who is really sort of a security guy but nobody is supposed to know it—the one you, Sophia, would like have as your own very *personal* security guy?"

Sophia sighed, and smiled. "I should have known you'd already know," she said. "Can you believe it, Azul actually *asked* for James to be assigned to him after that dreadful shooting in Nice when we lost—when Drazic was killed." She paused, and added, "That was the last time I saw you, Cat. I hate to sound like Azul, but where *have* you been?"

"I had a couple of follow-up assignments Simon gave me after you and Minister Dante left Nice," Cat lied. She looked away a moment, then into Sophia's eyes as she asked, "Why, um, why would Dante ask for James Devane after the incident in Nice? I thought Dante didn't like Devane, and you and I suspected he might actually be a bit jealous of him because of you."

Sophia nodded, her eyes big. "Yes," she said, "I know. But after that shooting and all—"

"What do you mean, Sophia?" asked Cat, dreading the answer.

"Oh, Cat," answered the young woman breathlessly. "When the shot was fired at Azul and absolute pandemonium broke out, James was the only security agent to get a shot at the assassin. He fired his gun up toward the roof of a nearby building and was pretty sure he hit his target. He was the first, and only, agent to react—until the French agents cornered the assassin and his partners in a room of

the building, and . . . killed them." She put one hand on
Cat's forearm. "Cat, it was so scary, that whole thing. But
James *acted*, and I guess Azul was impressed."

I'm impressed, too, thought Cat as she studied Sophia's
excited face. *American Agent James Devane shot American
Agent John Jameson . . . and now Dante has brought Devane
onto his team.* She had a sudden, daunting feeling in her
heart they were all being *used*, being manipulated by forces
they could not match or control. It was hopeless, senseless
to fight it. Man was simply too small, too powerless. Even
as these thoughts crashed around in her head, she heard
John Jameson's gentle, strong, calming voice telling her
about faith. Study Scripture, he had told her. Find the
truth there. Then listen to your heart, and cling to the
faith in a power greater than any other. She felt the blood
pounding in her temples, took a deep breath, and smiled at
Sophia. "Good, Sophia," she said, regaining her compo-
sure. "Having James close by will be a good thing for you.
As your new friend, I would caution you about Dante. He's
just a man, right? And men can get pretty territorial over a
woman like you. And as your new *girlfriend*, Sophia, I
would caution you not to act like some lovestruck sixteen-
year-old when you're around James. I repeat: make him
work for you a bit. Don't be so eager, and easy."

"Yes," replied Sophia, her cheeks reddening. "I remember your advice, and I have tried to stay, um . . . cool, you
know?" Then she stuck her tongue out at Cat briefly and
added, "I'm not some worldly woman like you, Cat, some
veteran journalist who probably keeps a man in every hotel
from here to Timbuktu."

"I wish," said Cat as she thought of John.

"I'll keep your feelings about Azul in mind, too, Cat," said the young woman. "And I thank you for being . . . you."

Cat smiled and shrugged.

"See you at the conference this evening, then," said Sophia as she turned to catch up with the others.

+   +   +

Slim Piedmont, lanky, unshaved, wearing what might be called a combat-photojournalist-utilitarian ensemble— khaki pants, shirt, and belt, scuffed suede hiking boots, a desert camouflage headband, and the obligatory surfer sunglasses—sat in a wicker chair in the lobby of a small hotel on the right side of the Seine River and watched as Cat Early approached with a grin. At his feet sat his battered camera bag. He carried both a digital and a prized 35-mm Pentax. As he stood, he wondered about his luck with girls. He had been in love with Cat's sister, Caroline, and had been immediately smitten with Cat when she came into his life. Now Caroline was dead, and Cat had declared him her "best, most special friend *ever*," since she had met Johann Rommel né John Jameson, *his* agent friend. Maybe she was attracted to older guys, he thought. He pushed those feelings aside as she hugged him tightly, keeping him close to her for a long wonderful moment before finally stepping back and holding him at arm's length for inspection. He saw there were tears in her eyes.

"Slim," she said, "look at you. You look great. I mean, you could use a shave, and your hair still looks like an explosion in a silo, and your clothes—"

"Good to see you, too, Cat."

"How'd you know I was here?" she asked.

"Hey, I'm an investigative journalist in addition to being one of the finest combat photographers in the world," he answered nonchalantly. "I just did some digging, that's all—tapped into my sources, the whole investigatory thing, you know."

"You booked a room here because you know this is where I always stay when I'm in Paris, you mean," she said. "And you checked with the front desk every morning, noon, and night."

"Well . . . yeah." He hesitated, then asked quietly, "How's our . . . friend?"

She did not know what answer would be the safest, so she said nothing.

"Cat," he said as he glanced around the lobby to make sure no one was listening. "We were together that morning in Nice before the assassination attempt on Dante, remember? We both know our friend traveling as Johann was there for a specific reason, and it wasn't to make sure Dante had a nice breakfast soufflé, okay? Next thing you know, *bang*, the rifle shot, ol' dead-eyes Drazic falls even deader than he *had* been, and everybody goes crazy. I go into my action-photog act, and when things settle down, I can't find you anywhere. You know that young 'diplomat,' James Devane, Cat? He's a pretty good guy. He didn't tell me outright, but I got the impression those young Muslims the French killed in that apartment were ringers—and he shot at the *real* shooter and thought he might have winged him. You're gone, Johann's gone, and over a week later you come waltzin' in here la-dee-da." He made a face, then rubbed one knuckly hand over it as he added, "So I ask you again, how is our friend, Cat?"

Cat studied his eyes for a long moment, searching in them for anything that wasn't genuinely open, honest, and caring. She was reassured. "He's fine, Slim. He's nicked up a bit, not sure of his next move, but . . . fine." She looked around the lobby now, then said, "But I do not know where he is at this moment, Slim. He knew I had to come here, and we . . . parted."

Slim grinned and let out a breath. He was pleased. "It's not that I worry about the big guy, know what I mean?" he said. "But you know, he's—he's—"

"I know, Slim."

"Hey, Cat, let me get your bags."

They headed toward the stairs. "Have you been covering the conferences over at that big hotel, Slim?" asked Cat.

"Nah," said the young man. "Too many gadflies, popinjays, paparazzi, poofenwiffles, and pistol-packing, proactive security types. Honest, working film-burners like me can't even get close. Can't sell shots of Azul Dante standin' around lookin' like royalty surrounded by all the fawnin' leaders of the world anyway—there's already too many. They'll be sellin' postcards of the guy, next." He turned suddenly, and added, "He's smart, though, Dante. Can you believe Sarcom is on his team now—our boss, Hiram Sarco, ol' 'never fair and totally off-balance'? And did you hear what he did yesterday? Invited representatives from *Muslim* countries to take part in these meetings—made some noises about how the mujahideen and Izbek Noir have 'perverted' the real lessons in the Quran. Well, *duh*. So I guess some prominent Muslims might show up. Uh, by *prominent*, do I actually mean filthy rich Muslims, like Saudis?" He sniffed, and turned to Cat as they got to her room. "Like I said, the guy is smart."

"Come with me tonight, Slim," said Cat on impulse.

"To the kasbah?"

"No, silly. To Dante's big press conference. There's a reception afterward. I can get Dante's secretary, Sophia, to clear you."

"Isn't she that porcelain hottie that liked my hair?"

Cat sighed and shook her head, "That's her, but don't waste your time, Slim. She's infatuated with a guy already."

"How could she be infatuated with anybody but me after she's met me?" he asked, indignantly. He pulled his shirt away from his bony chest, looked at it, and asked, "Do I have to wear somethin', you know, like—civilized?"

"Please," she laughed, "for me?"

"Yeah, yeah."

"Slim," she asked as he turned to go, "what in the world is a poofenwiffle?"

He just waved one hand over his shoulder as he walked away.

+   +   +

The main, spacious lobby of the Château Brozek was as far as they were permitted to go, so Tommy Church and Piet Dardon decided to take a look around. It was the first time in Paris for both of them, and in spite of the times and circumstances, they found it exciting to be there. They had ridden in the third car of Khalid's little caravan from the countryside and into the sprawling urban areas of Paris. The Saudi did not travel lightly, but the staff members of the hotel were ready for him. He and his entourage had stayed there in the past, and even though rooms were at a premium and the town was flooded with an international array of dignitaries, Khalid was greeted like the wealthy royalty he was. Once out of the cars and in the lobby, Khalid had explained to Tommy and Piet that his luggage and his aides would have to endure a comprehensive security examination—the bags, the credentials and weapons of his personal security—that would take some time. He would not be bothered with this, of course, but would retire to his room for a nap. He wished them good luck and walked away with a wave. Tommy noticed that Khalid wore a tailored business suit, no robes or head-covering while "amongst the infidels," he supposed.

Tommy and Piet knew already they would not be staying at the same hotel as Khalid. They were little frogs, and the whole pond was awash in big boys. An American student Tommy had spoken with in London told him about a smaller, less expensive hotel within walking distance—if you were a pretty good walker—of the center of things. It was called the Mont Vin, and was popular with journalists and others on a tight schedule and budget. He and Piet would hike over there, but first Piet wanted to look around the big hotel, which to Tommy looked a bit too fancy. He admitted to himself it was interesting to look at all the different people, knowing that some of the most powerful world leaders were there. He kept watching the banks of elevators, thinking any moment Azul Dante himself would come walking out, smiling and waving at the peasants. He didn't know very much about police or security people, but he saw what he guessed were lots of them, wearing their staring scowls, watching everything and everybody. He followed Piet around, wondering why the quiet young man was so interested in the elevators, the exits, the little side lobbies that led off to various conference rooms. The place was big enough to have one whole floor dedicated as a convention area, and others for shops, salons, and restaurants.

Finally Piet stopped in the center of the main lobby, tilted his head, and appraised a huge three-dimensional mural that took up one entire inner wall. It was made of beaten metals, copper, silver, bronze, brass, tin, and to Tommy the motif seemed to be about a medieval fair, or battle, some pageantry. Banners swirled through it, and pikes with small flags, figures in helmets leaned toward one another, and what looked like a twisting dragon with a spiraling tail hung over it all. Here and there were lances, arrows, and curved swords, and some of these helped give the work its three-dimensional look, as they were affixed to the various layers of metals. It seemed strange to Tommy that such a thing would be made to hang in a hotel lobby, but he figured, *Hey, what do I know about French hotels* or *French art?* He stood patiently behind Piet as the young man walked from one end of the work to the other, intently examining each of the pieces. He didn't know why Piet was so taken with the thing, and was going to suggest they get out of there and try to find their own hotel, when a couple of the serious types in suits approached. First one spoke in French, but Tommy wasn't sure what he said. Then the other spoke in another language Tommy did not understand. It was a question, and their tone was barely civil.

"Perhaps you speak English, then," said the first one as he stared at Tommy.

"Yep."

"We asked you, sir, if you and your friend are guests here at the hotel."

"No," replied Tommy, "we came here with Khalid, uh . . . the Prince? We came with him."

The two security men glanced at each other. Piet said nothing.

"But you are not guests here?" repeated the first.

"Just admiring the artwork," said Tommy. "Is that okay?"

"Of course," responded the man coldly, "but I'm afraid the hotel is very sensitive to persons . . . loitering . . . in the lobby at the present time. I'm sure you understand, sir."

Tommy looked at the man's face, and that of his companion. He felt Piet, who stood close, tense up, so he nudged him with his elbow and said tightly, "C'mon, Dorothy, we don't want any of *these* apples." The young man said nothing, but followed Tommy as they turned and walked across the lobby to the large sets of doors leading down wide steps to the sidewalk below. The two security men watched them blankly as they went.

"Tommy?" asked Piet in his soft voice after they had walked a little more than a block. "Who is Dorothy?"

"Ah, she's just a little Kansas gal who found herself in unfamiliar surroundings," laughed Tommy. "Sort of like us, but with fancier shoes."

Faseem, keeping Piet's face impassive, said nothing. But she decided this Dorothy person must have been important to Tommy if he still remembered her *shoes*.

An hour later Cat Early saw the lanky American and his smaller companion standing at the front desk of the Vin Mont. She had hurried out to buy a pair of shoes for the outfit she had borrowed for the evening, and as she entered the spartan lobby, she heard Tommy's plainly American accent and glanced at him. She turned toward the stairs and hoped maybe she'd get a chance to speak with this guy in the next day or so, maybe catch up on news from the home front. She was particularly interested in how world events were played by the media back in the States. She had no time now, though. She looked at his face once more, so she'd recognize him, and saw the person with him turn and pick up a bag from the floor. It was only a glimpse of movement, but she was struck by the appearance of the figure. The tall American, frayed jeans, cowboy boots, easy grin, was clearly and unapologetically male. The one with him, though— she wasn't sure. Boys' clothes, sweatshirt, sunglasses, baseball cap, and all, but the word *androgynous* came to mind. She headed up the stairs, and thought, *Well, Cat, this is Paris, what's the big deal? Boy, girl, whatever—not my business anyway.*

+   +   +

Mike Tsakis, CIA Field Agent Supervisor, looked at the display on his daughter's cell phone as it buzzed. He stood in the neat kitchen of his small home in Virginia, not far from Langley. The incoming call originated from a country and area code he did not recognize, and he muttered, "Finally." He held the small phone awkwardly between his left shoulder and ear, as he stood over the breakfast dishes in the sink, and grunted, "J. Cricket."

"It's me, Pinocchio."

"I thought you were all hung up."

"Nah . . . I got no strings to tie me down."

Kids' word games, thought Tsakis, relieved, *to keep us safe*.

"Is this two tomato cans and a tight string?" asked John Jameson, "or a boom-box ensemble?"

"This is still a secure line, John," said Tsakis with a grin. "So where are you?"

"I'm on the road, north, out of Italy." There was a pause, then in a different voice, Jameson asked, "Who took out Guido, Mike? I got the word yesterday."

Tsakis hesitated, then replied, "Apparently it was some of our teammates, John—under the orders of my boss." He knew he would not have to explain further about Benjamin Carter, and he knew he did not have to tell Jameson he would have prevented it if he could have.

"Understood."

"He's figured out that was you in Nice, John," said Tsakis. "So he feels justified in targeting you as rogue."

"I don't blame him—I *am* rogue."

"You traveling alone now, John?"

"Yep," responded Jameson, "I'm revising as I go along, as you can imagine, Mike. I don't believe going back to

Noir, whether to make another attempt on him or just maintain my credibility, has value. Being on the front takes me away from the *real* action—the *real problem*."

Tsakis knew Jameson referred to Azul Dante.

"I'm alone," continued Jameson, "and moving fast, so I figure to head for France and kind of . . . linger for a bit. Bunch of bigwigs are there, or headed there—including our *real* boss."

"Yes," agreed Tsakis. He thought of Clara Reese, glad she was in the Oval Office when they needed someone with guts. He knew she would probably sign an agreement with Dante's coalition—but he believed she would do nothing to hurt her country. "What about your bona fides?" he asked. Jameson's Johann Rommel identification had to be blown sky-high by now, he figured.

"All fresh, excellent quality, and squeaky clean . . . Irish lineage."

Tsakis would not ask for the name, even on a "secure" line, and he knew Jameson would not expect him to.

"I'll sit back a bit, nearby, and watch," said Jameson, referring to the activities in Paris. "If I plan to act in any way, I'll let you know."

"John," asked Tsakis, deeply worried, "who *is* this guy?" He referred to Dante.

"Not sure," replied Jameson as the number *seven* resonated in his heart. "But I believe if you'll go to the last few chapters of that book I suggested you read, you'll find some tantalizing parallels."

"I'll do that." Tsakis thought of the Bible, the feelings that had begun to overtake him as he explored it. "You be careful."

"I will, Mike," said Jameson. He thought of Cat Early, worried about her. He thought of Slim, also. He laughed softly and added, "I like Mr. Cricket's initials."

"Yeah, me, too," replied Tsakis with a grin. "And do you remember the suggestion ol' Jiminy sang about?"

"Always let your conscience be your guide?"

"That's the one, John."

"Works for me. *Ciao* for now."

CHAPTER TEN

Shannon Carpenter, Ted Glenn, and Thomas and Rebecca Church sat on the grass in the shade of a tree behind a small town hall in a quiet community a day's drive from the New Christian Cathedral. They were surrounded by perhaps thirty people, and they were talking about faith. The meeting had been arranged by one of the local preachers, in coordination with Reverend Henderson Smith, assisted by Ivy Sloan-Underwood. The group included members of three different churches, and a few people who attended no church but were looking for answers. It was to be one of the first "formal" missionary outings undertaken by members of the New Christian Cathedral, whom Nateesha Folks had dubbed CNTs, Christians Not Taken. The mission: Spread the Gospel.

Ted Glenn, a bit shy at first, had opened the meeting with a prayer of thanks and a short speech about why they were there and what they hoped to accomplish. Something unprecedented was happening to the world, to mankind, he had stated—everyone there knew it. Was it Biblical? Was it the hand of God? Was it simply the natural order of things, like the ozone layer, meteors, the earth's orbit around the sun bending slightly? There had been earthquakes, tidal waves, burning rain, the worldwide failing of crops, mountains of ash dropped into oceans turned to blood—war, pestilence, famine. There had been leaden skies streaked with colors some said came from the apocalyptic horsemen. And, he added matter-of-factly, it had all begun with the loss of millions of souls, including all the world's children, in the blink of an eye—the *uplifting* of those souls.

"Our premise," he went on, "our *reason*, our message, is that—*yes*—these things that have happened to our world are in fact the work of our God, *as they are described in Revelation.*" He looked around at the faces watching him intently. He saw a mix of old, young, of man, woman, the various hues, colors, shapes, sizes of his fellow human beings. Everyone was dressed casually: jeans, pullovers, some of the women in walking shorts, others in simple dresses. "Most of us here called ourselves Christians before the disappearances, and we"—he used one hand to encompass his little band from the Cathedral—"still do. We have had the good fortune to attend sermons given by Reverend Henderson Smith, who you are familiar with." Several in his audience nodded their heads. "He has been hammering away at us since the first days of chaos," said Ted, "hammering at us not to lose faith but to regain it, and to find it through Scripture—"

"Do you know the word *reconcile*, sir?" interrupted an

older man, leaned and hardened by his years, who stood at the far edge of the group.

"To make different pieces fit?" replied Ted. "To bring ideas together—in explanation? How do you mean it, sir?"

"I don't mean to be blunt," said the man, "but I don't have time for polite back-and-forth nowadays. What I mean, sir, is how do you reconcile all we were ever taught about our merciful and loving God with what He is doing to us today? He is destroying us, if these are in fact the end times as described in *Scripture*, He is destroying His own children. He is destroying our world, He has increased the suffering, pain, confusion, and sadness a thousand-fold. We, who have read His Bible, who have worshipped and prayed to His Son all of our lives . . . He is destroying us." He took a breath, his face reddened, "So I ask: How do you reconcile that?"

Ted Glenn looked at the man and sincerely wished Reverend Henderson Smith was there.

"Um, if I may," said Shannon Carpenter quietly. She sat beside Ted, a Bible in her lap.

All eyes turned to her, and she went on, "We do understand the word *reconcile*, and all of us here understand your use of it. We also understand the feelings that drive you to ask, because we have all asked ourselves the same thing. I know I'm not the only person here who lost my children on *that* day." She watched the faces, the eyes, confirming it. "How could my God, the God I had been taught all my life was a good and loving God, do such a terrible, *unforgivable* thing." With the word *unforgivable*, she thought of her friend Ivy. She shrugged. "I don't know—"

"So we can all leave right now," said the man caustically. "You sit there with that Bible in your lap. Well lady, I got one just like it at home. You know what I find when I open it nowadays? *Stuff and nonsense*. You come from that big cathedral, you out here spreadin' the good gospel from the Reverend Smith, but you *don't know*, do you?" He glared at them.

Everyone was already uncomfortable with the confrontational tone of the meeting, and they were shocked when Shannon said in the same quiet voice, "Do I look like God to you, sir?"

The man did not respond.

"Am I God?" Shannon asked, this time turning her gaze on the group. "Am I God?" She shook her head and smiled. "No. I am Shannon, a simple human woman who has tried to live her life without hurting anyone, who has tried to be a loving mother and wife, and who has tried to be a believer in a God who made things *right*. That said, sir"—she looked directly into the man's eyes—"no . . . I do not know. That is why I drove from Ohio to Selma, Alabama, for crying out loud. That's why I came to hear Reverend Smith talk about the Bible. I am quite sure God's message, God's plan, even if dumbed down to the simplest terms, is almost beyond my comprehension. That is why I carry myself through this quest with the one thing you don't have to be a rocket scientist to have—"

"Faith," interjected the man sarcastically. "We are to have that indescribable, intangible thing called faith, and if we have it, all will be eventually learned—"

"Excuse me," said Thomas Church, Rebecca beside him, "anyone mind if I jump in here?"

Everyone looked at him and waited.

"I am a former wishy-washy sort of believer," said Church with an awkward grin. "Eventually I morphed into a hard-core agnostic. You know, didn't believe in anything, basically. Without boring everyone with my personal story, let me just say that in the days since the disappearances, I've made a cautious, intellect-based journey. I'm an analytical sort, so I started with a simple choice: Either there *is* something, or there is *not*. By that I mean we live in the flesh, we are man, the base animal. We are intelligent, and afraid of death. Let's say because we are afraid of death, we created a structure of religion. We did this intellectually, millennia ago, as a way of explaining the unexplainable. In our minds we created a God and an afterlife, a place that might be heaven if we played our cards right. When our poor bodies of flesh no longer sustained our life, we surmised, then our *souls* would live on, because our souls are part of God." He unconsciously scratched his beard, his eyes searching the faces of his listeners. "But"— he held up one finger—"this belief was a fraud, because *we* created it, okay? The argument goes, we did not understand death, feared it, so we concocted this nice story of God and heaven and all that. It's been called the 'opiate of the masses,' right?"

No one said anything. Rebecca had a small smile on her face as she watched and listened to her husband. She knew the labyrinth that was his keen mind, how he wandered down many paths before reaching his destination.

"So," said Church, "back to the two premises. Since the one argument says intellectual man made up religion, then there really is nothing after we die. We are lumps of meat, biological accidents in an accidental world, and when we die it is as if a lightbulb is shut off—there is simply nothing. We are not, and never were. We are not even *aware* of our nonexistence, because *there is nothing*." He sat back on his heels, stroked his beard, took a breath, and finally said, "Or... there *is*." He saw the older man who had first questioned Ted Glenn fidgeting a bit, eyed the stony stare on the man's face, and added, "Please bear with me, my friend. This question was important enough for you to be here, and to ask—so stay with me while I try to get to it."

The man nodded.

"Okay," continued Church, "I then took look at choice number two. God is real. Actually, even for a skeptical pessimist, the evidence of an intelligent, overseeing, controlling, creating force, or presence, is everywhere in our world. *We* exist, and within us is an intellect that *tells* us we are not alone, but a part of something far greater. I won't go into a long dissertation about the miracles of our world, the earth and all of its physical wonders. Nor do I have to say anything about children, the creation of them, the birth, what they are, what we see in them, in their eyes, their hearts, their lives—"

Several hands shot up, and several people tried to speak at once, including the man who had asked the first question.

"I know, I know," said Church as he held one hand up and waited for his audience to quiet down. "Perfect example of what bothered us in the first place. How could a loving God take the *children?* Answer—again—I don't know, either." He kept his hand up, and quickly added, "But wait.

Just because I don't know, or Shannon doesn't know, or
Ted here, or even the good Reverend Smith—just because
we don't know the how and why of it doesn't make God
any less *real*. Stay with my premise for a little longer,
please. So I choose the proposition that God *is*. At this
point I don't have to begin dissecting every comment or
written word man has uttered through the ages to find the
real God, the *only* God. All I have to do is believe, to have
faith. As it turns out—and I will state this as a recent
scholar—there *is* a written document confirming God, His
Son, and the basic premise of man and his relationship
with his Lord. The Bible—"

Thomas Church was interrupted by the slow applause
of the older man.

"Excellent," said the man with a tight grin on his face.
"You hurry through a nice argument, only to lead us back
to the Bible, which I must state once again *tells us nothing,
proves nothing*."

"Perhaps," said Rebecca Church. She reached down,
plucked a blade of green grass from a clump near her right
knee, and held it against her lips. "Or perhaps the Bible
holds the key within it, and every person's locked heart can
be opened by the key that lies somewhere within the
words. Each of us here have wounded hearts, troubled
hearts. We are all searching desperately for reason, for answers. Why *can't* some of the answers, some solace, be
found in the Bible? It is a document that has withstood mi-
croinspection for thousands of years, a book that has
transformed the lives of millions and millions of intelligent, searching, skeptical people. Besides"—she leaned

forward, her eyes bright—"*what do you have to lose?* You want reconciliation? Reconcile the fact that you are the lump of meat Thomas mentioned, destined to become *nothing*. Quit whining about it, and wander off into your own personal darkness."

Everyone sat in shocked silence. Thomas stared at Rebecca, loving her immensely.

"Or," continued Rebecca, "buckle down. Yes, there's a hard rain falling on us. Yes, these are scary times, and it may well be the end of the world as we know it, the end of man. Choose a way for yourself, a way that, if nothing else, has the *potential* for bringing you light, for bringing you to a life after this life. It doesn't take a scholar to know this is an imperfect world. If we accept the premise, as students of life and of God, that God created an imperfect world where man suffers pain, loss, sadness, and fear, and eventually dies—then we can accept the fact that *it is part of God's plan*. Why do you think angels want to be like us?"

"What?" said the older man, his fists bunched up. He wasn't the only one thrown off balance by Rebecca's sudden change in direction. Ted Glenn thought of Ron Underwood's wondrous friend, Stan.

"Angels are *created* beings," said Rebecca. She had a sudden thought, her eyes went wide, and she said to the group, "Oh, I'm sorry. I'm assuming no one here has a problem with angels. Anyone?"

One woman sitting between two men in the front of the group laughed and said, "Works for me."

"Angels are real," said another. There were several nods in agreement.

"Okay," said Rebecca. "Angels want to be like us because they are created spirits, perhaps a form of life between human and divine, whereas we are *physically born* into this tormented world. *We are forced to learn and grow simply by living our lives here, where we are tested by the very physical, emotional, and spiritual landscape of this world of conflict.* How can we know what is good, what is just, what is beautiful, what is truth, what is love, unless we have experienced for ourselves what those things are *not?* God did not make a mistake when He created this hard, unexplainable world. He created it for *us*, as a first step toward knowing *Him*. This carries over to the now . . . to these terrible and frightening days. Now is *absolutely* the wrong time to turn your back on faith." She stopped and ran the fingers of one hand through her long hair. Her eyes went out of focus, and her voice softened as she went on, "It's there, in the Bible. He gave us His Son—Jesus, we call Him. His Son came here and lived as a man, and He died hard, died hard to show us in one simple, terrible lesson, that when we die—we *live*. *We live*. Now is the time for study, now is the time to go right back to that Bible, and I don't mean maybe. Now is the time for faith in God." She sat perfectly still for a moment, then blinked, shrugged, and said, "I'm done."

Thomas Church took his wife's hand and squeezed it.

"I, uh, I marked a few passages in that Bible Rebecca mentioned just now," said Ted Glenn after a moment, "in Revelation, Thessalonians, Daniel, and uh, Matthew. Everybody all right with, you know, reading a bit of it so we can open it up for more discussion?" He looked directly at the man at the edge of the group who had asked the first question, and spoke to him, "Friend? Will you stay? We don't have the answers, but we're looking. I'd consider it a gift if you'd stay and look with us."

The man stayed.

+   +   +

Later, after the meeting broke up with a final prayer, the little group of CNTs—Shannon, Ted, Thomas, and Rebecca—sat down in a small diner for lunch and a break. They were, each one, emotionally drained, and Ted was the first to admit, "Man, there's more to this spreading the gospel than I thought."

"You ain't just whistling Dixie," agreed Church with a grin. Then he added with a rueful shrug, "I'm not even sure if I ever *have* whistled Dixie."

"I thought he was, you know, one of those, apparitions," said Shannon quietly as she sipped iced tea. The others looked at her. "That man—the older, lean and hard man. His eyes were fierce, and he was so *angry* with his questions, mocking us, taunting us—like he *wanted* confrontation." She pursed her lips, remembering Ivy's tormentor. "I thought he was like a . . . tempter, a *demon* maybe, specifically sent there to undermine what we were trying to do."

"Whoa," said Rebecca, "that's spooky." Ted Glenn had told her and Thomas the story of the two strange men in the Cathedral parking lot the day Ivy came back from the hospital and Ron was spirited out of jail by the *other* one, called Stan.

"What do you think?" asked Shannon to them all.

"I have to admit it crossed my mind," said Ted, "but I don't think so—"

"Me neither," Church chimed in. "Know why?"

They waited.

"He didn't ask any questions that I haven't asked a hundred times through the years—and I'll bet each of us can say the same thing to some degree. I believe he's just a man, like me, a frightened man, angry at the God he thought he knew. He's been hurt, probably lost a loved one." He shook his head sadly. "Nah, he was just human, like us—hurting and lost."

"But he stayed through the whole thing," observed Rebecca, "and in the end I saw him sitting with that young woman with the blue scarf at her neck, reading the Bible she held for them both."

They were silent for a moment.

"You know what we didn't do?" said Shannon.

"*Didn't do?*" repeated Rebecca.

"Did not do," said Shannon again. "We did that whole talk and Bible study—sent out here as missionaries for Reverend Smith and the New Christian Cathedral—and we did not mention Azul Dante and the 'new' way of looking at things *once.*"

"What are you saying, Shannon?" asked Rebecca.

"I'm wondering if we, as a group, made an unconscious decision," replied Shannon, chewing her lower lip. "A decision not to go into any *new* interpretation of Scripture, and not try to bring Dante into the conversation in any . . . leading . . . way."

No one said anything for a moment, each examining his own thoughts.

"You know Ivy and I have discussed it," added Shannon after the pause. "She was the first to actually express doubt about Reverend Smith's obvious desire to accept a sort of new way of looking at things, doubt about the relevance of Azul Dante, doubt about"—she hesitated—"Dante's Prodigal Project."

"Whoa," said Rebecca, "I thought the Prodigal Project was all about the churches, all about supporting faith here in America and around the world. Even before Thomas— found me again, I had already read good things about it. Its affiliation with so many strong churches is its biggest attraction, millions of people are immediately involved, and in these times of darkness, its very structure is supposed to help us find answers, maybe even salvation. Right?"

"Certainly that's how it would appear," agreed Ted Glenn. He rubbed his jaw and added, "I know Thomas has told you about the *seven*, Rebecca. I'll tell ya, even if I wasn't close to Shannon—her being one of the seven—I'd still have reservations about Azul Dante, the Project, and Reverend Smith's, uh, revised look at the Bible. I mean, I'm no scholar, but sometimes a person seems to try *too hard* to sell somethin', and when they do, it makes you wonder, you know? You can sit there in the cathedral and watch the reverend giving these sermons—and I believe he is, in fact, a good man—you can almost *see* him struggling to make the pieces fit. I'd be the last man to tell any preacher what to do, but I've felt a couple of times like going up to him, grabbing him by his shirt, laying that Bible up against his head, and tellin' him to *relax*. The Bible is Scripture. It is *the Word*. I get a little nervous when anybody starts, uh, messin' with it."

They looked at one another, and no one said anything until Thomas Church cleared his throat and said, "I think we'll just stick to the basics while we're out being missionaries, okay?" He smiled. "If we are in fact God's servants, as we like to think of ourselves, we will do His bidding anyway. We didn't know how this first attempt would play out today, and we will continue to pray on it, then speak and teach from our hearts. Agreed?"

The waitress came to their table with the bill. "Anything else I can get for you all?" she asked in a quiet voice, her eyes downcast. She was a heavy woman with short hair, a thin wedding ring, and a frayed but clean uniform.

"You sound like you got the weight of the world on you, ma'am," said Ted Glenn. The others watched her closely.

The waitress lifted her face, studied Ted a moment, and said in a barely audible tone, "My children were took—my husband, too. But not me, I weren't took with 'em. I went to church like they did; me and my husband tried to raise them kids right. Now they's gone, the world's on fire, and I'm all alone. I walk into my trailer, and it's so scary *quiet* . . . but I can hear myself, you know? I can hear myself askin' why wasn't I took, *Why wasn't I took?*" She looked at them watching her, laid the bill on the table, and shook her head. "Sorry . . . but you did ask . . ."

"You ever seen one of these?" asked Shannon with a smile as she held up her Bible.

"Got one just like it in our truck," replied the woman with a sigh. "It's was my husband's. Now you gonna tell me everything will be put back the way it was if I read it with you, and get down on my knees and pray with you?" She pointed down with one hand. "Girl, my knees are *raw*, okay?"

"Nothing will ever be as it was," answered Shannon. "But let me ask you this: Is the love for your kids and husband still in your heart? Or is it gone?"

"It's just the air that I breathe," said the woman, a heavy tear precariously balanced on the corner of her right eye.

"That love is real? You know it? There is no doubt?"

"It's real," said the woman, "prob'ly the only real thing I've known in my life."

"That love . . . is from God," said Shannon. "The Bible tells us that God is love, and you are not alone, and you are not forgotten, and if you will trust in Him and let His love fill your heart, you will be with your children again someday, and you will live forever—because of *Him*."

The woman cried softly, the fingers of her hands laced together tightly.

"Don't turn your back on your faith," continued Shannon, "not now. Sit with me a few minutes, will you? Sit with me, and we'll talk." She reached out and took the woman's hands, "Let's look at that old Bible, and see if we can't find some hope—some *hope*."

The woman did not reply at first. Then she looked over her shoulder, caught the eye of another waitress, and said, "Cover for me a minute, will ya, Doreen?"

While Shannon sat side by side with the waitress in a

corner booth, their heads together, the others went out into the parking lot to wait. On their way out, a rough-looking man grabbed Ted Glenn's wrist, pulled him close, and asked shyly, "I . . . heard what that gal said to the waitress there. I, uh . . . I got a few questions myself. Do you think you could, I mean . . . sit with me for a coupla' minutes, and . . . talk?"

In the parking lot, Rebecca struck up a conversation with two young women who seemed to be lost, and soon they were sitting at a picnic table under a leaning pine tree. Rebecca had her Bible open on the table, and the three studied it intently.

Thomas Church smiled and took a deep breath. *Yep*, he mused, *we'll just stick with the basics.* The number *seven* rang in his heart.

CHAPTER ELEVEN

First there were children's voices, many of them but muted, as if in the distance. As the sounds got closer, the children could be heard laughing, shouting, singing, calling out—playing. Then, out of the lightening darkness, came the forms, shapes, curves and angles—images of children. They ran and jumped, spun, danced, and chased one another, girls with long hair flying behind them, boys with laughing eyes. Some ran close, their faces split into irreverent grins, teasing and pointing. All of the races of man were represented in the children, all of the shades, textures, hair colors, physiques—all the differences, and all the same. They were alive, the children, full of energy, noisy, active, colorful. Punctuating the soft cacophony were the sounds of infants, cooing, humming, joyful sounds of life. Then, at first almost imperceptibly, the sounds began to fade. They stretched, as if in the distance, becoming faint and tantalizing as they pulled away. Soon the images showed only lifeless playgrounds, slides, monkey bars, baseball diamonds—all empty, like the curved seat of a swing. Here lay a Frisbee, there a football, skateboards, bicycles, and strollers—unused, unridden. As the images lost focus, becoming indistinct shapes of gray and black, one tiny sound fluttered out of the montage, the unmistakable voice of an infant child. "Mommy?" it said.

Now the black and gray shapes began to come into focus once more, and suddenly jumped into sharp clarity with a jolt. The shapes were the bodies of the fallen, the harvest of global war. They lay sprawled in the cold and impossible twists of the dead, limbs flung out to the sides, legs curled under torsos, fists clenched, some whole, some in parts, many torn and gutted, many charred, blackened. Where there were faces, they wore the masks of horror— the expressions of those who died violently, who cried out in anger and fear as their bodies were ripped, their blood drained, their lives ended. The eyes that were open stared unseeing through opaque slits, into a reddened and undefined blackness. There were dozens, then hundreds of these splayed dead, some in military uniform, most in various civilian garb. There were hundreds, then thousands, men, women, again all the races of man represented, all equal within violated and rotting flesh. These shapes were scattered across various landscapes, thousands, then hundreds of thousands. Many fell along the roads, and in the cities among broken buildings and overturned cars. Trains lay on their sides, the dead passengers half out of the windows and draped across the tracks. Others filled ditches that ran alongside dirt roads that stretched into the hazy distance, here one clutched a rifle, here another a guitar, yet another clung desperately in death to a small dog—equally dead. On the fields of battle and the fields of the farmer lay the dead. The images traversed the demonic acreage, sweeping, then focusing on dusty, dried, and browned crops burned by an unforgiving sun, left to wither unwashed by cooling rain. It was parched earth, scorched earth, plowed by a grim reaper, yielding only the produce of pestilence and famine. Man, in these images, was lost.

Came a steady heartbeat, rhythmic, sure—the heartbeat of man, of life. New images came, images of men and women, healthy, alive, busy. Grocery shelves were being stocked with goods, fresh produce filled slatted boxes, fruit, vegetables, and rice overflowed containers. Streets were clean, traffic moderate, here and there construction repair going on at a rapid pace. People smiled; they waved at one another. A farmer on a tractor lifted his hat to a trucker in a big rig. The images were of progress, industry, farming, distribution, life. Behind these images, blending in, came the multicolored flags of many nations, unfurled, curling in a pleasant breeze. Over this, slowly, drifted the flag of the Prodigal Project. A rich, sincere voice intoned one word: *"Hope."*

"Hope."

"Hope."

Millions stood, staring up, their faces hopeful, their eyes bright. Shoulder to shoulder, black to white, red to yellow, they stood, listening. Over these faces, over the flags, with a soft rising sun behind him, stood the proud and determined figure of Azul Dante. He wore an eggshell-hued linen suit and seemed to be surrounded by a golden glow. His face was set in an expression of reverence as he glanced skyward, then strength as he turned his gaze upon the multitudes gathered before him. As he began to lift one outstretched arm, his hand open, palm up, a ripple flickered through his image—the subliminal repetition of four words, which was spoken by the voice of a man, then a woman, then a man in this language, woman in that— over and over in all the languages of man, four words: *"He is the one."*

It began in a subtle way, a piece here, a story there. It was unheralded, without hype, and it was initially a low-volume resonance. But it was like water on a rock, a constant, rhythmic pattern of image, sound bite, and written word. It documented the writhing horror that had overtaken the world since the day of disappearances, a hard primer and reminder of what had befallen man. It was steady and pervasive, successfully designed to penetrate even the most deadened senses, the hardened crust of layered denial. It was a Sarcom media blitz, a sensory assault, almost unavoidable anywhere on the planet Earth. It filled the radio waves, the print outlets, and—most important—televised and cable broadcasts across the globe. It showed what the world had become. It showed what the world was fighting to regain. It showed the Prodigal Project over all nations.

And it showed Azul Dante . . . THE ONE.

✝   ✝   ✝

"Ivy . . . wake up."

She heard the voice and knew immediately what it was. *No!* her mind screamed. *NO!*

"Yes, Ivy. Yes," said the voice. It was a pleasant voice, beguiling, confident—male arrogance plucked from vocal cords in knowing throat.

Oh, she thought, *it's a dream . . . okay.*

She felt someone take her hand in a warm, strong grip. Then she bolted up as a jabbing pain in one finger seared the nerve endings through her skin.

"What?" she said through a clenched jaw. She sat in her bed, in one of the apartmentlike dorm rooms next to the cathedral. She wore her thin nightgown, her brown hair was sleep tousled. She looked at her left hand, saw the plain gold band on her ring finger, and saw the drops of blood spurting from the tip of that finger. The blood left a bright red trail across her palm, and several drops fell onto the bedsheets. *"What?"* she said again. She sat up in her bed, fully and instantly awake.

The dark figure of Thad Knight, her tormentor and tempter, sat next to her on the edge of the bed, a serene smile on his angled and handsome face with its rugged jaw, sensual cut of a mouth, and piercing black eyes. His thick black hair was windblown and reckless, his brow slanted in appraisal. He wore what at first appeared to be black slacks, boots, and a black pullover shirt that clung to his muscular torso tight enough to enhance every edge. His bare arms rippled with strength, his big hands and long fingers promised a knowing and capable touch. The black fabric of his clothes was made of a light satiny material that changed shades as it caught the muted light in the room. What looked black was actually a deep bloodred, then briefly red-orange fire when he moved. He made sure she watched as his sinewy tongue snaked out from between his lips and quickly licked up a drop of her blood that rested there.

"You are a tasty morsel, indeed, Ivy Sloan-Underwood," he said, "and you're like a lot of sweet things in this world—one taste only makes you want more, know what I mean?"

"Get out," said Ivy in a constricted voice. "Get out of my room. How dare you—"

"I see you are sleeping all alone, Ivy," said Knight in his sibilant, unhurried voice. "Your husband, Ron, is here, he wants you—I mean he wants you like a husband should *want* his wife, and yet you make him sleep in another room while you sleep in this cold bed—alone. And you *want*, also, don't you, Ivy? I can feel it. I *know* it. You want, you *desire*." He shrugged and ran his left hand lightly from her shoulder down the bare skin of her right arm, down to her hip. "That's why I thought I should come to you tonight. Perhaps I can still your longing—perhaps I can play the song your starved body so desperately wants to sing. Oh, listen to your heart, Ivy! Thump-*thump*, sweetness! Yes . . . I hear you, and I'm right here . . . ready, willing, and able beyond even *your* carnal dreams—"

Ivy shrank away from him. She shuddered, aware of his discerning truth, aware of the aching hunger suddenly enflamed, almost overpowering in her need. She clutched at the bedcovers and pulled them over her shoulders. She stared at him, her face hot, and rasped, "Get out, get out, get . . . *out.*"

He just smiled.

She looked at her bloody finger again and asked, "Why did you cut me? You hurt me. Did you *bite* me? Why?"

"Oh . . . that's something I remember from demon one-oh-one," he said with a shrug. "Make you feel a little pain, leave a little blood, so you'll know this wasn't some twisted dream or something. Like if you thought it was a dream, you'd stupidly dismiss it, dismiss *me.*"

"You sicken me, Thad Knight," she said quietly. "You sicken me and frighten me, and I want you to go and leave me alone. What more can you do to me? What more do you *want?*"

He let his eyes travel appreciatively from her tousled head, across the front of her gown, down to her legs. "Besides the obvious, you mean?"

She said nothing. She felt revulsion, but in that instant her mind filled with the uncompromising image of him, her—*them*—entwined, holding tight, her eyes wide, her mouth open, her skin on fire. She felt her own traitorous body begin to warm, her mouth went dry, her hands shook. "Stop!" she cried at him. "Stop it!"

"If you say so, Ivy," he said.

She began to calm. Tears welled in her eyes. She waited.

"That's not really why I'm here, anyway, Ivy," said Knight. *As if I'd share myself with a human pig like you*, he thought. "No . . . we've got other things to discuss this evening."

"I've got nothing to discuss with you."

"Ah, Ivy," said Knight as he stood, "such a feisty little urchin."

She wiped the tears from her eyes with the back of one hand and stared at him.

"We'll discuss . . . Ronnie," he said as his grin widened.

"Yes . . . we will not discuss your physical wantonness, Ivy. We'll discuss your son, *okay?*"

"Get away from me!" she cried. "Don't say his name, don't say his name—leave me, leave him—leave us—*please.*"

"But, Ivy," he chided, "do you think I would come to you again if there wasn't some reason, some *purpose?* No, no. There seems to be something going on with the number *seven*, Ivy, know what I mean?" He leaned close, his menacing face only inches from hers. "You and six others, Ivy. Seven of you—you are like an itching powder, you know? Like an irritant." He shrugged. "You don't bother me, understand? But you *are* bothersome to my boss. I don't understand the whys and hows of the thing, but you and the number seven are becoming a real pain." He leaned close enough for his sulfurous breath to wash against the skin of her face. "You and your friends want to play? Then, let's play." He took a step back and straightened, his fists on his hips.

She watched him.

"Still love your son, Ivy?" he asked with a smirk. "Still love that twisted, helpless little boy, so distorted and warped, he had to live in a wheelchair, so damaged, he couldn't even speak to you? You still love that incredibly pathetic excuse for a human child? The child that ruined your life?" He licked his lips, his smirk becoming an evil grin. "Oh, yeah, Ivy—you remember all those unanswered prayers? The ones you used to whisper in the dead of night, the ones that asked why, why, *why?* You were young, beautiful, female. Men adored you and pursued you—and you wanted to be caught, didn't you? You wanted to *know*

those men. But you had a boy who needed full-time care,
I mean, twenty-four–*seven*, didn't you, Ivy? Your boy
needed you, and your husband no longer interested you
because he thought the boy was a gift and wouldn't stop
trying to get you to appreciate the"—his mouth twisted as
if something bitter fell against his lips—"*love* he saw in
your son." He stopped, his eyes furious. "Remember all
that . . . *Ivy?*"

Ivy cried. She hugged her knees to her chest, rocked
back and forth on her bed, and cried as she stared at him. It
was all true, she knew, and that's what made it so cruel. She
took a shuddering breath and said, "You are the beast, and
the beast is nothing. You cannot take from me anything I
haven't already taken from myself. You can't scourge me
any more than I've scourged myself. Go. I am not interested in you or your venom."

"Wanna bet?"

She stared at him.

"Ah, brave Ivy," he said, "brave and foolish. We both
know all I have to do is turn up the heat a bit and your
body will sweat itself right out of that nightgown and into
my arms—"

"Who wants it more, Thad Knight?" she managed,
"me . . . or you?"

He laughed, and a small framed photograph of her son,
Ronnie, which sat on a slim bookshelf, burst into flames.
She wanted to reach out and grab it, but her arms became
leaden at her sides. The fire flared, then went out, and the
photo stood undamaged. She stared at it, then at him.

"Like that little trick, Ivy?" he asked in a mocking tone.

"I like nothing about you."

"Would you like another chance?" he asked. His voice changed, his posture, his entire countenance changed. With that breath he became warm, sincere, his eyes caressed her, his empathy for her pain was palpable, it reached out for her, encircled her fear and anger, calmed her. "Would you like another chance to be a mother for Ronnie—a loving, caring mother who accepted him as the perfect child he could be?"

"Stop," she said. "Don't do this to me again." She hesitated, slowly lifted her face until her eyes met his. She licked her lips, and asked, "What do you mean—'perfect child'?"

"Do you remember our first deal, Ivy?" he asked. He knelt on one knee in front of her, and took her hands in his. He exuded confidence and admiration. "My boss had planned to make Ronnie whole for you, to fix Ronnie's imperfections—which came as no fault of *yours*—to bring a normal, happy little boy to your arms. If you remember, Ivy, what came next was not my fault, or my boss's doing, no. What came next was that horribly cynical and uncaring day when *all the world's children, including your Ronnie, were taken in the blinking of a selfish eye*." He sniffed. "We did not do that to you. We had an agreement, and my boss fully planned to honor it."

A full-scale war raged within her mind and heart. The truth was there. She was neither blind nor a fool. But the promise, the dream, the possibility of what he described was a siren call within her, a siren call she could not turn away from. Her eyes showed the fury, the agony, the uncertainty, and he drank it in as he watched her. Finally, the tortured substance that formed her wracked and defiled center made her ask quietly, "What chance?"

He turned his face so she could not see his reptilian and evil smile, cleared his throat, turned back to her, and said softly, "Look at me, Ivy."

She slowly lifted her gaze and was captured by his eyes. She was held there, immobile, and within seconds she began to feel a fullness, then a swelling, then a warm weight in her belly below her rib cage. She felt her body changing, flowering, expanding in a sweet and wholly encompassing way. Something was forming in her, forming as a child will form in a woman, life that takes from her blood, from her heart, from her very substance . . . life. She stared down at her belly, then at him.

He smiled. "Feel it, Ivy? Feel *him?* It's real, I can assure you—and, no, I'm not capable of doing such a special thing, such a miracle. I am but the messenger, the facilitator, do you understand? But it is real, Ivy, and this is your second chance—the second chance to know and love a child who is whole and beautiful, and a second chance to prove to the most powerful one that you are indeed his servant."

Oh, God, she thought. Then, she prayed. *Oh, God, help me. I feel him, I feel my Ronnie inside me, my child, my child, Lord. How can I resist this? How can I refuse? I want my child—I want to know him again, to be his mother, to be his loving and grateful mother. Oh, God, how can I fight this? I was Ronnie's mother, and You took him from me, You, Lord, and now I can feel him forming again, coming to my arms so I can love him forever, Lord.* She began to cry, softly at first, then stronger, until she began to sob. *Help me, God, help me*. She knew she could pray for God's help, but she also knew if she were to defeat this, it must come from *her*, and she forced her mind to seek the truth.

Thad Knight watched her, relishing her struggle, drinking in the searing pain that ate like acid through the walls of her heart. These were the moments he existed for, and he drank them in like a fine bile. He saw her glance again to the small photograph of her son, felt a cleansing rush of soft cool air, and thought, *No. She can't; she's not strong enough.*

But the strength came to her with that cool rush of air, with the image of her son's smiling face, her beautiful, innocent, loving child—the strength came. She straightened on the bed, her chin lifted, she balled her fists up and lay them against her chest. "Liar!" she spat out at him. "Liar— you are a lying, scheming, nothing beast. Nothing grows in my womb, but *hope*, and despair. You cannot create life in me, and neither can your *boss*. God creates life, God *is* life. You are *nothing* . . ." The artificial fullness in her belly was gone immediately.

"I am more than you, wanton failure of a woman," he responded calmly, "and I can—and will—return anytime I like, to prove it to you."

"You know nothing of love, Thad Knight. You think you know me, but you know *nothing*."

He looked at her, his eyes cold and flat. "I know the number seven, Ivy," he said in a hiss. "*Sevvvennn*. I know that's what is going to guarantee your torment forever."

She blinked, and he was gone. She was alone in the

room. She fell back on the bed, sweat soaked and exhausted. "Oh, God," she whispered, "let me be Your deserving child. Let me be Your deserving servant. Oh, God . . . thank you." She fell asleep.

A few hours later, early sunlight filled the room, and she heard a bird singing outside the window when she awoke. She kept her eyes closed for several minutes, building the courage to look. *It was a dream*, she told herself. *It was a dream, it was a dream . . . it was a dream.*

She opened her eyes. The ring fingertip and palm of her left hand were streaked with crimson blood, and there were drops of blood on the sheet near the edge. She counted them. There were seven.

+ + +

"He's all right, Henri," said James Devane quietly. He looked at Slim Piedmont, who stood at a security clearance table outside the large banquet hall in the hotel. The young combat photographer had managed to borrow a nicely cut black suit, shiny black tassel loafers, and a muted silver-and-gold tie that he wore with a crisp white shirt. The tie was a bit too thin to be fashionable, and the knot was askew, but Devane figured for a photojournalist, Piedmont was cleaned up the best he could be. The flap had begun when Piedmont showed the French security man, Henri, his event pass—which had come from Sophia Ghent. The pass was in order, so Slim could enter the banquet hall, but the young man had two cameras in his battered bag, and Henri had been told no bags except the women's purses, and no cameras. Authorized photographers would document the affair. Slim had tried to tell the Frenchman he *always* carried his cameras, felt *naked* without them, understood the "no photo" rule, and would obey it. Henri was tired of pushy Americans and nervous about making a mistake. His boss, like *all* the security bosses, was uptight about this summit meeting with so many of the world leaders—targets for the mujahideen, terrorists, and your garden variety wackos—gathered in one place. Heads would roll if something went wrong, and Henri and his peers were out to make *sure* nothing went wrong.

"Each of the cameras were scanned for organic substance downstairs," said Slim to Devane, referring to the color images of explosives. "And this guy even pulled the lens off the thirty-five—"

"Just so you know, Mr. Piedmont," replied Devane as he placed one hand on his French compatriot's shoulder, "Henri was one of the men involved in the action in Nice, so he's understandably cautious." He saw Henri straighten a bit.

Slim, aware of what Devane was doing, nodded and said, "Yes, I was there, too. The French guys did a heck of a job." He looked at Henri and shrugged. "I'm glad you are on our side, sir, and I do not mean to cause trouble—"

"It is nothing," said the French security man with a Gallic shrug of his own. "And if James says it is *bon* . . . then it is good, no?"

"And you Miss . . . Early?" said Devane as he turned to Cat, who stood beside Slim. He thought she looked attractive in her simple black evening dress trimmed in silver. Her black shoes had a filigree pattern in silver, and she carried a small matching handbag. Her hair was pulled back and pinned on one side with a small crystal brooch, and her makeup was simple, with a hint of blush. "You are with Mr. Piedmont, no?"

"Yes," she said with a smile.

"Sophia has spoken fondly of you," he went on.

"And of you, Mr. Devane," replied Cat. "And how are things on the *diplomatic* front these days?"

He grinned and waved them toward the open doors that led to the banquet hall.

As they moved through the people who stood dressed in their finery, sipping wine or champagne, Slim leaned toward Cat and said, "Those security guys take the fun out of these things."

Cat thought of John Jameson, squeezed Slim's arm, and said, "Just doing their job." She waited as Slim grabbed a couple of glasses of bubbly from a passing waiter and added, "Why are you so testy, Slim? Besides the fact that you are wearing a tie, you were forced to sort of comb your hair, and you are hobnobbing with popinjays and poofenwiffles?"

Slim sipped a bit of his drink, looked around at the faces, many familiar on the world political scene, and pursed his lips. "The Sarcom blitz about our man of the hour, Dante," he said. "I don't know—it bothers me."

Cat had seen it, of course, first in the print venues she contributed to, then on television. As a journalist she had been impressed with the sheer volume of it. But she suspected she knew why Slim didn't like it. It was a hard sell, almost *too* hard. She looked at him and waited.

"A lot of my shots are being used," he said to her. "In

the stills and in the video montages. Professionally I have no say, of course. I submitted them, and was paid. But—"

"You should be proud, Slim," said Cat. "You do good work, and your shots have enough of an impact to be used to good effect."

"But that's the thing, Cat," he said, glancing around the room again, fighting the urge to get out the thirty-five and see what these people looked like through the viewfinder. "My shots are being *used* by Sarcom, and Sarcom has an agenda." The images, many of them battlefield shots, were personal, and intimate, in his mind. They were captured moments in the life—and death—of his fellow human beings, not to be taken lightly. He shrugged. "Don't want to be part of anybody's *agenda*, that's all."

She watched his face, liking him greatly. "C'mon, Slim," she said with a wink. "You are my escort—so escort me around the room so I can talk to some of these luminaries and get enough for some kind of story." She hoped to speak with Sophia and maybe get a quote from Azul Dante. Perhaps, as her boss, Simon Blake, insisted, Dante would agree to another one-on-one interview. "Besides," she added as she leaned close to him, "I'm not sure what a poofenwiffle even *looks* like."

He made a face, then grinned and replied, "A poofenwiffle piously projects a perfectly pomaded pompadour when parading pompously with pandering and prolific promoters of promise."

"Of course," agreed Cat.

CHAPTER TWELVE

My God, my God, why have you forsaken me? Why are you so far from saving me, so far from the words of my groaning?

The Reverend Henderson Smith, on his knees on the carpet in his room, read the words from the twenty-second Psalm, and trembled. He stared at his Bible, and at his fingertips, which held the edge of the page. They were covered in a fine ash. The book had become ash, he thought, but still it did not fall from his hands, did not disintegrate and fall in drifting flakes to the floor. The Bible felt warm to his touch, and the right sleeve of his pajamas was singed and charred. The tears in his eyes were hot and bitter, his tongue felt like a twist of sawgrass in his parched mouth, and his lungs were filled with gaseous smoke.

He had been visited by Andrew Nuit.

Nuit was a specter embodied as a sweaty, porcine man who favored linen suits and weak Christians, the tempter who had made Smith an offer he could not refuse regarding the reverend's selfish desires to be the head of a large, affluent church. Andrew Nuit had been seen on the day of the disappearances, happily carrying a can of gasoline into Smith's old plain wooden church and burning the structure down while he stood in the flames laughing demonically. Since that day all Smith's dreams had come true. He was in fact the pastor of one of the largest New Christian Cathedrals in the country, supported by funding from the Prodigal Project. He had influence and respect, all the media and electronic accessories a Bible-touting preacher could want, and a rapt and frightened audience hungrily devouring his every word. But he had made a deal that twisted his heart, and he knew it. He knew it, and fought it, but could not stop himself from acting on it. The sermons he had loved to give, the gospel he had given everything to promote, now crossed his lips like acidic bile, the words like knives in his tortured heart, his tongue scaly and writhing around the truth.

He had awakened in the middle of the night, his nostrils filled with the stench of burning flesh, and knew without opening his eyes who was there with him. The heavy, sweating man sat on a straight-backed chair next to the bed, the sooty cloth of his trousers stretched tight across his thick legs. Nuit had smiled, which caused the folds of his cheeks to almost bury his beady black eyes. "Henderson," he said amicably, "you are beginning to worry us— that would be my boss and me."

"How?" Smith managed to get out.

"Oh," said Nuit, "this whole thing with the number seven. You are part of seven—that much we know—and the seven are part of . . . something." He leaned forward, and the chair creaked from his weight. "But *you*, Henderson, you can't be part of something when you are already part of *us*, right? I told my boss, told him ol' Henderson Smith wouldn't let us down, not when he made a deal. We *do* have a deal, don't we, Henderson?"

Smith, his eyes wide, had nodded. Images of the cathedral flashed in his mind, the congregation all staring up at him in admiration, his voice booming out across the airwaves, his face looked to for guidance, his handshake sought after as an affirmation of hope.

"Good stuff, don't you agree, Henderson?" asked Nuit. He saw the things Smith saw in his mind.

Smith nodded again.

Nuit took a deep breath and sighed. "Be a shame to throw it all away just to be part of some seven something—know what I mean?"

The images changed in Smith's head. He stood naked, mocked by a throng of laughing and pointing people who all had laser-beam eyes that allowed them to *see him*. They saw what he was, saw the dried leaves that were the words that fell from his snakepit of a mouth. They saw his heart, a twisted, shrunken thing the color of liver, not beating so much as *clenching* in an arrhythmic series of spasms. They saw what he was, and he was shamed.

"Henderson?" Nuit had said with a leering grin. "See our problem? I mean, you understand the word *loyalty*, right? You got to choose sides, baby, and we thought you *had*."

At that point in the visit, Henderson Smith had reached

way down inside himself, thought of Nateesha Folks, of Shannon, Ted, Thomas Church, Ivy and Ron, and tried to fight. He had picked up his Bible from the nightstand, held it in front of Nuit, let it fall open, and began to read, "The Lord is my shepherd, I shall lack nothing, He makes me lie down in green pastures, He leads me beside quiet waters, he restores . . ."

The thing that was Andrew Nuit, who had begun to squirm uncomfortably as the words were read, stood suddenly, waved one hand at Smith, and said, "*Bah!* Be *silent*, you pathetic little man!" He gritted his pointy teeth, and suddenly the Bible in Smith's hands became a sheet of rippling flame. Smith cried out and dropped it to the floor. "Do you want to live in these times counting on your *faith*, you fool?" asked Nuit as he took several deep breaths. "Have any of those words in the Book, the promises, come true for you? Will your faith in some future promise help you more *right now* than the most powerful man on earth who is here and already *at work?* Choose, Smith, you helpless little worm—*choose*."

In a blinding flash, Andrew Nuit was gone from the room, leaving behind his sickly, greasy stench.

Smith had sat there, sobbing, watching his Bible burn. Then, as he studied it more closely, he saw that while the Book appeared to be on fire, it was still there. He had hesitated; then reached into the flames with his fingers and picked it up. His fingers felt the warmth, and his skin became covered with ash but did not burn. The words remained on the pages also. He heard a soft knock, knew it

would be Nateesha, and sobbed. As the woman opened the
door and stepped in wearing a robe and a concerned look
on her pretty face, she saw the flames licking at his fingers
and gasped. She stepped toward him, and said, "Oh, no—
not again? I heard you cry out, thought you might be
dreamin', but that *smell*—"

He looked at her, then down at the words he sought,
and read, "But I am a worm and not a man, scorned by
men and despised by the people. All who see me mock me;
they hurl insults, shaking their heads: 'He trusts in the
LORD, let the LORD rescue him. Let Him deliver him,
since he delights in Him." He began to cry, his head down,
the Bible held loose before him.

"No, Henderson, oh, Lord, no," said the big black
woman. She knelt in front of him and took the Bible from
his trembling hands. As she did, the flames subsided and
were gone. Gone, too, was the ash, and the smell. "Here,"
she went on, "you've got to turn the page." She put one
hand gently on his cheek, and after a moment he covered it
with his. She smiled at him, and read from Psalm 24:
"There earth is the Lord's, and everything in it, the world,
and all who live in it; for He founded it upon the seas and
established it upon the waters. Who may ascend the hill of
the Lord? Who may stand in this holy place? He who has
clean hands and a pure heart, who does not lift up his soul
to an idol or swear by what is false. He will receive blessing
from the Lord and vindication from God his Savior."

He looked into her eyes and was calmed. After a moment, feeling the stirrings of courage, of suppressed joy
held in careful check, and knowing they had both been

raised on these words, he said, "Nateesha, what about over on the next page—those words aren't bad, either," and as he began to speak, she spoke the words with him. "The Lord is my light and savior—whom shall I fear? The Lord is the stronghold of my life—of whom shall I be afraid?"

They stopped and looked at each other. Then he leaned to her and they hugged tightly.

"My God," he said quietly, "what would I do without you?"

+   +   +

The large ornate hotel lobby was bustling and crowded by nine in the morning. In addition to the throng of reporters covering the historic summit meetings, the platoons of security people from all over, the various aides and staff members, there were many spectators hoping to get a glimpse of greatness. The hotel restaurants were still busy with the breakfast crowd, the front desk was trying to juggle requests, the business center was a beehive, and traffic out in front required a special police task force. The real working meetings between Azul Dante and the world leaders had been going on for several days, and the big party the evening before signaled their successful conclusion. On this morning Dante was scheduled to visit wounded soldiers from the front at a nearby hospital, and later hold a "prayer vigil for peace" on the steps of the famed Notre Dame.

Dante had sent a spasm through the ranks of security personnel by announcing he wanted the hotel lobby opened to the public on this morning. Certainly security

people were to be on their toes, his memo stated, but the
severe restrictions were to be relaxed. He was not there to
be seen only by the world leaders and others "with access,"
his memo chided, but by the common folk, as well. His
every move on this day would be broadcast live, worldwide, and the crowds of followers and well-wishers would
add to the pageantry. The restaurants, shops, and especially the lobby would be monitored, but open to anyone.
There was no formal announcement to this effect, but
people who began arriving at the hotel early soon discovered they were in fact welcome, and—with certain limits—
could mill and mingle around throughout the spacious and
heroically decorated lobby so they might see Dante and
others as they left on their rounds. The spectators came
from all over the world, and many wore colorful, regional
garb. Prudent Muslims, of course, refrained from wearing
their traditional religious clothing, especially the women.
There were few, in any case, because of the political cli-
mate, Prince Khalid being one. The women from India
caused an increased blood pressure in the security people,
dressed in their ornate and silky saris with head-cover.
None were veiled, however, and the material was too light
to effectively conceal any weapon. They were closely observed by the nervous security agents anyway.

While Cat Early waited for Slim at the smaller Hôtel
Vin Mont—he had called to say he'd grab some coffee and
bagels for them and come to her room—she thought about
the night before. She had managed a brief conversation
with Azul Dante while he stood with Sophia Ghent and

others at the party. He had seemed particularly interested in where she had been since the "incident" in Nice, and she had given an awkward explanation having to do with a short road trip to research a story. He had been polite, but distracted, and she had not even bothered to ask any questions during the press conference that followed, content to listen to others. As she was leaving with Slim, Sophia grabbed her arm, pulled close, and whispered, "Azul wants you to be in the lobby in the morning, Cat. He would like you to ride with him as he visits the hospital, and then the cathedral later, so you can do another of your fine interviews. You will sit with us in his limousine, yes?"

"Of course," Cat had answered. She knew as a professional she should be pleased, and she was, but she could not shake the feeling of being manipulated, and guessed Dante was not finished with *his* questions. Seeing the excitement in the Sophia's lovely eyes, she asked, "How's it going? You know—you and Devane?"

Sophia had quickly glanced around, pulled even closer to Cat's ear, and whispered, "We are meeting later tonight, after everything calms down. We will have coffee, and . . . talk . . . in the lounge. It will be for only a few minutes, because of the crazy schedule, but I'll take what I can have of him—for now."

And they had parted.

Cat had told Slim of the invitation, and he said he'd wait with her in the lobby, maybe get a few shots, and then he'd meet her later in the day for the happening on the steps of Notre Dame. He did not want to take photos of politicians visiting combat-wounded soldiers, he explained.

He did not have to tell her he considered the wounded to be unique representatives of honor, or that they were almost sacred in his eyes, and Dante visiting them was cynical and demeaning—she already knew.

She heard a knock on her door, then Slim's voice, "It is I, bagel boy, the man from la muncha."

+   +   +

In the small, functional lobby of the Vin Mont, Tommy Church sipped the rich hot coffee he bought in the small restaurant, and thought about his travel companion, Piet Dardon. The quiet young man had awakened before Tommy and knocked on the door to Tommy's room fully dressed and ready while Tommy was shaving. Tommy had answered the door with a towel tied around his hips, grinned, and said, "C'mon in, Piet—I'll be done in a sec, and we can amble downstairs and see what these people call breakfast here in *Pairee*." Piet had shyly entered the room, his head and eyes down like usual, and told Tommy he wanted to walk a bit before going to the Château Brozek as they had planned. Would that be all right? Tommy had shrugged, and told Piet to meet him near that huge metal wall mural in the lobby. Tommy told Piet he had spoken with an American photojournalist the night before—guy named Slim—and had learned the tight security was to be loosened a bit so Dante could be seen by the adoring masses. Tommy suggested that Piet not push his luck, however, and told the young man to lose the sunglasses and the hood of his sweatshirt before going into the hotel. Piet had nodded. Then, as he turned to go, he tentatively put out his small hand and lifted his big eyes to Tommy's. They shook hands, and Piet said in his curiously soft voice, "I have enjoyed our time together, Tommy Church, and wish you all the luck in the world." Then he turned and left.

Tommy thought that was odd.

Tommy heard a voice behind him ask, "Are those real cowboy boots, or are you a wanna-be?"

He turned to see an attractive woman wearing a simple pantsuit, standing with the guy named Slim he had met the night before.

He grinned. "They're real, but I *am* a wanna-be. I wanna be on a horse."

"But you're here in Paris because?"

Tommy shrugged. "Because of a bunch of reasons, ma'am. Mostly because I'm tryin' to live life, it seems the world is comin' to an end, ol' Azul Dante is bein' sold as the one who might save us all, and I kinda wanted to get a look at him for myself."

Cat shook the offered hand and introduced herself.

"My name's Tommy Church, ma'am," said Tommy. He grinned. "Hey, Slim. How'd a guy like you get to be with a fine woman like Cat, here?"

Slim pretended a yawn. "Ah, cowboy, she's like all the others—won't leave me alone."

"We're going over to the convention-center hotel this morning, Tommy," said Cat, watching his eyes closely. "Why don't you walk with us, and I can pick your brain about what's happening back in the States. Slim and I are journalists, so we have access to media outlets, of course— but I'm interested in the grassroots perspective."

"Well, sure," responded Tommy. "That'd be fine. My latest info is a couple of days old—last time I talked with my sister in Virginia, you know. My dad's with a church called the New Christian Cathedral, in Selma, and he's been out preachin', of all things, so I've been getting' the skinny from him, through her."

Cat, without realizing it, gripped Tommy's arm tightly as she stopped and turned to him, closely watched by Slim. "Tommy," she asked, her mouth suddenly dry, "what—what's you father's name?"

"Thomas Church."

As he said the name, Cat felt a ripple of energy surge through her, and the number *seven* rang in her mind. She took a breath, smiled at the young man, and said after a moment, "I'm really glad we met, Tommy."

"Well . . . me, too, Cat," Tommy replied.

"Don't let her get your spurs spinning, cowboy," said Slim as they began walking down the sidewalk. "She says that to every guy she meets."

+   +   +

The girl, Faseem, in her guise as Piet Dardon, watched her feet as they strode without hesitation into the noisy and busy lobby where *he* would be. She felt she was having an out-of-body experience, while still *in* her body. She had known she was driven by an unseen hand during the weeks leading up to this day, but had felt it more in her subconscious. On this morning it was *conscious*. She was an observer of herself, a passenger. She tried to resist, of course, tried first to simply remain lying on the bed in her hotel room, tried to simply not get dressed. To no avail. Soon she was standing before Tommy, saying good-bye, and longing to grab him in a hug that would last both their lifetimes. But she could not, did not. Then she was off, and soon she stood before Azul Dante's hotel.

Once inside, she made her way without hesitation to one of the fashionable boutiques on the second level. There were a couple of salesgirls and a few customers, but no one paid her any attention. She walked to the dressing rooms, opened the left one without knowing why, and stepped inside. She saw the bag lying on the bench and knew what it contained. Her intellectual self began to comprehend the workings of the plan—began to understand the dressing room, the clothing. There were dark whispers in her mind, tendrils of smoky thoughts that instructed her, guided her. Each time she consciously resisted these thoughts, her attempt was met with a stabbing pain behind her eyes and nausea in her gut. Even as these occurred, she found herself moving forward, doing what the voices told her to do. Once she forced herself to sit on the floor, her bunched fists hard against her forehead as she rocked back and forth and said, "No, no, no." But after a moment she stood, her hands relaxed, and she found herself once again reduced to observer as she pulled off her jeans, T-shirt, and sweatshirt to stand naked, frightened, and alone. Still she fought, trying to pray for strength, for deliverance from the controlling voices. But it was as if she knew not how to pray, and she sensed her pleading words being plucked from their intended path and scattered like dried locusts across a desert of grim silence. *It was as if she knew not how to pray.* She dressed and stood before the mirror. The image she saw reflected there was lovely, and she shuddered.

+ + +

Azul Dante stood in the elevator with James Devane, Sophia Ghent, Hiram Sarco, and Sarco's secretary, an obsequious young man named Richard. They all wore business suits in subdued hues, except Dante, who had purposely chosen an eggshell linen, with matching tie. He felt a swelling within his chest, a warming strength, a building density that vibrated in his muscles and tightened his skin. His mouth went dry in anticipation. As the elevator descended six floors to the main lobby, each of them silent in their own thoughts, Dante examined the range of human emotion and psyche that wallowed around him in the close confines. A barely contained tension flowed between Sophia and James Devane, a palpable male–female *awareness*. It was not unpleasant, and he let himself enjoy their base and ignorant attraction. The one with Sarco was a thin husk, and Dante discounted him. Sarco, of course, was consumed with Sarco. Dante felt Sarco's energy and excitement, but was put off by the man's cloying proximity. Sarco's excitement, Dante knew, came from *hunger*, the hunt for power, and this Dante appreciated. *Just a few more minutes, Hiram,* he mused. He allowed himself a little mind-travel. In his mind's eye he saw the dust-colored city of Jerusalem, the gray and craggy Old City, the sands, the palm trees, the worn brick pathways. He saw various peoples, their clothing for the most part khaki and black. He saw the wide, dun-hued steps leading to the Mosque of

Omar, the gleaming dome, the large heavy doors that opened to the cool and pleasing shadows within. He saw an old imam standing wide-legged in the square in front of the dome, staring at his feet. He widened his view and saw weapons—weapons of every type and size, assault rifles, rocket-propelled grenade launchers, machine guns, armored vehicles and heavy tanks. In the skies beyond hung attack helicopters, waiting. Almost all the observable weapons were Israeli, of course. This pleased him. His distant gaze went back to the Mosque of Omar, standing on the Temple Mount in the southeastern quarter of the Old City. Down below, through the foundation, through the packed clay, rock, and sediment that formed the Mount, down to the water beneath. He smiled. He closed his eyes, concentrated, and let out a small breath of air. At that moment there was an almost imperceptible shift, a gritty ripple that rocketed across the miles to the mosque. The old imam stared at his feet and wondered why they had gone suddenly numb.

Dante's concentration was broken by a muted bell as the elevator stopped on the lobby level. There was a moment's hesitation, and the doors opened.

CHAPTER THIRTEEN

Tommy Church managed to find a spot along one edge of the lobby of the Château Brozek where he could scan the crowd, the front desk, and the far wall where the elevators were. The hotel was buzzing with activity, jammed with jostling, excited people all waiting expectantly for the appearance of Azul Dante. Tommy had enjoyed talking with Cat Early and Slim as they walked over from their hotel, the day bright and sunny, and they had made tentative plans to get together that evening, if possible. They had parted at the front entrance to the busy hotel, and after a few minutes Tommy spotted them standing together on the other side of the huge expanse of lobby. He could not find Piet, however, and wondered if the shy young man had simply found all the bustle too much to handle. Tommy wouldn't blame Piet if he decided to pick a spot somewhere outside where he might get a glimpse of Dante waving to the crowds or entering his limousine. This throng was pretty intense, he felt, and wondered at himself for wanting to be there. He knew the chances of actually *speaking* with a world figure like Azul Dante were slim to none, and was not sure now what he hoped to gain by being there. He had just followed his heart thus far, he concluded, so he might as well continue on, and take what he could from the experience. He did admit to himself that it *was* pretty neat, just being there. He allowed himself a few minutes of people-watching, taking in the different groups, the varied clothing styles, the mixed cultures represented. He wished he could find Piet, though, and was worried about the young guy.

Suddenly a surge of energy coursed through the crowded lobby, everyone turned toward the elevators, and Azul Dante stepped out, smiling. The small group with him stepped out behind him, but all eyes were on Dante, who radiated power, strength, confidence, and *awareness*. He gazed pleasantly upon the crowd, and each person there felt he was looking directly into *their* eyes. It was as if he was surrounded by a golden glow, a special light that enhanced his figure and made him visible to everyone there. The glow carried with it a wave of positive energy, which swept through and over the people, filling their hearts with a rush of goodwill and calm. Each man and woman in the lobby felt an immediate and *personal* bond with him, felt a kinship, a *oneness*, and embraced it openly. Many had tears of gladness on their cheeks, pent-up fears and emotions allayed and released. *He was the one*, and they felt it.

Tommy Church felt it, was caught totally off guard by its intensity, and thought, *Whew, this man has got it goin' on.*

He watched as Dante took a few steps forward, then stopped, bowed elegantly, straightened, and waved, and he knew—as did everyone there—that Dante had befriended each one of them at that moment. The crowd broke into spontaneous applause, laughter, and glad expressions of support until Dante raised one hand, his eyebrows up, and waited. Realizing he was going to speak, the crowd quickly quieted.

"My friends," said Dante expansively, and his voice, though not loud, carried to every corner of the lobby. "My brothers, my sisters—good morning!"

They were cheers, and cries of "Good morning," in many languages.

"It is a fine day, is it not?" Dante continued, "and I thank each of you for being here to see me off on my rounds. You are a gift to me, and your being here indicates your support, and validates my mission. *You*, of course, are the reason I even exist, good friends, and I am grateful for you—and looking forward to working on our mission together. It is a new morning, a new day, and a new world is ours to build!"

He stepped forward, waving and smiling, moving through the cheering and applauding crowd, tense security agents doing the best they could to clear a path for him, all the while watching the hands. They pressed to him, reached for him, the hands, all hoping for a brief touch, human nerve endings on outstretched fingertips longing for a moment's contact with something larger than life. The innocent hands were a nightmare for the security agents, for even in such a fawning crowd as this might lurk the hand that held the knife, the gun, the bomb, a sweaty, frightened, hateful hand that would bring death instead of adoration. But Dante moved among the people seemingly unmindful of such things, reaching out, touching, waving, smiling at every face, making eye contact with each turn of his head. He strode across the lobby, through the sea of leaning, cheering, happily crying faces, unhindered and uninhibited by fear.

As Azul Dante and his small entourage moved closer to where he stood, Tommy felt the projected wave of emotion and excitement wash over him. He was fascinated by the spectacle, amazed at how much raw *power* Dante exuded, immediately glad he was there. He wished Piet was there, too, to see it, to witness such an awe-inspiring, fulfilling event. He pulled his eyes away from Dante for a moment and quickly scanned the crowd once more, hoping to spot his young friend. Near the huge panoramic metal sculpture that dominated one side of the lobby his eyes swept the faces, then suddenly stopped, backed, and focused. He took a sharp intake of breath, and thought, *What?* He had spotted Piet, but it wasn't Piet at all, it was a lovely young woman from India, her pale yellow and white sari draped around her, the filmy scarf covering her black hair, one side of her face, and one big brown eye. It was the eye that had made Tommy stare. He knew those eyes, because they had bothered him since the first time he had gazed into them, dark and mysterious pools, which made him question his conscious acceptance of Piet—*the young man*. With an immediate and jolting clarity he understood his own misgivings and recognized why he had never reconciled his feelings about Piet's occasionally bothersome attachment to him. Piet was a girl. She was a girl, and now she stood within a few feet of Azul Dante, dressed in East Indian garb and wearing a distant, dreamy expression on her pretty face.

Tommy did not like this one bit, and he began to push his way through the crowd toward his friend. He did not know what was going on, but knew instinctively it wasn't good.

Veteran combat photographers and veteran security agents develop a sense of *the moment*. It is a wispy, intangible, undefined reality that sometimes sign-posts a violent physical action a moment before it occurs. This allows the combat photographer to capture that rare and once-in-a-lifetime shot *as it happened*, and allows the security agent to perhaps *act* in time to stop, deflect, or absorb the violence before it reaches their charge.

Because of that sense, Slim Piedmont, without really knowing why, but not questioning it, raised his camera and focused on the beautiful young Indian woman who turned toward the sprawling metal wall sculpture behind her as Azul Dante moved close.

Because of it, James Devane, the American agent, suddenly tensed, pushed Hiram Sarco's wispy secretary aside and shouldered toward the slim young woman in the yellow and white sari as she turned.

Dante was in front of his small group now, with Sarco slightly behind and to his left, Sophia behind and to his right, his broad smile and beaming countenance radiating over the surging crowd. His steps were carefully timed, of course, and he was fully aware of the young woman to his right as her long willowy arms shot out toward the wall sculpture. Her pale hands grasped tightly the smooth wooden handle of a large, curved, forged and hammered-metal scimitar that was but a piece in the three-dimensional mosaic, and with a barely audible grunt yanked it from the intertwined pieces of metal that formed the artistic tableau. It sprang to her grasp, separating from its mountings with a sharp *ping*. She spun with it in her hands, raising it over her head as she did, and pierced the restless air of the lobby with a scream as she lunged forward two steps, the gleaming blade whistling down in a rapid and relentless arc.

Slim was quick enough to capture in series the attack. His photos showed a smiling, seemingly unaware Azul Dante, his carefully combed salt-and-pepper hair highlighted by the overhead lights, his face turned slightly away from the wall, his eyes bright. Behind him in the first image could be seen the arms, hands, and gleaming blade as the sword swept toward his head. Behind, slightly out of focus, was the serene face of a lovely young woman with black hair. The next image actually captured the moment the sharp edge of the weapon as it hit the top of Dante's head, on the right side. As the blade dug into the hair, flesh, then skull of Dante, his expression became twisted and distorted with pain, his eyes wide and staring, his mouth an elongated grimace. The next frames show Dante's head turning down and to the right from the force of the blow, the blade cutting in, cleaving the skull as bright crimson blood and grayish tissue exploded from the deep cut. The glaring color of the blood lay stark and visceral on the pastoral cloth of Dante's eggshell linen suit. Dante's eyes rolled back, and he collapsed even as the young woman, now in sharp focus, stood over him, her hands still grasping the handle of the bloody scimitar. Her face was that of a young girl, captured in a troubled dream.

James Devane was not quick enough. He was perhaps one step too far from position when he first saw the girl spin with the weapon. He hurled himself at her, already knowing he could not stop that hissing, inexorable, deadly arc of the blade as it fell on its target. As he dived at her with his left arm and hand outstretched, his right instinctively reached under his jacket for his automatic pistol. Within the microseconds of the action, his trained mind examined the pros and cons of using the firearm in such close and crowded quarters. There was the sure chance that one of his bullets would find an innocent, and that he accepted. More important, he knew, even if he shot the attacker in the head or heart, it was already too late to prevent the fall of that sword. He made his lunge for her in desperation, saw the explosion of blood, immediately comprehended no man could survive such a wound, and knew he would fail.

There occurred one of those strange cessations of time, a frozen moment during which all movement seems to happen in slow motion, where all sound becomes muted and distant. Depending on the position and proximity of the observer, people saw and heard different things. Some heard the metallic *ping*, some heard the girl's grunt, almost all heard her piercing scream as she lunged. Some actually heard the sickening, gritty sound of the blade impacting and cleaving Dante's skull. Then there was that spectral pause, a collective holding of breath. Just for a moment.

The scream filled the room. The sword fell upon Azul Dante, cutting into his head, inflicting a mortal wound. The blood exploded. Dante collapsed. The young woman attacker was tackled to the floor, and as she fell, the heavy scimitar slipped from her small hands and *clanked* onto the polished tile floor. Now—pandemonium. Now—panic, screams, falling, pushing, shoving, turning, running. Screams. Shouts. Cries of fear, of helplessness, of anger and loss. The room erupted in an explosion of people all reacting differently to a close and brutal onslaught of violence—violence directed against the one whom a moment ago had walked in and filled the room with a storm of positive emotion and promise. *Promise.*

"Oh, God!" someone screamed. *"How could this happen?"*

Cat Early watched in macabre fascination as Azul Dante, his shoulder and the right side of his face now cloaked in blood, went loose and fell onto the floor. She, like most others there, had become frozen in place as the blade fell, and only when she heard the clicking of Slim's camera, and felt him moving forward against the surging mob, did she begin to move also. She saw Sophia Ghent on her knees, holding Dante's upper torso on her lap, openly crying, one whitened fist held against her teeth. She saw the agent, James Devane, tackle the frail Indian girl who had committed the impossible act, and fall to the floor in a jumble as other, slower, security people piled on. She watched as one beefy security agent in a dark suit and sunglasses kicked the gleaming sword away from Dante and those with the girl. He toed it across the floor until it rested against the wall under the sculpture it came from, and he stood there pointing his pistol at it, glaring at anyone who came near. Amidst the running, pushing, falling people moving away from the bloody scene, she saw a lanky figure shouldering and shoving his way *toward* it. She realized it was the young American she had met, and she watched with a sinking feeling as he threw himself onto the security agents in an effort to get to the girl. Several of the agents, determining they were being attacked, countered Tommy's lunge by kicking and punching at him. Even from where she stood she heard Tommy yell, "No! Leave her alone! She doesn't—!" Then he fell amidst an avalanche of blows, his arms reaching for the girl, who lay in the fetal position underneath James Devane. Cat crouched and cocked her head to the side to look at the girl's distant expression, and concluded the girl was out of her mind.

Then she looked at Hiram Sarco.

Sarco stood rigid behind the seated Sophia, the sprawled Dante. He seemed to her larger than she remembered, his shoulders straight, his great round head slowly turning this way and that, his face dark and glowering. His hands were balled into fists at his sides, and his mouth twisted as he leaned his head back and spoke in a rich and booming voice that washed over them all.

"Do not fear!" Sarco cried, and the words echoed from

the walls, out into the street, and around the huge square in front of the hotel. It was as if his words became the very air, and completely permeated the atmosphere. "Do not fear this act! Good people of this new world! Do not fear those who might destroy he who will save us! *He cannot be destroyed!*"

Cat Early heard these words coming from the energized and surreal figure of the newly empowered Hiram Sarco, glanced back at the broken, bleeding skull of Azul Dante, and thought, *Looks like he's destroyed to me*. She had been on too many battlefields, had seen too many fatally wounded men. *No way any man can survive that.*

"It appears he has fallen!" cried Sarco as he strode across the lobby. The entire series of glass front doors to the hotel were suddenly flung open, seemingly by the power of his words. Many people fell to the ground, or crouched hugging one another in fear. Sarco stopped just outside the doors, on the top of the wide steps that looked down to the street and the square. Thousands stared up at him, frightened, confused, hungry for someone to lead them. "It appears he has fallen!" he shouted again. "But hear me, good people, hear me and learn! Now is the time for you to bring his faith into your hearts—make it *your faith in him*. Make it your faith in *the one!* He will not fall if you have faith, and *believe in him!*"

A woman's wailing voice lifted above the cowering crowd: "Oh, God—oh, my God. How could this happen?"

Sarco, his face dark and angry, his eyes reddened and fierce, lifted his arms above him, his fists in the air, and cried out, "Don't waste your time, and Azul Dante's *promise*, beseeching one *who is not there—one who only has power in your IMAGINATION! Call only upon the one who is Here, the one who really can CHANGE THIS SAD WORLD!*" He turned slightly, and with one arm flung behind him, pointed into the hotel lobby. His mouth opened, and appeared fiery in his dark face. "In there lies *the one*, seemingly destroyed. Don't be fooled! Don't lose faith! Call on *him*, and you will be rewarded."

"But his enemies are many!" cried a desperate, frightened voice from the crowds below. "We must fear them!"

Hiram Sarco turned once more, then lifted his face to the heavens, raised his hands even more, opened his fists as he splayed his fingers skyward, and cried, "Do not fear what has happened. *Fear this!*"

As his words boomed across the square a sharp, rattling hiss—much like the sound of a huge fireworks rocket—seared across the blue skies, and streaks of fire arced across the curved expanse. The fiery, molten fingers raced in random directions from one edge to another, down from the middle, and laced together in a jagged, monstrous crisscross pattern above the earth. Here and there globs of fire fell onto the roofs of buildings, into the streets, across the square, igniting all they touched. In the din and tumult it was not at first observed—and would only later very cautiously— that the burning globs fell for the most part on mosques, synagogues, and churches. Even the revered Notre Dame was hit, though the burning globs struck only a few gargoyles, which seemed to embrace the flames before exploding into sooty lava. Hiram Sarco, immediately aware that he was only a conduit for this display, aware he was acting in concert with an unseen hand, that his body and voice were temporarily not his own, felt a surge of raw, animal, pleasure—and knew in his heart he had chosen wisely. The searing display in the skies lasted only a few moments, and as it abated, he turned and strode back into the hotel lobby.

"Seal and secure all doors, all entrances!" Sarco shouted, and agents from all the varied security teams jumped at his command. "Remove everyone from the lobby!" He saw the emergency medical team had already been summoned, and were in fact lifting the unconscious Azul Dante onto a gurney, his head wrapped in what appeared to be a bloody sheet. The faces on the EMTs were glum, and one shook his head at Sarco, as if to say *no way*. Sarco glared at them. "Take him upstairs—to his suite!" he shouted. "There's no time for the hospital, and it would never be secure!" He saw the hesitation on the faces and strode toward them, pointing with one hand toward the elevators. "Call for the best doctors, get whatever medical teams you want here, but take him upstairs *now!*" The EMTs looked at each other and shrugged. They knew Hiram Sarco could call for all the king's horses, and all the king's men if he wanted to. Dante was lost anyway. James Devane, standing over the handcuffed girl, and the handcuffed and bloody young American who had tried to pull her from him, nodded at the EMTs. He, like them, felt it really didn't matter if Dante went to the best hospital in the world, into his bed in his fancy suite, or onto a park bench down by the Louvre—Dante was a dead man.

* * *

Sophia stood, the front of her suit darkened by blood, her face ashen. She swayed for a moment, took a deep breath, and regained her strength. She turned toward the supine figure of Azul Dante on the stretcher and looked at him with tears in her eyes. She looked back at Devane and said softly, "James?" He reached out with his right hand and with the backs of his fingers brushed the skin of her cheek. "Go with him, Sophia. Stay with him. I'll be there in a few minutes." She nodded and reached out for Dante's lifeless left hand, which dangled off the edge of the gurney. She walked beside him as the EMTs moved him across the lobby floor toward the elevators.

At that moment two members of the French security group rushed up to Devane, holding an unzipped backpack. One of them showed it to the American, and said, "This was found in a dressing room in one of the boutiques, and the salesgirls there told us they saw this one"—he sneered down at the girl on the floor—"go into the room dressed like a *boy*." He held the backpack open for all to see, and went on. "In here we found pants, a shirt, a heavier shirt with a hood, sunglasses, and a hat. We also found these pieces of identification." He held up two passports and some other papers. "Our little assassin apparently holds dual citizenship—French and Jordanian. He, or *she*, is Piet Dardon."

Devane did not want the investigation, or the interrogation, to be conducted in the lobby of the hotel, so he put one hand up to stop the man, and shook his head. Then he leaned close to the girl, who lay with a calm expression on her face. Her delicate sari had been torn at the neck in the struggle, and she held the edges against the skin of her chest with her manacled hands. Gently, Devane asked, "Is that who you are? Piet Dardon—from Jordan?"

"Don't answer him!" cried Tommy through his bloody, torn lips. He lay only a few feet from the girl, his hands behind him. His shirt had been torn also; his hat was gone. He wheezed with each breath of his bloody nose and guessed it was broken. "Don't say anything! You don't have to—" Tommy was at a total loss, found it impossible to understand what had just happened, accepted that, and put it aside for the moment. He was aware of an immediate and consuming loyalty to the girl, a loyalty that dominated and controlled him. He was able to accept this, and had acted on it, because his driven heart was filled with a sure sense of purpose, of *right*. There was something very important taking place, and he was convinced neither he nor the girl were there by happenstance. He had seen something in Azul Dante's expression as the man fell, bloody and cleaved, something sinister—and *knowing*. It had frightened him and filled him with resolve. He wished his dad were there with him.

A security man standing over Tommy kicked him savagely in the ribs, then knelt down and used his thumb as a pressure point behind Tommy's left ear. Tommy grimaced in pain, and kicked his feet trying to spin around. Another agent pounced on him, then another, and there were more blows until Devane shouted, "Enough! Stop!" The agents stood back, breathing heavily. One of them pointed at Tommy, who lay gagging, and said through clenched teeth, "My partner and I saw this one with the cowboy boots yesterday, right here in this lobby. He was with that small one who cut Minister Dante. They stood near here, after they had searched around the entire lobby. They stood here, looking at this sculpture on the wall." He took another breath and added, "They are together. He is her accomplice in this."

Another agent interrupted, his eyes wide, "They came with that Saudi! That Muslim! They arrived here with that, uh, that—Khalid—the Saudi! He's a Saudi Muslim, and she's a Muslim, too!"

"Find him," said Devane, calmly. "Hold him in his suite until we can interview him."

Three or four agents turned away, one spoke urgently into a small radio.

The girl let out a soft moan, and everyone stared at her. Devane watched as her eyes seemed to jump into focus, then dart around in confusion and fear. To Devane it looked as if she were awakening from a bad dream. He saw her look down at her handcuffed hands, then over at the bloody and beaten American on the floor a few feet away. A look of vague recognition and acceptance clouded her face, and she closed her eyes.

"Are you with this American, my child?" asked Devane in a gentle voice. "Did you arrive here with Prince Khalid? Are you Piet Dardon—from Jordan?"

She opened her eyes and looked at Devane. She shifted her gaze from him, to Tommy, then across the floor where the bloodied scimitar lay. She took a deep breath and laid her head onto the floor.

Devane heard shouts from the other side of the lobby and turned to see security agents shoving and arguing with newspeople. He recognized Cat Early and Slim Piedmont. There were many cable-feed, video, and television cameramen gathered around, too—and all their cycloptic eyes pointed at him. Before he could speak, however, Hiram Sarco strode across the lobby from the front desk and said in his oddly strong voice, "Gentlemen! The lobby has been cleared of the innocents. It is safe, and secure now. The journalists and camera crews will be allowed to stay. All media people will take their orders from *me*, understood? The world needs to see what has happened here today—as it is even at this moment." He knew the entire incident had been broadcast worldwide as it happened, and even as he spoke millions of viewers would see the action. What had occurred in the skies was seen globally, of course. He pointed at the thick pool of dark blood on the floor, already beginning to congeal, and at Tommy and the girl. "Focus the lenses on the scene of this horror," he commanded, "and on the perpetrators of this fruitless crime." He turned in a slow circle and glared at all who watched him. "The cameras will tell the story," he said.

Devane, while not in agreement with Hiram Sarco, had more important matters on his mind. He knew the French would want to control the incarceration and interrogation of the all suspects in this assassination, but also felt he *must* lead the investigation. He was Dante's appointed personal security head, and this *was* personal. One of the suspects appeared to be American, and that was another reason. There was something else. He had looked into the girl's eyes, and sensed—something. He leaned close to her once more, and almost whispering, asked, "Are you Piet Dardon—from Jordan?"

The girl looked into his eyes, and answered quietly, "I am Faseem. Please find John for me."

"I will try," responded Devane. He wondered who *John* was.

+   +   +

Over two hundred miles away, General Izbek Noir let an evil smile split his purple lips. He did not need a television to tell him the story. He had seen the atmospheric fireworks, of course, and found them to be striking. He understood their visual impact upon the peoples of earth—even his own soldiers had cowered and cried out as the fires streaked the skies—but dismissed them as nothing more than a stunt. His mind's eye, traveling on a plane not understood and unrecognized by mortal man, witnessed the attack on Azul Dante. He saw the cleaving of the skull, the wondrous blade in the hands of a vile female vessel, and comprehended the act. *Of course*, he mused. Again, the entity that was Dante impressed him with his adherence to what was prophesied—using it to his, Dante's, own advantage. A bothersome voice whispered to him, only for a moment, wondering if Dante was using prophecy—or if what was happening was as it was *written*. He shrugged it off. He knew that Dante, like himself, had within him something in common with lowly man—the ego. He had long ago dismissed written prophecy, *the Word*, as something irrelevant to what he was, what he planned, and suspected Dante had already made the same decision.

He stroked his angular jaw with his long pointed fingers, his eyes glowing, and mused, *It will be interesting indeed to see how this all plays out.*

CHAPTER F⊕URTEEN

"My brothers and sisters," intoned Reverend Henderson Smith, his voice deep and solemn. "Clearly, it is time for prayer. We have all seen with our own eyes this horrible and completely devious attack on the one man who might lead this convulsed world out of darkness, Azul Dante. Here we have the man who not only created the worldwide Prodigal Project, dedicated to the resurrection and redemption of man's world, but who also was very close to building a coalition of world powers that would smite the heathen mujahideen and their leader, Izbek Noir. What should have been a triumphant day for him was carried on live television across the world, so—depending on the time where the viewer was—the world saw the attack as it happened, or since then on the replays. I say triumphant day, for him, for *us*, because Azul Dante had just brought together the most powerful of world leaders—including our own President Clara Reese—and they formally agreed to join him in his efforts to save the world. He was on his way to visit wounded soldiers from the front, then onto the steps of the Notre Dame Cathedral for a moment of thanks." He paused, let his eyes scan all the faces watching him as he stood high in the reaching pulpit of the New Christian Cathedral, then used one hand to wipe his eyes. "But no," he said with a heavy voice, "no . . . before he could begin his work in *our* behalf, he was *cut down*." He let those words echo throughout the church. "He was cut down, fellow believers, his head deeply wounded with a heavy sword. The chances of his survival . . . dim."

Many who sat in the pews had tears in their eyes. Some openly wept. All were mesmerized as they listened to Smith, hoping he could explain the unexplainable, hoping he could give them hope again each time it seemed to be taken away. Ivy Sloan-Underwood and her husband, Ron, sat next to Ted Glenn and Shannon Carpenter. Beside Shannon sat Rebecca, then Thomas Church. Thomas's and Rebecca's faces were pale, drawn, and Shannon held Rebecca's hand tightly in her own. They listened to Smith, but there was no peace in their hearts. They were, each of them, in tumult, torn and pummeled by forces and emotions raw, powerful, and consuming.

"And what of Hiram Sarco, Azul's new right-hand man, his assistant and partner in the building of our new world? We should pray for him—a prayer of *thanks*," said Smith as he pounded one fist onto the top rail of his pulpit. "We should be thankful Hiram Sarco was there, was ready to step up and be strong when needed. And what of that magnificent display of celestial pyrotechnics? Some have attributed it—all those streaks of fire making odd patterns across the skies—to some unknown power unleashed by Sarco in his anger over what had happened to Dante." He shook his head reprovingly. "No, no. Brothers and sisters, I see it differently. Yes, there was fire in the skies, and it appeared as Sarco stood on the steps of the hotel where Dante lay grievously wounded—but I believe it was there as a message from *God*. It was a *sign*, a signal of how displeased He was about what had happened." He shrugged. "Perhaps Sarco was the conduit, I don't know. What I *do* know is that even with all that energy and wondrous power, mercy was shown, too. Yes, mercy came with the very little amount of destruction those fires caused. Yes, buildings were damaged, yes, some unfortunates lost their lives—maybe a few thousand, total, *worldwide*." He stopped, took a long drink of cold water from the heavy crystal goblet near his left elbow, and unconsciously wiped his lips with the back of his left hand. "It was scary, and it caught our attention—and that is what I believe it was meant to do. Now look outside, and look at what the news shows us is happening out there." He waved one hand toward the far walls of the church, the windows, beyond. "Deadly riots in some parts of the world, panic everywhere, people in the streets fighting with authorities, a run on the few banks still working with our government's help. Why—it's very much like the aftermath of the disappearances, am I right? People in *fear*, in *panic*—chaos ensues, total lawlessness, looting in the grocery stores, gas stations raided—all of it. Just when the world was beginning to believe there might be some *hope*, some *reason*, that hope and reason embodied in Azul Dante and his selfless works, it has been brutally, violently, inexplicably *taken*. So now poor, foolish, ignorant man returns to the mindless beast he was before being shown the light—doesn't he? Panic—riots—and with this, Izbek Noir sees a chance and exploits it, sending his howling mujahideen in a merciless attack which is even now punching its way into Turkey." He took a breath and nodded. "I don't have to tell you—this is a dark day, indeed."

Thomas Church stared up at Henderson Smith and wondered again about the reverend's message. It seemed obvious to him that Smith had a definite slant on things he was trying to sell, and it bothered Church. He could not figure the need for it. Clearly what had happened to Azul Dante was a disaster, and did not bode well for the future of man. Dante did in fact seem to be building the right kind of partnership with world leaders, and his coalition forces *were* the best hope against the mujahideen hordes. This completely despicable attack by what first reports were saying was a young Muslim woman was a major setback for man, thought Church, but there was more to it—and Smith was not going there. This Hiram Sarco, mega-corporate-conglomerate communications mogul, was far less impressive spiritually than Dante. The images of him standing on the steps of the hotel, reaching for the skies and calling down the wrath of God's fires was—to Church—a bit overdone, overdramatic, over the top.

He felt Rebecca squeeze his hand, and glanced at her. There were tears in her eyes, and she chewed her lower lip. Only the ones seated with them knew they had seen their son, Tommy, on the television shots of the attack on Dante. Over, and over again, there was the young woman, there was the sword, the blood, the violent tumbling to the floor of the lobby. Then, within a second or two, there was Tommy, shouting something, lunging, diving for the girl— as if to protect her. Tommy could clearly be seen reaching for the girl before several security agents fell on him, punching and kicking. Then, a few minutes later, the images of the waiflike young woman with short black hair, her sari almost torn from her, her small hands manacled— and Tommy. His face was beaten, bruised and bloody, his nose swollen, his lips smashed. His hands were in handcuffs, and he stood beside the girl, looking down at her, surrounded by jostling and surly security agents, their faces furious. The various talking heads on the TV were already calling him "the female assassin's accomplice." They had given his name, and the fact that he was an American. They made him sound suspicious, and sinister—traveling across Europe with seemingly no specific purpose, showing up in Paris where Dante's important talks were taking place. The fact that Tommy had arrived there with a Muslim Saudi prince, and had been seen with the girl "casing" the lobby of the hotel, was frantically reported, as was the information that Tommy had been working on the Saudi's horse farm in central France prior to their journey to Paris. That the girl had multiple IDs, and had been traveling as a man, caused the reporters' voices to reach almost hysterical levels. The last images of Tommy and the girl showed them being roughly crammed into the back of a police van, on their way to a nearby prison for "interrogation."

Without saying anything, both Thomas and Rebecca Church knew their son Tommy would not have acted as he did without good reason. Tommy was not an "assassin," or an "accomplice." Their hearts told them there had to be an explanation. Tommy had told Sissy—their daughter, his sister—he was going to Paris to try to see Dante. He sounded upbeat and excited about his adventure. They knew, they *knew*, their son would not be part of something evil, or even criminal, and because of that they knew there had to be an explanation. They planned to leave for Europe the next morning.

"So, my brothers and sisters," continued Smith as he looked down upon his congregation, "I say again—it is a time for prayer. All of us here are *directly* affected by this wounding of Azul Dante, and even though to us his wound certainly appears fatal—who here will deny the reality of miracles? Is it not *possible* Azul Dante might come back from the brink of what appears to be a sure death? Yes—it is possible. But it won't happen because we *hope* it will. It will happen only if we *pray* it will. We must, each one of us here today, pray for Azul Dante, for his recovery. *We need him.*" He looked down at the pew where Thomas Church sat with the others. A troubled look crossed his face, and a spasm of fear pierced his heart. Through his dried lips he heard his own voice say, "Some of us in this church today might say a little different prayer, perhaps a prayer of forgiveness. We might ask ourselves what it is we believe, if what we believe is right for this world. Some of us here today will have been very personally touched by what happened in Paris, and we might want to examine our hearts, examine our *loyalty*." He paused and stared down at Thomas Church, and those who sat with him. They stared back, and Henderson's heart was racked by in-decision and self-doubt. "Now, brothers and sisters," he managed to say quietly, "let us pray."

While Reverend Henderson Smith led a prayer that asked for a miraculous healing of Azul Dante, Nateesha Folks—who stood almost directly behind and below him in the choir loft—heard his words and watched his face with tears in her eyes. She wept not for Azul Dante, but for Henderson Smith. During the prayer, Thomas Church, holding hands with Rebecca, who held hands with Shannon, and her with Ted Glenn, quietly stood and made his way out of the pew, to the aisle. They were fol-lowed by Ivy and Ron Underwood. Their faces were grim as all of them walked out of the church.

+   +   +

"Cat," said Slim urgently as he quickly opened his hotel room door so she could come in, "thanks for indulging me." He looked up and down the hallway, then closed the door and locked it. "Wanted to show you something . . . interesting."

Cat saw he held a manila envelope in one hand. She waited. She was very tired, emotionally drained. After Azul Dante was taken to his room, and after the girl and the American, Tommy Church, were driven away in the police van, she had hurried to file her eyewitness stories for Simon Blake. He would forward them to the various publications that carried her byline. She did one video segment also, standing on the street as the police van drove off. She gave an accurate, unadorned account of what had happened, and did not resort to speculation. After filing, she had spent the rest of the day unsuccessfully trying to contact James Devane—regarding the incarcerated "assassins"— and Sophia Ghent—regarding Azul Dante. She, like many others working the story, spent the hours holding her breath in anticipation of the inevitable announcement that Azul Dante had died from acute trauma to his brain. She stood in Slim's room now, saw how edgy and fatigued he appeared to be, and waited.

"Do you remember me telling you about the . . . anomaly . . . I discovered when I was with that freaky General Izbek Noir?" asked Slim, his eyes bright. "He kept me there supposedly as his personal shutterbug biographer— but apparently only when he *wanted* me to be. I think I told you about it, because that's how John Jameson and I first began our friendship."

Cat hesitated, then nodded. "You said the images you took of Noir were fine as long as he knew you were photographing him, like he was posing heroically, but when you snapped *candid* shots of him when he was unaware or disinterested in you, the images were like, blurred—or muddied somehow." She dropped her bag to the floor and rolled her shoulders to ease the tension in them. "You felt it had something to do with Noir's actual, um, *physiology*, or physical embodiment."

"Exactly," said Slim, "and when Jameson didn't look at me like I was a complete nut case, I knew *he* suspected something . . . strange . . . also."

Cat sat on one corner of the unmade bed, looked at the small bar-refrigerator under the television cabinet, pointed, and asked, "Got any good soda in yours? Mine only has fancy water, hard liquor, and prune juice."

He said, "Yeah . . . I think so," opened the fridge, and pulled out two soft drinks. He handed her one, they both took long drinks, and Cat held hers against her forehead.

"Good," she said.

"Anyway, Cat," continued Slim, "Azul Dante is *very* photogenic, as you know. I mean, it's no secret among the media troops—especially us still-camera troops—that it is apparently impossible to take a bad picture of the guy. I mean, he's a publicist's dream. He's got no 'bad side,' never gets mugged stuffing his face with a huge bite of salad or anything, and always has a sort of composed and *knowing* expression. Yes? No?"

"Yes," agreed Cat. She knew it was a standing joke within the media ranks: *a fat raspberry award to the first newsie to get an unflattering shot of Azul Dante.*

"So, look at these I managed to get today."

Slim handed her a half-dozen photos. "Some I printed off the digital myself—had the thirty-fives done fast by a back-alley guy I know here. I shot with both—did it without thinking," he explained.

Cat examined the shots. They captured the moment the girl began to swing the big-bladed sword down toward Dante's head. The girl's expression was slightly out of focus in the first shot, better in the second. They were clear enough to show a placid, dreamy look on her, as if the horrific physical act of violence her body was committing had absolutely nothing to do with *her*. More telling was Azul Dante's face, and she saw immediately what Slim had discovered, what bothered him. Dante's expression was that of a person who knew *exactly* what was taking place: When the girl is behind him, sword raised in that millisecond before she brought it down, Dante's eyes seem to be glancing down, and to his right, as if looking behind him. His eyes close as the cutting edge of the blade first touches his head, and his face is slightly tilted back . . . as if in anticipation. There is no fear, or even *surprise* in his expression. Then, as the blade cuts into his skull, his face reacts, scrunching up in a spasm of pain, the eyes squinting tightly, the twisted lips curling around the open mouth. The next shot, for Cat, was the most dramatic. It showed the blade deeply embedded in Dante's skull, an explosion of blood and tissue forming a halo around the back of his head, and his body already collapsing. But his face at that moment was composed, accepting, almost serene. Cat looked through each of them once more.

"Whoa," she said quietly.

"Whoa," echoed Slim.

As Cat held the photos, Slim used his fingers to spread them out in her hands. Then he pulled one a bit, and said, "Take another look at this one, and tell me the first word that comes to mind to describe his expression."

She gazed at the most dramatic shot, with Dante's skull cleaved. "Composed," she responded.

"Good," agreed Slim, "Now study it more, and relate it to a human condition that is the other side of pain, or fear."

She held the photo, staring at it. When it came to her she was startled, and her mouth went suddenly dry. She turned to Slim, and said, "Sensual—*sensual pleasure.*"

Slim took the photos from her, nodded, his face troubled rather than triumphant, and said, "That's what impacted me, Cat. It's like he knows it's coming, he's waiting in excited anticipation. As the blade cuts into him he feels, uh . . . *pleasure.*" He rubbed his jaw, "Is that *possible?* Are we seeing something into this that's not there?"

"No," replied Cat, her voice tight. "You see it, I see it, we see it because it is *there.*"

"So Azul Dante knew it was coming—like he had some kind of welcomed premonition, some kind of *death wish?*" He paused, took a long pull from his soda can, swallowed, and added, "*That's* how he's gonna save the world, by *dying?*"

"It's been done before," said Cat softly, almost to herself. "Two thousand years ago. But by an entirely different— and infinitely *better*—kind of man." She wanted to get back to her room, back to her dead sister's Bible. "Slim," she said as she put one hand on his forearm and squeezed, "you did good, and you are not wrong to be concerned about this. I would keep it to yourself, understand?" She thought of the number *seven,* and was disquieted. "These are weird times, Slim, and as your friend, I'll tell you I believe there are, um, dark forces at work in our world."

"Took a few shots of that fireworks display in the sky, and of bigmouthed Hiram Sarco standing on the hotel steps calling fire down on the rest of us mere mortals," said Slim with a nervous grin as he handed her another print, "I don't know much about signs, portents, or atmospheric cataclysms—but check out the *patterns* left by the fires."

Cat look at the photo, her face became pale, and she whispered, "Pentagrams?"

Slim nodded, "Yep . . . and the others?"

She looked again. Hesitated, and said, "Three curved lines, like claw marks, sort of—"

"Rather *beastly*, is what I thought," said Slim.

Cat could feel her heart pounding in her chest. She wished John were there.

+   +   +

James Devane listened to the tape. The young woman's voice was listless, apathetic—to him it sounded as if she was almost disinterested, unfazed by the intensity of the interrogators. She had been taken to a maximum-security prison on the outskirts of Paris, ostensibly part of a military facility, but known in intelligence circles as a terrorist-suspect holding area. Her questioning had begun immediately following her arrival—after she had been thoroughly searched, her torn clothing replaced with pale yellow prison clothes, fingerprinted, photographed. She had not resisted the search or the questioning in any way, and had given her name as Faseem during an examination by a medical doctor. Devane could not *order* the French authorities to handle their prisoner in any particular way, but he had strongly suggested they give her decent treatment— handle her with tact and patience rather than subject her to the brutal interrogation he sensed many of the security agents wanted. Oddly, Hiram Sarco had—speaking as Azul Dante's *partner*, and guardian—conveyed the same thing to the French: Question the girl, but go easy. The tape had been delivered that morning, and he listened to it in his car as the driver took him to the prison.

"I am Faseem," said the girl's voice on the tape, "I am from Saudi Arabia. I was a girl, then I was a soldier, then a boy, and now I am the girl, Faseem, again." She spoke in English, as did her interviewer.

When asked if Prince Khalid was her leader, the girl responded, "I have no leader. I am adrift."

When asked about the young American, the girl's voice softened, and she said only, "He is a cowboy, a man who speaks with love, kindness, and respect to horses, and to persons adrift."

It was when the name Azul Dante was spoken the first time by the interviewer that the girl's voice changed so dramatically, Devane sat up in his seat. He stopped the tape, rewound it, and listened again. The interviewer asked why she had attacked Azul Dante.

"I am a soldier of Allah," answered the girl, her voice strained, deeper, the edges of the words stretched with a malevolent hiss. "I am a Muslim warrior committed to serving the one true God—none other. Azul Dante is a charlatan usurper of Allah, and tells lies to the ignorant unbelievers of the world. There is none but Allah, and Dante is of the other God—the one with the Son. Dante will save the world for the infidels, because of his God, so he must be destroyed. I worship Allah, I pray for the mujahideen. I am a Muslim—a soldier of Allah."

After that the interviewer tried questions about the plotters' support system—where did they get their operating funds, where did they stay, how did they travel? The girl seemed confused, her answers vague. The interviewer asked how she had prepared the huge sword to be so easily pulled from its place within the artwork on the wall, and the girl answered, "What sword?" The interviewer, growing frustrated, tried the same series of questions again, and the girl began to hum a simple tune, which seemed to infuriate the interviewer. Devane listened, but could not remember what the tune was—something from childhood.

When his driver parked the car in the small walled compound of the prison, Devane sat for a moment before going inside. He reviewed what he had heard on the tape and found he was relieved, though still mystified, *not* to hear the girl mention what she had asked him to do. He had hoped no one had heard her say it to him, and apparently they had not. Good. He could not explain why, but he wanted at least a *part* of this "assassin" to himself.

As he opened the door to get out, the driver—a burly black former U.S. Marine—looked at him over his right shoulder, and said, "Sir."

"Yes, Goodwell?"

"I know you've been listening to that cassette while we rode over here, so I'm guessing you haven't heard what's on the radio—I mean the *broadcast* radio. I've been trying to improve my French, so I scan the dial when I'm driving. It's all over the stations, sir."

"What is?"

"That interview with the girl—all the questions they asked her about her attack on Azul Dante, all her answers about being a Muslim soldier, supporting the mujahideen—all that—"

"They just interviewed her late last night," said Devane incredulously, "and I just got the tape myself this morning."

The big Marine shrugged. "I know this isn't the way *we* do business, sir, but apparently that Hiram Sarco fella made the tape available. One announcer I heard said something like Sarco felt it was important for the people of the world to hear the truth from the assassin's own mouth." He scrunched up his face and shook his bullet-shaped head. "He's the man with the plan, I guess."

"Thanks for telling me, Goodwell," replied Devane, exasperated. "Sit tight. I won't be long." He turned and walked toward the entrance gate.

He was further surprised by the attitude of the agent-guards who kept watch over the new prisoners. The Saudi prince, Khalid, had been questioned in a polite, almost perfunctory way, then left alone. The young American, Tommy Church, had been treated for his bruises and cuts by a doctor, put into a cell not far from the girl, and not questioned at all. Devane had the feeling the French authorities apparently had all the information they thought they needed, and were simply holding the three for now. When Azul Dante died—which he surely would, given the severity of his wound—then the three would be tried for his murder. One agent even told Devane it would be the old "Give them a fair trial—then hang them" kind of thing. This is not to say security was lax; it was on heightened alert. The "word" was Muslim sympathizers would make an attempt to break the three suspects out of

prison, or stage terror attacks upon the civilian populations of Europe, or take hostages to trade. This was a
Muslim deal from start to finish, went the official word,
and it wasn't over yet. Devane was grateful, however, for
the general attitude, when he learned he would visit the
girl in her cell alone. The door would be guarded, but
there would be no French interviewer sitting with him.
Anything said in the cell would be taped, of course, but
he could not prevent that.

The girl sat on the edge of the steel bunk that hung
against one wall of the concrete cell. She did not look up
when the heavy door was swung open, or when Devane
walked in. She looked childlike in the prison blouse and
pants, her small feet resting on floppy straw sandals. Her
short black hair was tousled, and she sat with her elbows
on her knees, her thumbs pressed against her lips. Only
when Devane sat on a small stool across from her, and
spoke, did she raise her eyes.

"Faseem," Devane said gently, "do you remember me?"

The girl's eyes seemed to focus slowly, then her face
brightened in recognition, and she nodded.

"How are you feeling?" asked Devane with a smile.
"Do you need something to drink, or a snack perhaps?"

She shrugged.

"Tell me why you are here," said Devane. "Do you
know?"

"I—hurt someone," answered the girl after a long hesitation.

"Azul Dante."

Her face tightened, her jaw was thrust forward, she sat
straight on the bunk, and in a hard voice, she responded,

"Yes. *Him*. I destroyed him. I am a Muslim—I am a follower of the brave mujahideen, I am—"

"You are the girl, Faseem," interrupted Devane, still using the gentle voice. "You traveled here with Tommy—"

Again the girl's face changed. A small smile crossed her lips, and she replied, "Yes. I am here with Tommy, my friend. He is good; he is not bad." She looked down at her feet. "I do not have fancy shoes, but I know I can make him . . . like me."

"Are you Piet Dardon . . . from Jordan?" asked Devane carefully. He did not know what she meant about the shoes, and left it be.

"Only pretend," said the girl easily. "Only so I can leave the horror behind, and travel to the free world and meet someone like Tommy." She shrugged. "I found Piet and the others in the fields of dead. I used his passports and money. Piet did not mind, because he knew I was leaving the horror behind and going to find Tommy."

"Do you remember saying something to me, asking me to find someone for you?" asked Devane.

Her eyes went far away, but her face remained relaxed. Devane had determined her countenance only changed at the mention of Azul Dante . . . as if she had been brainwashed, or programmed with drugs in some way. She still smiled as she responded, "Yes. I asked you to find John for me."

Devane lowered his voice, and leaned close to the girl. He wanted a bit of a head start on this part. "Who is John, Faseem?"

"John is one who saved me. He saved me from the Muslims, and from myself. He gave me the gift of my life." Her smiled broadened. "He is big, a dark man, strong, with the muja—but not of them."

"But who *is* he?" pressed Devane, his mouth dry.

"He is a man. A man in the desert with a gun in his hand, and the Christ in his heart. He is a man of the Book, a man I am supposed to consider *infidel*." She looked directly into Devane's eyes. "He has the watcher's eyes, like you, eyes that see, and *hear*. You have a heart like his, don't you? And you know the Christ, too."

Devane said nothing.

"It will be all right," said the girl.

"Where is John now?" asked Devane.

The girl shrugged. After a moment she said in a tiny voice, "He gave me the gift of my life, and now I must ask for his hand once again. He must come for me, and Tommy, so we may live."

"But where is he?"

The girl's expression darkened for a moment, and she looked frightened. She took a deep breath and let out a sudden sob. She took another breath, then one more, and her face brightened again. Her eyes grew big, and stared off into a distance Devane could not fathom. "It will be all right," said Faseem. She reached out and placed one hand on Devane's right forearm. As her fingers squeezed him tightly, she smiled into his eyes and said, "John has the Christ in his heart, like you. John will come for us."

After a few minutes, Devane signaled for the guard to let him out. As he left he saw Faseem, her thumbs against her lips, rocking back and forth on the bunk, humming the simple tune he had heard on the tape.

CHAPTER FIFTEEN

Tommy held his old backpack tightly to his chest, looked at the hard, watchful man in the dark suit who had given it to him, and said, "Thank you."

"No problem," said James Devane. After he left the girl's cell he had conferred briefly with the guard marshall, and learned Tommy Church had been cooperative and calm during his intake procedure, and since he was placed into a cell not far from the girl's. They were in a special wing of the compound, normally used for terror suspects. The staff was highly trained, and the facility was well maintained. Devane wanted to make a positive impression with the young American, so he asked to see the prisoner's personal possessions. In the backpack, beside some personal items, photos of what Devane guessed to be family members, and one shot of a brown and white horse. Also in the pack was an old Bible.

Devane learned from the guard marshall, to his relief, that Tommy had not been subjected to any comprehensive or "adversarial" interrogation. Nor had the guards used any of the more subtle methods of "softening" a prisoner prior to interrogation: disorientation, constant lights and blaring music, sleep deprivation, or any psychological drugs. After his initial interview and medical examination, the young American had simply been placed in his cell and left alone. The guard marshall told Devane the young prisoner asked only to be allowed to visit with the girl—denied—to be allowed a phone call—denied with a chuckle—and requested the American Embassy be notified of his arrest. This had been done. As if to defend his professionalism, and guessing Devane might think he was handling lightly this prisoner who was the accomplice of the assassin of Azul Dante, the guard marshall stated he was treating Tommy Church as had been "suggested" by Hiram Sarco. Devane assured the man he understood his position.

Devane looked at Tommy, who stood before him in the cell. The lanky young American stared back, his right eye swollen black and blue, his lower lip puffy, split, the skin reddened. The doctor's report stated Tommy apparently had at least two cracked ribs, and various abrasions and contusions. He asked, "What kind of horse is that in the picture? I know they have a name for that, uh, breed."

Tommy grinned, and winced as his lip stretched. He wheezed slightly when he spoke, and Devane guessed his nose might be broken. "You went through my stuff, huh?" Tommy responded, "Well—I appreciate you bringing this to me." He patted the backpack. "That horse was one I owned before—before the disappearances. He's called a pinto or 'paint,' basically a quarterhorse, not too big, but plenty of heart."

"Family in the other shots?"

"Yep."

"Can you tell me their names, where they are?"

Tommy looked into Devane's eyes, hesitated, then answered, "My dad, Thomas Church, my mom, Rebecca. My sister—we call her Sissy—and her husband, Mitch." He shrugged. "Back in the States."

"Did you know Faseem was going to kill Azul Dante?"

Tommy sighed. He paced back and forth a moment, then asked, "So, he's dead?"

"Not yet. Doesn't look good."

"Okay," said Tommy. "No, I did not know . . . she . . . was going to do *anything*. This will probably sound dumb to you, but I didn't even know *she* was a girl. She was with that Saudi fella when I first met him—they were having trouble with an Arabian, they can be flighty sometimes— had him turned-out in a small pasture by himself for one thing—" He paused, shrugged again, and added, "I knew him, or her, as Piet. Thought he was a quiet sort of guy, maybe had some troubles on his mind or somethin'. We came here together with that Khalid, but nothing was planned, you know?" He made a face. "Why are you askin' me anyway? These boys here have already gone over my whole life, and I'd bet they taped it, too."

Devane smiled and nodded. "I wanted to hear you say it, Tommy," he said easily. "You and I are Americans, and I guessed we might see things the same way."

"You're the agent that tackled Piet, uh, Faseem, after she hit Dante with the sword, aren't you?"

"Yes."

"I didn't want you to hurt . . . her . . . that's why I jumped in—"

"I know."

The two men stared at each other.

"I don't know too much about too many things," said Tommy quietly. "But I'll tell ya this much. I'm just a curious sort who traveled here from the New Christian Cathedral in Selma, Alabama, to get a look at ol' Azul Dante because he might be the most important thing to happen to the people of this world in a long time. That Saudi fella, Khalid, is a Muslim and all, but I don't believe he's a bad man, and I don't believe he came here to Paris to be part of some 'assassination plot.' And I know horses better than I know people, but I'll tell ya this—that gal you got shut up in here is no killer, okay? She was actin' weird all morning, like she was zoned out or somethin'—and if you saw her face when she swung that sword you'd know she was like, *not there*, okay?" He took a deep breath, nodded as if to himself, and added, "This whole deal is very strange. I know you are part of Dante's security, and you got a job to do and all, but mister, you'd better take a close look at this mess, because I don't think things are as plain as they appear to be." He hugged the backpack, and said, "I'm done."

Devane had watched Tommy's eyes while the young guy spoke, he had watched, and he had listened, and his heart told him Tommy Church was right. "Perhaps someone from the embassy staff will contact you," he said. "For now, sit tight. We'll see how this shakes down." He hesitated, "I'll see what I can do about you visiting the girl—might do her good."

"Thank you," said Tommy. "Can I ask your name, sir?"

"James Devane."

Tommy pulled his Bible out of the back and held it up. "Thanks for bringing me this, also."

Devane put his hand out, and after a moment Tommy shook it firmly.

As Devane walked the corridor with the guard, on his way out, he paused in front of the girl's cell. Very faintly he could hear her humming the same tune. He concentrated, trying to get it into his own head. A few minutes later, he leaned forward in the backseat of the car, and said to the driver, "Goodwell? Listen to this little tune, would you? I know I've heard it before, but I just can't place it."

"Sure thing, Agent Devane," responded the big man, looking at Devane in the rearview mirror with an amused smile.

Devane began humming the tune, and Goodwell gave a soft laugh, grinned, and nodded. "You don't remember that one, sir?" he chided.

"It comes from my childhood, Goodwell," replied Devane defensively, "and that was a long time ago."

"Yes, sir," agreed the driver. Then he added, "Maybe we should all get back to those days once in a while—"

"Goodwell," said Devane, "what is the tune?"

"*Jesus loves me,*" Goodwell began to sing softly, "*this I know . . .*"

Devane's serious face lit up, and he joined in, "*because the Bible tells me so.*"

+   +   +

The big, dark man dressed in laborer's clothes watched the shiny black sedan as the imposing driver eased the car out of the compound and onto the street. He recognized Agent James Devane sitting in the rear seat, and this confirmed he was in the right place. He had arrived in the Paris area the day before, had learned of the prison location, and made his way to the northeastern outskirts of the sprawling city. He had guessed the two prisoners would be held in a maximum-type facility—like this one designed to incarcerate terror suspects—and kept in close proximity to each other. Whether the Saudi prince, ostensibly another suspect in the attempted assassination of Azul Dante, was held in the same prison did not matter to the big, watchful man. It was the American he was interested in, and the girl.

No one took much notice when the working man strolled the sidewalks in the blocks surrounding the compound. The man wore black jeans, boots, a battered leather jacket over his long-sleeved shirt, and carried a canvas bag over his shoulder. Tucked into his waistband under the jacket was a large semiautomatic pistol. He had the dark stubble of beard on his jaw, and wore a sweat-stained hat over his shaggy black hair. His face was lined, and worn, and he seemed to blend in with the neighborhood, which was not affluent, but rather an area where immigrants and transients of all stripe passed through. A person who took a moment might see something unsettling in the way the man's eyes never stopped moving, the intensity of them, the grim set of his mouth, but most did not really *see* him. He stopped once at a corner café, standing at the counter as he sipped coffee and stared at the television mounted behind the bar. It was set on one of the news stations, and every few minutes showed a live shot of a hotel room, the figure of a man, his head in bandages, laying beneath the covers. The figure had an IV in each arm, and a doctor in a white smock hovered nearby. Arrayed behind the bed on light-boxes were large X rays of the figure's skull, the dramatic cut through the bone and into the brain a clearly visible ugly white line. To the watcher, this image was surreal, and he asked the young woman behind the counter in rough French what it was supposed to be. She told him, her eyes filling with tears, that the figure on the bed was Azul Dante, and this was what the news commentator called a "worldwide death watch." The screen then showed a news interview of Hiram Sarco, who seemed to be the man in charge at that moment. It was he who had suggested, the watcher learned as the program progressed, that a live camera keep vigil over Azul Dante as he clung precariously to life. "The world will want to watch—and *learn*," Sarco intoned.

Interspersed with Sarco and the hotel room, the news segments ran the video of the actual attack on Dante by the girl with the sword. Then came the faces of the three suspects, and also pieces of the girl's taped "confession." Although Hiram Sarco had denounced such acts, the news reported an upswing of attacks on Muslims in Paris by angry, near-riotous mobs. Several Arab-looking men had been hanged in a park, and several had simply been beaten to death. It was a macabre living theater, with an interacting, unstable, and panicked audience. To the big watcher, who finished his coffee and moved on, it all boded no good, and he felt the heat of resolve fill his belly. He had recognized the girl, of course. Seeing her face on the television had jolted him, then filled him with wonder. He was amazed that she had come so far, that she was a part of this, that the life he had given her was used to this seemingly dark and twisted purpose. He fought off a wave of doubt and confusion, the looked into his very center, at his faith. He knew the answers were there, he understood nothing was happening as a result of some far-flung cosmic accident. This realization made him take a harder look at the beaten face of the lanky American "accomplice"— this Tommy Church. The dark watcher stared at the name on the screen, and the number *seven* resonated throughout his being. *Of course*, he thought. From that moment he was committed to action.

He waited now until a bus stopped at the corner across the way from the maximum-security compound, and many people got off and on, milling around before heading off, laborers, office clerks, shoppers. He sat on a bench, reading a newspaper, watching.

"John Jameson," said the man quietly as he sat down on the bench.

The big man with the newspaper ignored the newcomer.

"John Jameson," repeated the man softly, and this time the watcher turned his head slightly and stared at the newcomer with fiercely intense eyes. He saw that the man who sat down was tall and fit, with a full head of dark blond hair, a handsome face with a surfer's tan, disconcerting sky-blue eyes, and an easy smile. The man wore a nice gray suit, a matching tie over a crisp white shirt, and shiny black loafers. Over his shoulders hung a sand-colored trench coat, and he held a black briefcase across his knees as he sat on the bench. "It's all right, John," he said as he leaned closer, "I know."

The watcher glanced around, saw nothing out of the ordinary, and roughly grunted, "No *parley-vous.*"

The newcomer glanced around also, then nodded, and said sotto voce, "I gotcha, John—you are deep cover, and on the run. Your home team is out to get you—you're a hunted man and a *wanted* man. You've ditched the Johann Rommel identity General Izbek Noir kind of liked, especially since there are Interpol arrest warrants issued in that name for the 'death' of that poor Drazic fellow. Now you're in Paris calling yourself Christy Brown—a likeable Irishman on holiday." He looked up and down the street with a coconspirator's stare, "Not to worry—I get the picture."

John Jameson felt himself coiling, tightening, the adrenaline raging though his body. He was within a hairbreadth of taking this guy out right there on the bus bench, but hesitated as he looked into the man's eyes. They were calm, patient, *knowing.*

"Who are you?" asked Jameson tightly, "Who sent you, Carter—or *Tsakis?*" He watched the man's face closely, knowing the man's answer would be the trigger.

"I'm Ayak," replied the man with a self-deprecating smile and shrug. "Well, I go by Stan while I'm on this mission, so my formal identity documents validate me as Stan Ayak—from the American Embassy staff." He glanced at his manicured hands and added, "Neither of those you mentioned sent me, exactly—but I must say of the two, I prefer that Michael Taskis. He is your friend, I believe."

Jameson, totally mystified, quite sure he had never seen this guy before and equally sure there was no way the man was some State Department operative, asked, "What organization are you with?"

"Oh," responded Stan with a small wave of one hand, "one of the newer *corps*, actually. Don't get me wrong, John, they did salt our ranks with some *veterans*, if you get me, but most of us are fairly new—like me."

Jameson was at a loss. The guy had access to *way* too much info, and Jameson had no clue who the man worked for. When it was crucial to know the players, when every move was literally a matter of your survival, another agent floating onto the scene completely out of the blue was extremely dangerous. "Look, Stan," he said as he turned slightly on the bench, pulled his right hand back, tightened his fingers into a claw, and shifted his weight a bit as he readied himself, "I don't know one single thing you're talking about, okay? Time for you to just get up, and walk away. Don't say anything, and don't look back—"

"I can help you spring Faseem, the girl," said Stan calmly. "And Tommy Church. You are here to break them out of that prison—"

"You don't know—"

"John," said Stan, and something in the change of his voice made Jameson pause. "There is no time. Have you seen what is lying in that hotel room, its head swathed in bandages? There is no time. We must act."

Jameson said nothing, but his face betrayed his inner conflict.

Stan, aware of Jameson's fears, took a deep breath, and looked all around once more. "*Seven*, John," he said, his voice urgent. "You, Cat Early, Ivy and Ron Underwood, Shannon Carpenter, Reverend Henderson Smith, and Thomas Church. The only one you know of the first seven is Cat, but I have met the others. Along with these are ones you have touched, like the girl, Faseem, and loved ones like Church's son, Tommy." He leaned even closer, his right hand on Jameson's left forearm, his eyes bright. "You are part of seven, John Jameson. Look into your heart— you know it. I'm aware of your faith, John, and your purpose, and I've been sent to help."

At that moment Jameson knew who, or what, Stan was. That it flew in the face of every pragmatic, realist, professional fiber in his body did not in any way diminish its authenticity. It came to him with a hot certainty, filling him with awe. He felt at the same time humbled, emboldened, and grateful. He understood he was the recipient of something very rare indeed—a real-time, physical manifestation and *validation*—of God's work, God's presence. "It's about time you showed up, Ayak," he said with a quick grin, his eyes wide, his heart pounding. He gestured toward the compound across the street, "Now—how do we get those kids out of that place?"

Stan smiled, "Tommy has asked to see a representative from the American Embassy." He raised his eyebrows, and waited.

"I love it," said Jameson.

+ + +

The news commentator fawned over Hiram Sarco, who sat back in his chair, one leg thrown casually over the other. They were doing a live feed from the spacious front room of Azul Dante's luxury hotel suite, as Sarco had made it known he would not leave Dante's side through "these dark and anxious hours." But the world deserved to know, he had said, to know, to watch, to learn. Before the interview began, the commentator read the litany of horror, disharmony, and fear that was the current world news. There was a global panic, the skeletal stock markets were teetering on the brink of a crash, runs on the bank—financial and physical—were taking place. There were riots in the streets in many cities, in countries all across the planet. People fought with and killed one another over food, water, and fuel. In strong countries like the United States, things were bad, but not out of control. The police forces, still bolstered by National Guard and Reserve units, kept a precarious order. Communications were still up, hospitals functioned even though stressed by the sudden influx of injured, and the larger transportation hubs were open. In countries already weakened by drought, famine, war, and mob-ravaged infrastructures, life was hard—and cheap. Men killed other men, and women, for their clothes or a small bag of stolen groceries.

On the war front, it appeared the mujahideen armies of General Izbek Noir were once again almost unstoppable. The mujahideen forces had blown out of northern Iraq and had gutted most of Turkey, leaving a sad and incarnadined trail in their wake. The dead numbered in the hundreds of thousands, and carrion birds dominated the ash-filled skies. The Coalition Forces of Azul Dante were ably led and doing the best they could, but they fought a fanatic enemy who willingly embraced death for an elusive and unsubstantiated promise of paradise, where they would be eternally served by the *infidel* slaves they had killed. Oddly, to military observers, General Noir seemed in no hurry to punch his way forward, content to consolidate his gains and let his troops amuse themselves with prisoners of war and civilian refugees caught as they attempted to flee. The horrific tales of witness-survivors had become commonplace, the rapine and destructive atrocities committed against the defeated had become almost unnewsworthy.

And now Azul Dante, man's last and best hope, founder and leader of the powerful Prodigal Project and its global network of believers, lay dying.

"Is there any sign of . . . change?" asked the news commentator with some temerity. "Anything at all?"

"No," replied Hiram Sarco, his lips pulled down into a frown. He looked directly into the camera as he added, "As you know, and as the good people of the world know, I have arranged for the world's best surgeons and neurologists to be flown here. Two from the United States were sent here by President Reese on *Air Force One*. They have gathered, have examined Minister Dante, and are standing by."

"Is surgery, um, scheduled?" asked the commentator. He read from a list of questions provided to him by Hiram Sarco's aide. "I ask this, sir," he continued, "because to me—a layman—and to many who witnessed the attack and the horrible wound, it appears that there is little that might be done, even by the best doctors. Such a terrible, deep wound—how can anyone . . . ?"

"The best are in attendance," sniffed Sarco. "They will do what they can."

"Perhaps we should pray for him, then," suggested the commentator, as cued. "We here, and the people in the street, in fact all of the people in the world. We should pray for Azul Dante, pray for a miracle that might save him, and bring him back to us. We, the world, we *need* him." He paused, looked at Sarco beseechingly, and repeated, "Perhaps the world should pray for him."

Hiram Sarco let it hang for a moment as he stared into the camera. Then he lifted his jaw, his eyes narrowed, and said in his curiously strong and vibrant voice, "Perhaps we should pray *to* him."

"Sir?" The commentator's cues had ended.

"Perhaps the world should pray *to* him," said Sarco again. He turned in his chair and pointed toward the master bedroom of the suite. "He *lives*," he intoned. "He lies there fighting for survival, when surely any mortal man would have died the moment the sword of that harlot Muslim swung into him. His eyes are closed against the sadness, lies, and hatred of man, yet if they *open again* it will signal his victory over the sword. He lays there, barely alive, displaying to the world an incredible power, an incredible *will*. The world is in chaos, the world is lost, and foolish man runs in panic and wails for help from the skies above. This special man, this entity without peer, this Azul Dante—he is the one. He can save us from ourselves."

He turned to face the camera square, his eyes burning. "You, out there—the people of the world," he said to his audience in the certainty that his words at that moment were being heard by billions across the planet, "hear me." He lowered his voice, and the undiminished strength of it was hypnotic in its force as he said again, *"Perhaps we should pray to him!"*

CHAPTER SIXTEEN

It began as the formation of a gathering storm, with low-hanging clouds, heavy air, and wind gusts that backed and turned, died away, then surged. The skies, though streaked and stretched by the gusts, had the look of coming snow in winter. But the wind blew hot and wet, indolent and foul, like the rancid breath of a great beast. It was unsettling, irritating, and put people on edge. Though the gusts began to increase in frequency and intensity, the weather still felt as if it hung on the brink of something far worse, and this brought with it uncertainty, and fear. Eventually the winds reached a volume and depth that began to permeate the minds of men all across the globe. It growled and chuffed, whistled and howled. And it moaned.

It was as if some mournful cosmic creature, tortured and lost, vented its sorrow and pain on the winds of the earth. The wind moaned, and it became a haunting, hurting voice that swept across the far reaches of the planet.

In some ways the wind manifested the feelings of a world racked with draught, famine, war, chaos, panic, and fear. It moaned, and the moan was the like cry of millions of souls standing at the edge of the abyss, their hearts gripped in the black hand of destruction. The brilliant white snow that capped the Himalayas was blackened and sooty as the moan fell down the peaks, rushing toward the lower altitudes, shaking the conifers and wilting the stands of smaller trees. It rolled like a heavy sigh across the oceans already fouled and thickened by dead and dying fish, the waters bloodred. It billowed across the Far East, the Pacific archipelago, and India. The vast reaches of China and Siberia felt its clinging breath, and the people of Africa felt it wash against their sunken cheeks and recognized the stench of the carnivore's mouth, razor teeth mildewed with rotting flesh. It hung over the massed armies in battle in western Europe, the intensity of it washed away the pitiful cries of the wounded, and it tumbled and rumbled throughout the main population centers, causing men and women to subconsciously tuck their necks down into their collars and cast their fearful gaze heavenward. It fell on the Americas, too, that howling, despairing moan, otherworldly and macabre in its cloying, cloaking omnipresence—tearing at the ears and hearts of man wherever he might be.

"It is an evil wind, Henderson," cried Nateesha Folks as she stood beside the Reverend Smith on the front steps of the New Christian Cathedral, "an evil wind."

"Yes," was all he could manage, his frightened eyes scanned the dirty clouds racing by overhead, the horrible moaning sound slicing though the pulsating chambers of his heart. The clatter of dead leaves blew past them, and Nateesha hugged him close as she cried into his left ear, "Henderson, Shannon told me that Thomas and Rebecca Church left this morning. They were going to try to get to Paris, to their son—"

Smith said nothing, shivering involuntarily.

"Ivy and Ron Underwood are staying here for now," added Nateesha, "but Shannon said she and Ted Glenn might leave for Israel in a few days."

"They can go where they want!" shouted Smith, suddenly angry. "They can leave and try to find whatever they want! They don't have to stay here—they don't want to listen to me anyway, or listen to *the Word!*"

The big black woman by his side, loving him, frightened for him, pulled closer, but said nothing.

"They can scatter like these leaves," said Smith, almost sobbing, "and they can moan like this evil wind, but they can't change what's happening, Nateesha! *They can't change what's happening now!*"

"Henderson." Nateesha leaned close to his ear, her warm lips against his skin. "They are only following their hearts, and the promise. They *must* follow the promise—"

"*What* promise?" cried Smith, turning to her, pulling at her. "Can't they see there really *was* no promise? We can wait, and wait, and wait—we can stand around wringing our hands waiting—*but the promise will not be fulfilled,* can't you see? Can't they see?" He glanced at the raging skies, then flung one arm back toward the interior of the church. "There is a new reality, Nateesha. Oh, yes, I been tryin' to tell all these good folks, haven't I? There is a new reality, and a new truth, and all anybody has to do is look on that television screen in there, look and see the figure of the one lyin' on that bed with his head split. *He should be dead*, Nateesha. *Can't you understand?* They've got those monitors hooked up to him—the camera right on them, you can see the little jagged line that is his heartbeat, *his heartbeat*. He *lives*, and he is the new truth!" There were tears streaming down his cheeks as he stared at the clawing gunmetal skies, his fists bunched at his side. "I have tried to tell them, but they will not hear me—"

"*He who has an ear, let him hear,*" said Nateesha in a tight voice, her mouth close to Smith.

"What—what did you just say?" asked Smith as he turned to look at her.

"*He who has an ear, let him hear.* Get back to your Bible, Henderson Smith!" said Nateesha as she began pulling on Smith's left arm, trying to drag him off the steps and back into the church. "Don't you be tellin' me about *promises!* You sound like that burning fool, that Andrew Nuit—"

The name jolted him, and caused him to take a quick breath. He turned with Nateesha, his eyes held by hers.

"Henderson," she said, "there is promise, there is hope. We got to go back to the Bible. We got to go back."

Smith, openly crying now, glanced once more at the mocking clouds. Then he let her lead him back.

✝   ✝   ✝

General Izbek Noir crouched on the cupola of a burned-out tank, gently stroked the charred skull of the dead tank commander, and looked at the blowing skies. The shrieking moans of the winds were like a rich and melodic choir in his heart, and he felt a fullness within him. He glanced at the empty eye sockets of the disjointed and melted corpse beside him and chuckled. "Ah, my friend," he said, "you went to your death just too soon, though it was a lovely death, was it not?" The hulk had been a French tank, manned by Turks, and he had personally blown it up with an antitank rocket. As each of the surviving crew members had attempted to escape from the flames, he had stood close, shooting them with a pistol, laughing demonically. He shot them only to wound, only to prevent them from escaping the licking flames. He sucked in the fumes as the men writhed and burned, screaming until their lungs burst, then curling into charred and marbled twists. It was life's sweet breath for him.

He looked toward the west, over his left shoulder, and grinned. The moaning winds pulled at his words as they escaped from his cut of a mouth. "Ah, Azul—it is time, it is time, you amazing and wondrous creature!"

+   +   +

On the outskirts of Paris, a few miles from the hotel where Azul Dante lay near death, John Jameson sat at a small table in the back of a nondescript restaurant a few blocks from the maximum security facility that held Faseem and Tommy. He leaned over a cup of coffee and listened to the moaning wind. He was deeply unsettled— and very worried about Cat. He wondered where she was at that moment, and for some inexplicable reason knew she stood at the very vortex of the storm. He wanted to be with her, he *should* be with her, he thought.

"You can't be with her, John," said Stan quietly, "not right now—"

Jameson looked at his new companion closely. Stan's expression, usually composed and confident, if seemingly somewhat amused, was tight, stretched. His sky blue eyes were bright, and his hand shook slightly as he held his chipped coffee cup.

Stan looked at his trembling fingers, then shyly at Jameson, and said, "Isn't it amazing the way feelings that impact your heart manifest themselves in subtle actions of your body?"

"You mean the way your hands shake when you are afraid?" asked Jameson gently.

"Is that it?" asked Stan, in wonder. "I'm *afraid?* I—I was not sure I would experience *all* of the facets of this level of existence when I took this mission."

Jameson put his right hand over the hand Stan held the cup with, and steadied him. "It's okay, Stan," he said quietly. "Fear is a common human condition—out there across the world right now, millions are staring at the skies, hearing that terrible, unrelenting moan, and their hands are shaking, not to mention their hearts."

"Well," sniffed Stan, "I suppose if I'm to be *authentic* in this role—"

"I'm worried about Cat," said Jameson as he glanced out the windows at the front of the place.

"You are one of seven, John," replied Stan, "and Cat is one of seven."

"So?"

"So," responded Stan with a small shrug, "so none of you are where you are, or have the light in your hearts, by accident. You know you must carry on, as will she, and it will be as it is meant to be."

Jameson said nothing. The winds grew louder.

Stan stared out the windows, his eyes far away. Suddenly he sat up straight in his chair, turned his head toward the center of Paris, and said in a soft whisper, "It is time. As it is written, it is time. Oh—my Lord."

+   +   +

James Devane came for Cat Early and Slim Piedmont. He told them he had been dispatched by Hiram Sarco, to bring them to the bedside of Azul Dante. He admitted he did not know why they had been summoned.

They were in the car driven by Goodwell, the former Marine. Devane sat in front, Slim and Cat in back. As they rode the short distance to the hotel, Devane looked at the streaking skies and said quietly, "This is an evil wind."

"Yeah," agreed Slim. "It feels like it's *lying* on us, you know? And that unending *moan*. It gets on your nerves."

"Strange," added Cat. She was greatly disquieted by the moaning wind and felt it pulling at the inner walls of her heart. To divert their thoughts, she asked Devane, "Have you seen the, um, prisoners? Can you say anything about them?"

Devane looked over his shoulder, into her eyes. "On the record? Yes—they are in a maximum security facility, they have not been harmed in any way, and they are being—"

"*Off* the record," said Cat. It was her decision as a professional, and she knew she could make it to a man like Devane only once.

He stared at her a long moment, then nodded, and said, "I don't believe the Saudi had any knowledge of a planned attack on Dante. I don't believe the American kid, Tommy, did either." He hesitated, then added, "And I'm not sure *the girl* did either."

Slim, for once, said nothing.

Cat held her breath.

"I don't know," said Devane. "It's like the girl—Faseem, a Muslim—it's like she was somehow *driven* to it. She has no real recollection of the act, and is passive and kind of lost, until you mention his name."

"Azul Dante's name?"

"Yep."

"So who drove her, James?" asked Cat, unconsciously using his first name as a validation of his partnership with them.

Devane shrugged. "I've got sort of a feeling, but it doesn't make sense. I'm not ready to say."

They all had the same feeling, and *none* of them was ready to say it.

As the car pulled into the sweeping circular drive in front of the hotel, Goodwell said quietly without turning his head, "Sir . . . there's one of Sarco's new security guys, see him?"

"Yeah," said Devane tightly. "First time I've seen one out of the suite up there. Must be here to watch over Cat and Slim."

"What 'new security'?" asked Slim as he opened his door and began to untangle his long legs.

"They showed up late last night," answered Devane, almost under his breath. "Sarco told us Dante had already arranged for their arrival before he got his head split. Supposed to be some 'very special people' Dante wanted as his personal boys. I'm still assigned, along with our little ragtag international group all stumbling over one another." He could not keep the tendrils of professional sarcasm and distrust out of his voice as he added, "They've got no documentation, no backgrounds, no agency validation. They all wear suits and ties, seem to be very well trained and mission focused. They carry the very best weapons for close-quarter combat, they speak in a language I still haven't placed, but have absolutely no communications gear—radios, I mean. Their head boy carries one, but I think that's so he can call one of *us*."

"Where are they from?" asked Slim as he carefully watched a tall, severe man in a black suit approach.

"Albania, maybe?" replied Devane out of the side of his mouth. "The Balkans?" He shook his head in frustration, and they headed up the wide steps and into the hotel lobby.

They rode the elevator in silence and stepped off into the foyer of the suite to be greeted by Richard, Hiram Sarco's aide. "Finally," he said petulantly.

Devane's cheeks reddened, but he said nothing. His face changed when he saw Sophia walking toward him.

"James," she said, her eyes bright, her face pale and lovely.

"Sophia." He held her hand for a moment, then let it go.

Sophia turned and greeted Cat and Slim with hugs.

"What's up?" asked Cat as she lifted her eyebrows and rolled her eyes toward the spacious living room and closed bedroom doors beyond.

"Don't know," whispered Sophia. "Hiram was with Azul this morning, and suddenly he, Hiram, wanted you two here, quickly." They began to walk across the room, toward two more of the new security men who flanked the bedroom doors.

"Cat," whispered Slim in Cat's right ear, "check out their eyes. Each one of them has that 'Drazic look,' if you follow."

"I know," Cat whispered back. All veteran security agents have closed, tight, impassive faces, and watchful, distrustful eyes. This she recognized, and accepted. But, like the former aide Drazic, these new agents had brittle coal-black eyes, emotionless, flat, *cold*. The eyes of dead men. She shuddered, took a breath, and tried to compose herself.

The bedroom doors were opened, and Hiram Sarco stood at the foot of what appeared to be a hospital bed. He wore a charcoal suit and tie, he had a crooked smile on his tight purple lips, and his eyes were fierce. "Please come in," he said in a funereal voice, and swept the room with his right arm. As Cat and Slim entered, with Sophia behind— Devane had stopped in the foyer—Sarco added, "You, photographer, stand there at the foot of the bed. You may shoot whatever you wish."

I'd like to shoot you, you pompous windbag, thought Slim. He nodded and began fiddling with his cameras.

"Miss Early," said Sarco, "you are to stand here, beside the bed, at Minister Dante's right shoulder."

Cat moved quietly to the side of the bed. She held her breath as she looked down at the figure of Azul Dante. He lay under crisp white sheets, his arms exposed and relaxed along his flanks. He wore what appeared to be light blue pajamas. The bandage around the top of his head was much smaller than Cat expected, there was no blood, and it appeared it had been placed carefully so as not to mess up his hair. Dante was clean shaved, with a smooth and healthy complexion. His eyes were closed. *Of course his eyes are closed*, she thought. *They have been closed since he was hit with the sword.* For some reason, she glanced at his hands and saw his nails were carefully manicured. She raised her eyes to take in the rest of the room, not wanting to miss any detail. She saw the bank of electronic medical monitors arrayed behind the bed. She looked twice at the displayed blood-pressure numbers. They were in normal range. She looked at the heart-monitor display, and saw it was almost a straight line, with only an occasional faint and feeble *blip* pulsing it. There was one older man in a smock with a stethoscope around his neck. He held a clipboard and carefully watched the monitors. She saw Sophia had quietly moved to the other side of the bed, her big eyes on Dante's relaxed face. Cat glanced at Hiram Sarco, who stood at her right elbow, but he, too, was fixated on Dante.

Sophia, Slim, and the doctor all turned their heads at that moment, listening. The moans of the winds outside seemed to be reaching a rapid, piercing, blanketing crescendo, and they were clearly heard inside the room.

The sound took on a heavy, palpable form, a musky, pervasive presence that weighed on them, clung to them. It had the cadence, tenor, and edgy richness of a wailing, satanic choir, calling out in sustained agony and despair. Somehow Cat understood that the howling winds were at that moment buffeting every nook and cranny, every heart and mind, everywhere in the world. It was an evil wind, indeed, all consuming, all controlling, and Cat had a sudden image of millions of people cowed, on their knees, their heads bent and covered with their trembling hands, their hearts crying out for relief from the unrelenting black roar.

The terrible, unending howl of the wind began to overtake them all. It became a physical thing, an undeniable *presence*, an atmospheric creature on the prowl, on the hunt. Cat, though focused on Azul Dante, felt her mouth go dry and licked her lips as she glanced at the drape-covered windows a few feet away. She thought she could feel the building tremble, and half expected the winds to come shearing through the brick and steel walls at any moment. She made eye contact with Slim, and saw he had the same fears. She turned when she heard a sob, and saw Sophia standing with her hands over her ears, crying. Hiram Sarco stared at the figure on the bed, his face a tight mask. Still the winds moaned, demonic, dominating. For one tilting moment Cat wondered if *this*, in fact, was the end of the world.

+   +   +

A few miles away, John Jameson crouched alongside Stan in the small restaurant. They had their backs to the street, and their backs were covered in glass. The front windows of the building had blown in, showering the people taking refuge inside with shards of knife-edged shrapnel. Jameson thought of Cat Early, and muttered, "Lord, watch over her."

Stan, kneeling beside Jameson, heard his small prayer, leaned close, and cried in the din, "How about good old Psalm Nineteen? 'The heavens declare the glory of God; the skies proclaim the work of His hands. Day after day they pour forth speech; night after night they display knowledge. There is no speech or language where their voice is not heard. Their voice goes out into all the earth, their words to the ends of the world.'"

Jameson saw the intensity on Stan's face, the open faith in his eyes. He nodded and smiled.

"He always was, always is, always will be," said Stan. "Got it?"

"Got it," replied Jameson.

In an airport parking garage adjacent to Hart's Field, in Atlanta, Georgia, Thomas and Rebecca Church sat hugging each other tightly in the front seat of Church's battered old Bronco. The black skies and tearing winds had been building for hours, buffeting them as they drove, and it was a slight relief to get under some cover, even though the winds were still able to overturn small cars and throw people tumbling to the ground. Rebecca's lips were against the skin of Thomas's throat, and she cried, "It's too much, Thomas, it's too much!"

"Hang on, Rebecca!" he said, patting her back, cupping

the side of her face. "This will pass, it will pass." He tried to remember a Bible passage, any passage, that would comfort her, but against the all-consuming roar of the wind, he could only say softly to her, *"In the Lord, I take refuge, in the Lord I take refuge ... in the ... Lord ... I take ... refuge ..."*

At the New Christian Cathedral, Henderson Smith and Nateesha Folks sat in the nave side by side. Nateesha rested her head on Smith's shoulder as she read from her Bible. Outside the winds crashed against the church, pushing and buffeting it, tearing at it, the noise a wild thing. Inside, the building was expectant, poised, waiting. Smith's face was drawn, and his eyes were big, but he was composed. He had drawn from the last of his inner reserves, aware he could do nothing now but wait, survive this day, then stand to see what came next. That Nateesha was with him, that she wanted only to read from his Bible, he recognized and acknowledged was a good thing. She had gone to Psalm 5, and he liked it.

"Give ear to my words, O Lord, consider my sighing. Listen to my cry for help, my King and my God, for to You I pray."

Shannon Carpenter had chosen the same passage. She and Ted Glenn were still in the dorm room provided by the Cathedral. They had made the decision to travel to Israel. She was drawn there, she had told him, and he said simply, "I'm with you." They sat together on the floor, Ted behind her, hugging her. She felt safe, warm, and protected in his strong arms. Shannon was frightened of the roaring winds like anyone else, but she somehow saw immediately they signaled an important, life-changing event—world-changing event. That change, to her, meant the plan was moving forward. She was part of that plan, part of *seven*, and Ted was with her, and it would be all right. She had been emboldened with a strength she had never known when she simply *accepted* her place as a child of God. He had a plan, she was but an infinitesimal part of it, and she accepted it.

She sat with her legs crossed, Ted close behind her, his chin on her right shoulder. She held her open Bible on her lap, and echoed Nateesha as she read, "Morning by morning, O Lord, You hear my voice; morning by morning I lay my requests before You and wait in expectation."

Ron Underwood stood a few feet away from his wife, Ivy, watching her with sadness and fear. They had been standing together at the back of the cathedral as the winds reached their crescendo, in the relative quiet of the lee side. But there really was no lee side, and soon Ron became frightened as tree branches, trash cans, lawn chairs, and other things began bouncing and crashing across the expanse of grass and trees behind the church. He had tried to pull Ivy inside the rear doors, near the dining room and kitchen area of the building, but she wrenched away from him, her eyes on fire, her expression a twisted grin. He watched her now, standing against the force of that horrible moaning storm, her hair whipped away from her face, her clothing almost torn from her body. He saw her lift her eyes, then her arms, toward the skies.

"Take me now!" she cried, her tiny voice immediately

torn away. "Take me now and be done with it! I'm ready—oh, God—I'm ready!"

"Ivy!" called Ron, but she either didn't hear, or chose to ignore him.

Suddenly a four-foot piece of lumber bounced and jerked across the grass, torn from a fence perhaps, or the eaves of a nearby house. Ivy had time to put her right arm up and turn to her left, then the board hit her, and she fell to the ground. Ron ran to her, grabbed her arms, and dragged her to the side of the building. He managed to get the back doors opened, saw many others huddled inside, and dragged Ivy into the hallway. He stretched her out on the carpeted floor and checked her over. She had a nasty cut on her right elbow, and a bump over her right eye. He put a handkerchief over the cut to stop the bleeding, and in a moment one of the women who worked in the kitchen crawled over on her hands and knees with a napkin filled with ice. Ron took it from her gratefully. She gave him a quick hug, and crawled back to her friends hiding under a long work table.

He placed the cold cloth gently against the swollen bruise over Ivy's eye, and looked down at her. She was out, and her face looked peaceful, lovely and relaxed. Tears filled his eyes as he looked at her and wished he could take away her pain, take away her anger. He thought of a passage from Psalm 32 he had been reading last night, and whispered it quietly as he held her. "Blessed is he," he said, "whose transgressions are forgiven, whose sins are covered. Blessed is the man whose sin the Lord does not count against him and in whose spirit is no deceit." He closed his eyes, hugged Ivy in his lap, and said the ending, "Rejoice in the Lord and be glad, you righteous; sing, all you who are upright in heart!"

+   +   +

The winds got to the guards. They were too much, those skies, that constant howling moan, the sheer *weight* of it. They, like their prisoners, were trapped, and it began to unnerve them. They sat huddled together in a front office, holding their weapons at the ready, their eyes wide, their minds almost overwhelmed with fear. The guard marshall, an older man, managed to stay on his feet, and forced himself to check on his prisoners. The Saudi, Prince Khalid, remained hunkered down in his cell, his hands over his head, his face pressed tightly into a corner of the small room. The guard marshall could hear the Saudi muttering something in a low tone, but could not make out the words. A short distance away the young American sat on the bunk in his cell, reading from his Bible. He looked up when the guard marshall opened the cell portal, saw who it was, and winked. It made the older man laugh and shake his head. He moved down the corridor to the girl's cell. At first he could not see her, then, by standing on his toes he saw she lay curled in the fetal position on the hard concrete floor, her fists against her face. She made a small keening sound, much like an injured kitten, and it bothered the guard marshall, who had raised two daughters before losing them, *their* children, and his wife in the disappearances. He listened to the keening sound barely discernible under the roar outside and made a decision. Without saying anything, he opened Tommy's cell, motioned to him, and led him down the corridor. Tommy followed, carrying his Bible, curious. The guard marshall stopped at Faseem's cell, unlocked it, held the door open a bit, and motioned Tommy inside. As Tommy moved past him, the man said quietly, "Stay with her awhile, yes?"

"Yes," replied Tommy.

Faseem's eyes brightened when she looked up and saw Tommy in her cell. He reached down for her and pulled her from the floor and into his arms. He hugged her tightly as she cried against him and said, "Tommy, I am so afraid. Are we lost? Are we lost?"

He sat down on the bunk, holding her small body easily in his arms. Her head was against his chest, and he kissed her hair as he answered, "No, girl—we are found." With one hand he brought his Bible out of the backpack, let it fall open on the bunk beside them, and said, "Shush now, girl. It's just a noisy wind, that's all—it's just the wind." He fumbled through some pages, then stopped, and read quietly to her, "Praise the Lord. Praise God in His sanctuary; praise Him in His mighty heavens. Praise Him for His acts of power; praise Him for His surpassing greatness. Praise Him with the sounding of the trumpet, praise Him with the harp and lyre, praise Him with tambourine and dancing, praise Him with the strings and flute, praise Him with the clash of cymbals. Let everything that has breath praise the Lord." He looked down at her sweet face, her eyes searching his, her small hands holding him tightly. "Praise the Lord," he said.

* * *

Cat Early felt a trembling in the room, a vibration in the air. The sounds outside possessed her, ravaged her heart, numbed her mind. It would not stop, and when she thought it had reached its apogee, it continued to grow, until it was the dominant force in her world—but for the figure on the bed, Azul Dante. She looked at his face, his closed eyes. She began to lean forward, her head cocked to the side, her eyes narrowing, and at that instant Azul Dante's eyes slammed open.

The instant Dante's ice-blue eyes opened, the howling, moaning winds stopped. They stopped, all across the world, with a jolting, wrenching, *suddenness*. They had been so all-consuming, and when they so instantly, *immediately*, stopped, the silence was like a cannon shot, and millions fell to the ground holding their ears.

Cat fell back from the bed, one hand to her mouth, the other over her heart. She heard Sophia gasp, saw Slim staring mesmerized at Dante's wide-open eyes—his camera resting unused in his hands. She did not turn her head as she heard Hiram Sarco say in a ragged voice, "He lives! He *lives!*"

At that same instant, five hundred miles away across the Mediterranean Sea, in the southeast corner of the Old City in Jerusalem, the Mosque of Omar, the Dome of the Rock, began to tremble. Everyone in the area had already sought cover, or lay prostrate on the ground under the demonic winds. In the impossible silence that came when the winds stopped, people began to feel the earth rumble and shake, and brick walls began to lean away from the corners.

Inside the mosque the old imam got up from his knees where he had been as the winds ruled the world, and shakily stood. He put one hand out to steady himself, looked at his feet, and saw the bricks beneath him sliding and moving, clattering into pieces against one another. "Nooo!" he cried. "No!" He looked up, toward the high dome, toward heaven, and cried, "Nooo!" as he felt the building begin to lean and turn.

At that moment, with a rumble and roar, amid a rising cloud of ancient dust undermined and launched billowing into the air by two thousand years of water, the Dome of the Rock collapsed. It fell in slabs of brick, mortar, wood, steel, and concrete that slammed in destructive force against the ground. It took with it all the landscaping, all the symbols, all the people inside who had sought refuge. The great and glittering dome fell at first in one great piece, but then split and folded until it disintegrated with a metallic, shrieking screech. The entire structure fell into unrecognizable rubble in a huge sinkhole over one hundred meters wide, and within seconds no piece larger than the palm of a man's hand remained.

Azul Dante lay with his eyes wide open.

"He is *alive!*" said Hiram Sarco. "He lives!"

In the Old City of Jerusalem, on the Temple Mount, *on the site of the First Temple*, the Dome of the Rock—the Mosque of Omar—was gone.

All across the world, man held his breath.

ALSO AVAILABLE
IN THE *PRODIGAL PROJECT* SERIES

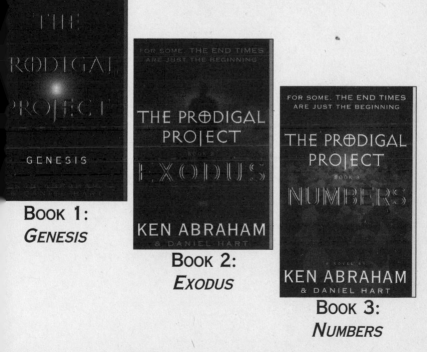